LEGACY

A DEADLY CURIOSITIES NOVEL

GAIL Z. MARTIN

SOL

eBook ISBN: 978-1-64795-019-4
Print ISBN: 978-1-64795-020-0
Legacy: Copyright © 2021 by Gail Z. Martin.

Cover art by Lou Harper
SOL Publishing is an imprint of DreamSpinner Communications, LLC

For my wonderful husband Larry and our family, Kyrie, Nick, Chandler, Zach, Cody, and Sarah. Much love and gratitude to you.

LEGACY
DEADLY CURIOSITIES BOOK 5

By Gail Z. Martin

CHAPTER ONE

"WHERE'S EVAN?" THE OLD MAN GLARED AT ME, HIS BUSHY WHITE eyebrows gathering like storm clouds. I'd never seen him before, but his question told me that he was acquainted with Trifles and Folly—and the store's previous owner, my great-uncle Evan.

"Evan passed away several years ago," I said gently. "I'm his great-niece, Cassidy Kincaide—the new owner."

The gentleman gave me the once-over. Given the gap in our ages, I couldn't blame him for being skeptical. My bet put him on the far side of ninety, while I was in my late twenties—probably younger than his great-grandchildren.

"Sorry to hear that," the man said, with a stoic nod in acknowledgment. He'd probably been tall in his younger days, and from his broad shoulders, I guessed he'd been muscular and craggily handsome before time and age thinned his frame and bowed his back.

The seersucker suit and bow tie suggested he was a true Charlestonian. He had a white-knuckle grip on a cypress walking stick with his left hand.

"D'you take after Evan?" He met my gaze, and I knew what he meant.

He wants to know if I've got Evan's magic.

On the other side of the store, my assistant manager, best friend, and sometimes bodyguard, Teag Logan, looked up and shot me a concerned glance, silently asking if I needed backup. I gave a barely-there shake of the head, and he went back to rearranging the silver tea sets.

"Yes. I'm definitely his heir," I replied. The wording could be taken more than one way because I had been the one Evan chose to inherit the shop. I assumed that whatever brought him to the store today needed special talents to handle.

"Good." He reached into his pocket, withdrawing a picture of a really old bottle of liquor. He set the photo on the counter. I could see binding sigils painted onto the glass and over the label, with more scratched into the glass itself. The top was sealed with wax and what looked to be threads of silver. As I bent to look closer, I saw what looked like a faint glow and a blur that might have been something moving inside the bottle when the photo was taken.

"You've heard of a genie in a bottle?" the old man asked. "Well, seventy-five years ago, my friends and I put a djinn in the gin." He laughed at his joke, but Teag and I exchanged a worried look.

Worried but not overly surprised. Because dealing with situations like this—that's kinda our job.

I'm Cassidy Kincaide, and I own Trifles and Folly, which has been in my family for more than three centuries, almost since Charleston's founding. Most people think of the shop as a great place to find a perfect piece of heirloom jewelry or old silver—and it is—but the truth is a lot more interesting. Since the beginning, we've also been part of an alliance between mortals and immortals to get dangerous magical items out of the wrong hands and keep the world safe from supernatural threats.

Great-uncle Evan chose me as his successor because I have the same special ability as he did—I'm a psychometric who can read the history and magic of an object by touching it. That definitely comes in handy when weeding out cursed and haunted items, but it's also useful when we've been trying to stop something really bad from happening.

Teag had crossed the room to get a closer look. A lock of straight, black hair fell into his eyes as he peered at the photograph. He looks more like a skater-boy, but he was all-but-dissertation on his History Ph.D. before he started working here and decided saving the world was more interesting.

"A djinn?" Teag repeated. "Like Robin Williams in Aladdin? Like in the Arabian Nights?" He sounded cautious and curious, which mirrored my feelings. I looked at the photo of the bottle as if it might bite, and because of my touch magic, I didn't want to get too close.

The old man chuckled, a sound that ended with a rattle deep in his chest. "Not quite." He shook his head. "Where are my manners? I'm Clyde Kenner."

Teag introduced himself and shook hands. "We'd love to hear the story about the bottle," I said. "Would you like to come into the break room and have a glass of sweet tea? You could sit down, and we'd have privacy."

Maggie, our part-time helper, came out from the back room just then. "Go." She scooted us with a flick of her hands. "I'll cover the front if customers come in."

Mr. Kenner picked up the photo and carried it with us into the little kitchen area. He set it in the middle of the scuffed table and sighed as he settled into a chair. I brought him a glass of tea, and he nodded his thanks.

"Originally, there were six of us," Kenner said. "We fought in Korea together. We were twenty years old, full of piss and vinegar, headstrong and stupid," he said with a sad laugh. "Best damn friends I ever had. Ben and Ricky didn't make it home," he added, sobering. "Carl, Eddie, John, and I were thicker than ever after they passed. Like being in each other's pockets would get us home safe."

Kenner paused to take a sip of the tea. It didn't ease the rasp of his voice, and I wondered if he'd been a smoker. He smelled of peppermint and eucalyptus, not cigarettes, but maybe the damage was done long ago.

"We had gone into Seoul on leave, four crazy kids a long way from home. We had too much to drink, got all turned around, and ended up lost in a part of town that doesn't get tourists. Eddie saw a strange little shop and said he needed to buy something for his mama for her birthday. So we all went in, and it was full of candles and statues and dried plants. I got this weird feeling like we shouldn't be there, but the guys wouldn't listen," Kenner recalled.

"Anyhow, Eddie told the lady behind the counter that he wanted something to bring good luck to his mama. She kinda gave me the creeps because I never saw her blink. She picked out a shiny black stone and told him it would keep his mother safe. Then Carl pointed to a fancy bottle and asked what it was. She said it would make our wishes come true. Carl thought it was a big joke, and he bought it." Kenner stared into the middle distance as he talked, and I knew that in his mind, he was decades and thousands of miles away.

"I'll never forget the look on her face when she told him that, about the wishes," Kenner said, shuddering. "She smiled, but I swear there was something evil about it. Like getting suckered into a practical joke, a bad one that's going to hurt."

Teag and I waited, letting him tell his story at his own pace. I already had the feeling that it wasn't going to end well.

"She told him to make the wishes count because there was no telling when the spirit would stop granting them. And she said it would be happy if we fed it alcohol." He shook his head at the naïveté of his younger self. "Carl was so excited. Like someone gave him a million dollars. He was joking with us when he paid her, and I didn't quite catch the last thing she said, but it was something about wishes having a price."

"What happened after that?" Teag asked.

"Eddie and I were freaked out, but Carl and John thought it was all a big gag. We went back to the base that night, and since we had a mission the next day, Carl wanted to prove that this magic spirit was a good thing. So he broke the seal on the bottle, and there was light and fog, and then this ugly little goblin thing was sitting on the floor," Kenner recounted.

"Carl ordered him to protect us the next day. The thing said it would. I gave it some of my beer, and it went away." Kenner's expression grew pensive. "The next day, our convoy came under fire. We were at the front. The Jeep that the four of us were in never got a scratch, but the one right behind us hit a land mine." He looked up, guilt still clear in his eyes after all these years.

"There's no way we should have been able to drive over that mine and not have it blow us sky-high," he said. "Except that goblin kept us safe—and it cost the lives of the men in the truck behind us."

"Doesn't that happen a lot in a war zone?" Teag asked. "You always hear stories about someone whose buddy gets shot when they're standing next to each other, or one tent gets hit and another doesn't?"

Kenner nodded. "And if it had been sniper fire or shelling, I'd be inclined to believe that. But our Jeep should have triggered that mine." He shook his head. "We all looked at each other, and we knew."

"What did you do?" I found myself holding my breath.

"Carl still wanted to prove this was a good thing—maybe more to himself than to us," Kenner remembered. "So he said we hadn't thought big enough. The next time we went out on a mission, he asked for the whole unit to be safe. We came under heavy fire. Got pinned down, had a hell of a fight. When the dust settled, our unit hadn't lost a man. But the unit we'd partnered with? They lost everyone."

I could see that although more than seventy years had passed since the incident, Kenner still felt responsible for those deaths, even though without the spirit's help, he and his friends might never have survived.

"Carl panicked. He wanted to take the bottle to the chaplain—a priest—and confess everything, maybe ask for an exorcism. Eddie—he was the smart one. He went to a fortune teller in the village outside our base and asked how to stop a spirit—hypothetically," he added with a bitter laugh.

"She said to get it drunk on strong liquor and shut it in a new bottle, then say a spell and seal it up just so. So we bought some home-made hooch and offered it to the little goblin-thing. We did what the fortune teller told us. And we made a pact to watch over it and drew up an order for it to be inherited as we died. I'm the last one, and I want to make sure it doesn't hurt anyone else. My time is short, so here I am."

He somehow looked even older with the telling, and I could see how the burden weighed on him. At the same time, Kenner had lost the tension that stiffened his shoulders and clenched his jaw, and I thought of the old saying about how confession is good for the soul. He had carried the weight long enough.

"Where is the bottle now?" I asked.

"That's the damnedest thing," Kenner replied. "I was working up my nerve to bring it here—I've been on borrowed time for a while, and I need to get my affairs in order. Strange things started happening, so I figured I'd better hand off the bottle sooner rather than later. And then this morning, someone broke in and stole it."

"Just the bottle?" Teag asked, eyebrows raised in suspicion.

Kenner nodded. "I'd kept it locked up tight all these years, but since I intended to bring it to the shop, I got it out. I should have known something was up. When the bottle was in the safe, I couldn't hear it anymore. Started up again as soon as I took the darned thing out."

"Hear it?" I asked, suddenly on alert.

"Not like it spoke out loud," Kenner said. "But it had a way of getting into your thoughts, into your dreams, unless it was locked up under a bunch of lead or iron. It slithered in and started to weigh you down like it wanted you to drown..." He shook his head as if he were clearing away bad memories. "Sometimes it screamed."

"Screamed? Did anything...unusual happen before the bottle was stolen?" Teag asked.

Kenner thought for a moment. "No, nothing." A pause: "Wait. There were strangers in the neighborhood. I saw a man in a fancy, expensive car that didn't belong. Most of us have lived there since the Sixties. Raised our kids, saw them grow up, threw retirement parties. Regular folks. Then there was a construction truck parked on the street, but I couldn't figure out where they were working. Seemed unusual, at least thinking about it now."

He sighed. "Maybe someone was casing the joint, as they say on TV. I couldn't shake the feeling that I was being watched, even though no one was around. But that's probably just an old soldier's paranoia."

Teag and I exchanged a look. It seemed likely to me that Kenner wasn't being paranoid—and I bet Teag felt the same way. Someone—or something—with magic could have had their eye on him. "Anything else?" I asked.

"Yeah. There was a commotion in the backyard, and I went to see what was going on," Kenner said.

"Commotion?" I pressed. "What do you mean?"

"It was the damnedest thing," he said. "I'd had a metal shed behind my house for twenty years. Didn't blow away in all the hurricanes. And that day, it just fell apart. Made a hell of a racket. I went out to see what happened. The shed had just collapsed. I figured I would have to call someone to haul it away. And when I came back to the living room, the front door was open. The bottle was gone. Left my TV set and my good watch that was on the table and just took the weird old bottle."

He leaned in like he was imparting a secret. "I think the spirit knew I was going to get rid of it."

"Did you mention the bottle or the story to anyone?" I thought it sounded more like someone had gotten wind of the bottle and took the chance to grab it.

Kenner scowled. "I don't need anyone thinking I'm not right in the head. I never told anyone—not even my wife, God rest her soul."

"Did you report the theft to the police?" Teag refilled Kenner's glass without being asked.

"Of course not. They wouldn't have believed me. But you do, don't you? Believe me?"

"We do," I replied. "And we'll do everything we can to find it—before it can cause problems." It might already be too late for that, but we had a stolen bottle with a captive djinn on the loose, and both possibilities sounded like a heap of trouble.

"We can make sure that once the bottle is found, it's handled properly so that no more harm comes to anyone," I told him, already thinking of a couple of allies I could pull in to help. "Thank you for trusting us with your story."

He grabbed my hand without warning, and his gnarled grip was tighter than I expected. His blue eyes turned fierce. "It gets into your dreams if you're not careful," he warned. "It wants to get loose. You've got to lock it up in a lead safe, on a bed of rock salt. Doesn't hurt to put a crucifix and a rosary in with it for good measure. The bottle with the sigils contains it, but to shut it up, you need to keep it in the safe. I painted the same marks on the outside of the safe that are on the bottle, just to be sure. You don't know what it's like to hear it screaming in your head."

I covered his hand with mine and hoped he couldn't see the worry in my eyes. "Thank you," I said. "We'll take it from here."

I walked Kenner to the door and thanked him again. He turned to me when we reached the doorway and laid his hand on my arm.

"Doc says I've got a month left, give or take. Told me to get my house in order. That was the last thing on my list. Now it's done, and so am I. It'll be good to rest. I hope Eddie and the boys have some cold beer waiting for me on the other side," Kenner said with a smile. Then he turned and walked away.

When I went back to the break room, Teag had pulled a woven net out of the gear bag we kept in the office. Teag's a Weaver witch, which means he can weave magic into cloth. I knew the net was one he had woven himself.

"Between the salted holy water and colloidal silver that the net was soaked in, along with my magic woven into the net, that should be good to contain even a very strong spirit once we find the bottle. Then we can put it in the lead safe until we can destroy it or hand it off safely," Teag said.

We'd put some sketchy supernatural items in the safe before to keep them neutralized, and I hoped it would work now until we could pass the bottle off to friends who could make sure it wouldn't hurt anyone again.

"I'll let Sorren and Donnelly know," I replied.

"He called it a djinn. What kind of spirit do you think it is?"

I tipped my head. "No idea. It could actually be a djinn...or an ifrit. Maybe some other kind of wish-granting demon. The folklore blends them all together. There are so many possibilities."

Kenner's gin genie wasn't the strangest thing we'd had to deal with or the most dangerous. Getting cursed and haunted objects out of the wrong hands is a big part of what we do, but saving the world comes in a close second. Fortunately, we had a network of good friends with special abilities that helped us deal with supernatural threats. The world was still here, and I counted that as a win.

"I figure that if Rowan and her coven can't figure out how to dispel it, Donnelly and the Briggs Society can make it disappear," Teag said. "But we have to find it first."

"Great minds think alike," I replied with a smirk. "If a time-traveling, dimension-hopping haven for vanished explorers and malicious magical objects can't handle it, we're in more trouble than I know how to deal with."

Considering the kind of threats we'd stopped, that was saying a lot. I hoped our record held.

Mid-afternoon, I declared all of us in need of a coffee break and went out to Honeysuckle Café, our favorite local joint, to retrieve caffeine for Teag, Maggie, and me. The weather was perfect for walking, cool but not cold, and low humidity, which is why I love autumn in Charleston.

I called Sorren and left a detailed message. I knew he wouldn't be awake yet, but I figured once night fell, he'd call me back. Maybe in his long existence, he'd seen something like the spirit bottle and would know the best way to handle it.

Since the day was beautiful, I took the long way to the coffee shop, the scenic route that led past St. Philip's Church and its two large graveyards. The tombstones dated back to the 1600s, in burying grounds surrounded by brick walls and wrought iron fences, under the gnarled branches of ancient live oaks.

Usually, the cemetery gave me a feeling of peace, despite being notoriously haunted. Today, I stopped in my tracks, heart rate rising, trying to make sense of what I saw. A pulsating black shroud covered the entire cemetery, glistening blue-black where the sun lanced through the shade of the live oaks.

I caught my breath, unsure what I was seeing, and I let my wand slip down my sleeve and into my hand, ready for an attack.

The "shroud" suddenly moved in a hundred directions at once as a huge flock of crows rose from the ground, flapping and cawing. I threw my arms up in front of my face as the birds took off, flying so close I felt the beat of their wings. For a few seconds, the din of their cries filled the air, and the sky around me turned black with their numbers.

Then they were gone, and I stared after them, wondering where they came from and where they were going. I realized that several other people stood staring at the sky, looking just as rattled as I felt.

That's not normal. I've never seen a flock that large. A darker thought occurred to me. *Crows are an omen. That can't be a sign of anything good.*

The birds didn't return, and after I collected my wits, I headed for the coffee shop once more, wondering if anyone there had also seen the crows. As I walked, the conversation with Clyde Kenner replayed in my mind. I felt certain that the bottle's disappearance on the very morning when he intended to be rid of it was no coincidence. More concerning was his admission that the spirit inside had been able to influence his dreams. I suspected that the bottle's wardings had weakened and that the djinn—or whatever it was—saw a chance to escape and took it.

Before I left the shop, I'd put in a call to Rowan, a witch friend of ours, and to a couple of other folks who might have some ideas on how to find, bind, and dispose of a troublesome—and dangerous—magical creature. With luck, we could track the bottle and its occupant down before anything world-endingly bad happened.

I was so deep in thought that I almost overlooked the ghost bike.

Charleston is a reasonably friendly city for cyclists, but any time there are cars and bikes sharing a road, tragedies occasionally happen. The "ghost bikes" are a memorial project that takes old bicycles and paints them white, then fastens them to a signpost or some other permanent object close to where an accident occurred, along with a memorial plaque.

As a memorial, they're a visible reminder to share the road. But for those of us with extra abilities, they're a connection to the other side. My friends who can see ghosts sometimes sense the spirit of the unfortunate cyclist nearby, even though the bike used for the memorial isn't the one involved in the wreck. I do my level best not to touch the bikes. Even so, they tend to act as a bellwether for me, letting me know if the supernatural world is troubled, which usually means problems are headed my way.

The air around me was still as I approached the white bike chained to a telephone pole, and there was no one else nearby, no rush of wind from a passing truck. But as I came closer, the front wheel spun…slow, lazy circles at first, then faster and faster until the spokes blurred.

I stared at the bike as the wheel gradually lost inertia and slowed again and felt a chill go down my back. *First the crows. Now this?*

When I arrived at Honeysuckle Café, I took a deep breath to let the aroma of freshly roasted goodness wash over me. The café is one of my happy places, and I focused on the smell of baking muffins and the friendly banter between Trina, the owner, and Rick, her theatrically-inclined barista. They play off each other so well; I wouldn't be surprised if a lot of the patrons come back for the "show" as much as the excellent brew and pastries.

"Cassidy! Good to see you. What can I get for you?" Rick asked.

I rattled off my usual, plus orders for Teag and Maggie, and he nodded, expecting it.

"Hey, have people mentioned anything weird lately?" I tried to sound nonchalant, but Trifles and Folly has a reputation, and even if most folks think we take care of haunted heirlooms, people who know me lump all the spooky stuff together.

"How weird? You mean like how a big flock of crows flew into town and doesn't seem to want to leave?" he asked over the noise of the espresso machine. "Can't tell you how many people have commented on them. I mean, everyone sees a crow now and again, but a flock of hundreds? Does that count?"

I took the cups as he set them on the counter. "Yeah, actually, it does."

"Then my good deed for this hour has been done." Rick made an exaggerated bow.

I laughed and thanked him, even as my mind filed away the news for later. Trina was running the register when I stepped up to pay. She grinned when she saw me.

"So, did you feel it?" she asked as I tapped my card on the scanner.

"The coffee? Haven't drunk it yet," I replied.

"No, the tremors. I guess that answers my question." She jerked her head toward the TV in the corner, and I read the closed captioning as the news anchors discussed "yet another" minor tremor shaking up Charleston. We hadn't had a major earthquake in more than a century, but that one had been bad enough that everyone keeps waiting for another like an unfulfilled prophecy.

"Did you notice it?" I asked.

"Only because I was looking at a pitcher of water on the counter that was sloshing for no good reason," Trina replied. "Sometimes a big truck going by will do that, but we usually hear them coming. Otherwise, I never would have felt it."

"How many does that make?" I tried not to show the worry building in my gut. One omen could be passed off as an oddity, but the ghost bikes *and* the crows *and* now tremors? I didn't know whether the cosmos was warning us about the missing genie or something else, but I was afraid we were going to find out soon.

"Over the last couple of months? Three or four, at least," Trina answered my question about the minor earthquakes. "They're getting closer together, which might or might not mean something. I guess we'll find out!" Her smile and upbeat tone let me know Trina wasn't too worried.

I didn't have the luxury of thinking on the bright side because omens occur for a reason. It wouldn't be smart to ignore warning signs.

"I hope two of those drinks are for Teag and Maggie," Trina teased. "If you drink all three, you'll be shaking enough on your own that you'll never feel a quake."

I promised I'd see her again tomorrow and headed back to the shop with the drinks. The omens weighed on my mind. They appeared to be recent, which meant we might have a chance to get out in front of whatever was causing them. As much trouble as the gin djinn might cause, I didn't think he was dangerous enough to warrant omens, although he might make a bad situation more complicated.

We needed to figure this out before a big supernatural problem landed in our lap. That meant I needed to check in with some friends in the paranormal community and see what they were encountering.

Rowan was waiting in the break room when I got back to the shop. I offered her my untouched latte since I felt bad I didn't know to bring one for her, but she waved me off and stuck with the glass of sweet tea Teag or Maggie had poured for her. They accepted their coffees enthusiastically, grateful for help avoiding a mid-afternoon slump, and went to watch the front while I met with our guest.

"Something weird is going on," Rowan said when I sat. Rowan is in her early thirties, blond and pretty in a girl-next-door way, too perky and pleasant for anyone to suspect that she's a powerful witch and the leader of a respected—and in some circles, feared—coven.

"You mean besides a runaway genie?" I thought about the worrisome omens and hoped I was just paranoid.

"That—and other things. I'd make a joke about there being a disturbance in the Force, but it's almost exactly like that. Something's changed about the way magic *feels,* and I don't think that's a good thing."

I frowned and tried to think whether I'd noticed a change. Then again, I hadn't tried to use my gift for anything substantial in the past day or two. "Since when? And what does the shift feel like to you?"

Rowan pursed her lips as she thought, eyes narrowing. Magic is always difficult to put into words. It's also highly individual, so two people with similar abilities might have different experiences. Usually though, there's some common ground practitioners can find to understand each other.

"It's like a boundary I didn't even realize was there before is...

looser now." She chuckled. "Maybe it's the way a dog feels when the power goes out, and the Invisible Fence turns off."

I had to think about that analogy for a minute. "When you said 'boundary,' you meant something protective, not limiting?"

She nodded. "You know how when there's a noise that's always in the background, you don't notice it until it goes away? Sorta like that. A hum of power that's always been there, so it didn't stand out—until it's not."

"Is it gone?"

"It's weaker—which makes it noticeable. But I don't know what it is, what it does, or where it's coming from. If it's very old, it might have been part of the magical background of Charleston for so long, no one even thinks about it," Rowan added.

"That doesn't sound good. And here I was worried about crows and ghost bikes."

She looked up. "You've noticed the omens too? You're not imagining things. I've heard people say that the monk ghost is back down at the Battery, and the boats are calling in reports of seeing the Charleston Light again."

Since the original Charleston lighthouse was destroyed in the Civil War, time and tides had moved the spit of land where it once stood, so anyone following its guidance was in for a dangerous surprise. And to my knowledge, the solemn ghost of a plague church monk had never hurt anyone, but like the Pawley's Island "Gray Man," seeing him wasn't a good thing.

"And I guess we're getting tremors now?" Shit. Bad stuff was piling up, and we didn't have a clue about what was going on.

Rowan nodded. "Major storm warnings too, although it's not the usual season for them. The people on TV are saying it's 'climate change,' but I think there's something supernatural behind it."

"Any ideas what would trigger all those omens? Or summon storms?" We'd faced down some big bads, but nothing before warranted apocalyptic foreshadowing.

"The coven has been trying to figure out what changed, but we haven't come up with an answer yet," Rowan told me. "So hunting an

AWOL djinn comes at a bad time—not that there would ever be a good time. Let's just hope that whoever stole him wants to win the lottery instead of re-making reality."

"You think the spirit in the bottle is that powerful?"

Rowan shrugged. "No way to know until we try to catch it. It's possible—but they vary in strength. So if the old man kept it trapped in a makeshift bottle for seventy years, maybe it wasn't that strong."

"Or they got lucky," I said.

"Or that."

"Do we know when the magic started to change?" I asked. "We can help research what might have happened to cause that."

"It's gotten stranger over the past month, but looking back, I think it started a few months before then," Rowan said. "And I've got no idea what kind of trigger we're looking for. It's got us stumped—and that worries me."

"About the same time the tremors started," I said. Something else prickled in the back of my mind, forgotten yet important, but I couldn't snag it right now.

Rowan waved off another refill of tea, and I finished my latte. "What about the bottle spirit?" I asked. "Any ideas on how to track him down?"

She shrugged. "It would help if we knew what kind of creature it actually is. What works on some won't work on others—and if it turns out to be really dangerous, it sucks to be throwing spells at it and hoping they stick."

"Do those spirit-creatures leave traces? An energy trail, or a reaction to it by people with a gift?" Even if the djinn stuck to the kind of twisted deals Kenner had told me about, people were likely to get hurt.

"Maybe. We can look for unusual energy pulses—but with the other weirdness going on, that might be harder to track than usual. And if the spirit is strong enough to cause problems but not at a world-ending level, we might have to watch for unlikely incidents and follow the trail."

"Let's hope for the not-world-ending part," I said. "Unless you think the omens might be a warning about the spirit going loose?"

Rowan shook her head. "I guess it's possible, but I don't think it's likely. From the story Teag told me about the bottle's last owner, the spirit brought bad luck, but not on a huge scale."

"Maybe the person didn't wish for a big disaster. But if he had, could the spirit have made it happen?" That was the question I'd been mulling over since Kenner told us about the bottle.

"Aren't you a ray of sunshine?" Rowan asked in a droll tone. "Let's not borrow trouble—we tend to have enough without imagining more."

She finished her tea, and I walked her to the door. "I'll let you know if we find anything," she promised, and I assured her we'd do the same. After Rowan left, I found myself feeling even more worried than on my walk back from the café. If Rowan and her coven didn't have a ready answer, I dreaded what it might take to prove the omens wrong.

The sun had barely set when Sorren's ring tone sounded on my phone. "Cassidy—I got your message. That's all...most disturbing. Are you and the others safe?"

I picked up Baxter and settled into my favorite corner of the couch. "Yes—at least for now. What do you make of it?" I respected the experience that came with a very long existence and hoped Sorren knew what the hell was going on.

"Trouble," he replied. "I'm in upstate New York—their news doesn't cover much south of the Mason-Dixon Line. So I hadn't heard about the tremors. The omens you mention are worrisome, especially with a big storm in the offing. I don't like it one bit."

"Neither do we," I confirmed. "It all seems unnatural—even by our standards."

"We know the Pendlewoods aren't behind it," he said as if thinking out loud. "The Etheridges have been laying low for quite a while—for a family of witches, they seem to be more focused on white-collar crime than sorcery. As powerful as the Charleston witches are, I don't think they alone would do something that would trigger harbingers of doom."

"That's pretty much what Rowan said," I told him. "And then there's the missing bottle spirit."

Sorren swore under his breath. "I'll come back as soon as I can. I know you and Teag can handle yourselves—and you've got plenty of allies. But I'll feel better when we're there to help."

I didn't say it, but that would make me feel a lot better too.

"I'll look into the bottle spirit," Sorren added. "And I'll let you know if I find anything. In the meantime—pull in your friends. You're stronger together."

The call ended, and I buried my face in Baxter's soft fur. Life was about to get a lot more exciting—and not in a good way.

CHAPTER TWO

"I KNEW AS SOON AS THE PAPERWORK CAME THROUGH THAT YOU needed to have a look at the place," Alistair McKinnon told me when we got out of our cars the next morning. Teag and I had followed Alistair. Alicia Peters, a friend of ours who was a gifted medium, rode with us.

"Are there rumors about it being haunted?" I asked as we stood in front of a colonial mansion built just before the Revolutionary War on Edisto Island. The two-story brick home was large for its era, stately and symmetrical with a pitched roof and matching chimneys.

"Its name is Custos Sanctum," Alistair said, looking up at the mansion's facade with an academic's sense of wonder. "It means 'guardians' sanctuary.'"

"Odd choice, isn't it?" I asked. "Gideon Sullivan was a sea captain, not a military commander."

"Gideon Sullivan was many things, including an enigma," Alistair replied. "He was the second son of a wealthy shipping magnate, a sea captain who successfully navigated dangerous routes for nearly two decades. Yet if legend is to be believed, he consorted with privateers and is said to have made a deal with the devil."

Teag raised an eyebrow. "Privateers—or pirates? There's a difference—at least technically."

Alistair chuckled. As curator of the Lowcountry Museum, Alistair
knew his way around old houses and interesting antiques. He had a
trim build and a full head of gray hair despite being in his early sixties,
as well as a penchant for bow ties. "There's supposed to be, in theory.
In practice, that dividing line could be subjective."

Alistair didn't know the full extent of everything we did at Trifles
and Folly, or that for more than three hundred years, the shop had been
a front for a secret coalition of mortals and immortals who kept the
world safe from supernatural threats. What he did know was that my
touch magic and Teag's weaver magic had taken care of some problem
items. Alicia's ghost whispering had come in handy as well since
museums and haunted objects went together like PB&J.

Teag glanced at me. "You up for this?" He wasn't doubting my
abilities; he'd been my wingman long enough to pick me up off the
floor more than once when the images I saw through my psychometry
put me flat on my butt.

I nodded. "Yeah. I'll be fine." I'd gained more control of my gift
over the years, which included learning to protect myself. The agate
necklace I wore helped deflect dangerous magic, as did my silver and
onyx bracelet, the woven scarf Teag had made for me, and the ancient
agate spindle whorl in my pocket. They wouldn't stop every threat, but
together they worked against most.

"As you can see," Alistair narrated like a tour guide, "the house has
a commanding view of the ocean. The original owners planted the land
around it thickly with holly, bamboo, rowan, and ash trees. Closer in,
there's a hedge of juniper and hemlock that surrounds the house on
three sides, leaving it open to the sea in the front."

"Interesting choice of plantings," I observed. Every single plant he
mentioned had strong protective magic.

"Around back, there's a kitchen garden with fennel, mint, ginger,
sage, and basil," Alistair went on. "And the plantings closest to the
house have nettle, rue, alyssum, gardenia, geranium, and agrimony.
The deed and will specify the plantings must be maintained and are

never to be cleared away. Lots of iron fencing and custom wrought-iron gates with some interesting symbols too."

"So Sullivan planted a defensive magic garden," Teag said. "And I'd love to take a look at the sigils in the wrought iron. Wouldn't be surprised if they're the same kind of thing. What was he afraid of?"

Alistair shook his head. "No idea. But he had to have thought something powerful was after him, to put that kind of effort into a passive defense."

I glanced at Alicia. She probably didn't fit most people's idea of a powerful ghost whisperer in a pair of jeans and a twin set that flattered her curves in colors that set off her blue eyes and shoulder-length dark hair. While she looked more PTA than paranormal, I knew how skilled she was, and more importantly, the spirits recognized her abilities. "Are you picking up on any ghosts yet?"

Her eyes narrowed as she regarded the mansion. "Not yet."

"Why would anyone think Sullivan made a deal with the devil?" I asked.

"People said he could control the waves in a storm and turn them against attackers. You'd think that would be a good thing, but you know how people can be," Alistair said with a shrug.

A car roared up the driveway at a reckless speed, sliding to a stop on the gravel.

"McKinnon! You've got no right to be here, let alone taking strangers into that house."

The man looked to be in his late thirties, dressed with the expensive blandness that usually indicated a career in banking or investments. With his blond hair, regular features, and broad shoulders, he might have been handsome, but the hard set to his mouth and the entitlement in his manner told me he would be trouble. My mind dredged up a name from the social page pictures of a local magazine. Carter Etheridge, a hedge fund manager who liked to be seen with all the right people in all the right places.

"We've been through this before, Mr. Etheridge," Alistair said, with the chilly politeness that is the Charleston equivalent of telling someone to go to hell. "The lawyers have reviewed the paperwork. It's all in order."

I recognized the name. The Etheridges were one of Charleston's old families, known for their wealth—and the questionable magic they used to give themselves an unfair advantage. Even if his arrogance and entitlement didn't make me recoil, my intuition picked up a darkness that I knew better than to ignore.

"I have lawyers too, McKinnon. We will challenge the disposition of the property," Etheridge threatened.

Alistair looked unaffected by the threat. "You can certainly try, although it won't look good in the news, wasting the museum donors' money on legal costs. Your family has no claim on the property, and the bequest is more than sufficient to sustain the mansion without being a drain on the museum's finances. The fact that you want to force us to sell so you could flip the property for a huge profit isn't likely to win sympathy."

"This isn't finished!" It didn't take much to see that Etheridge wasn't used to losing, and his barely controlled fury had as much to do with ego as profits.

"It is for today," Alistair said in a no-nonsense tone. "You're trespassing, and if you won't leave, I will have the police remove you."

Etheridge flushed with anger, dropping the affable country club vibe and showing the red-meat predator beneath the mask. "I'll be in touch with your board of directors."

"They're well aware and have passed a unanimous resolution in favor of accepting the bequest," Alistair replied in a cool tone. "Good day."

Etheridge turned on his heel and stalked back to his sports car, peeling out with a spray of gravel that would have pelted us if we'd been closer. As it was, some of the stones pinged disturbingly against our cars, earning sour looks from all of us. Alistair sighed as Etheridge roared out of sight.

"Now, where were we?" He managed a wan smile.

I felt certain down to the marrow of my bones that the Etheridges were the worst people to acquire the old mansion. It crossed my mind that it would be bad if they found out about the missing spirit bottle. Whoever stole it might not have plans for world domination, but I wouldn't put that kind of thing past the Etheridges. Recognizing the new potential threat made me even more determined to find the missing djinn—or whatever it was.

We followed Alistair up the wide front steps of the mansion. As we walked inside, I sensed a frisson of something strangely familiar and shot a glance at Teag, seeing the same recognition in his eyes.

Magic.

My house, Teag's house, Maggie's apartment, and the shop were all heavily warded with magical protections, a necessity given the types of bad guys we went up against. We inconvenienced and angered people and creatures who were a lot more powerful and a lot less mortal than we are and who could accomplish their plans more easily if we were out of the way. The magic tilts the odds of surviving a bit more in our favor, although nothing is ever guaranteed.

"You said Sullivan never left the mansion grounds once he came back from the sea for the last time?" I asked.

Alistair nodded. "So the stories go. It's always made me wonder if he was disfigured or maimed in a way that he felt ashamed of. We're hoping that we'll find information in the house to tell a more complete story. Gideon's not just historically important for his own deeds, but he comes from a very prominent family. When we eventually open the house to the public, we want to do right by him."

Maybe he didn't leave because he had the property magically locked down to keep him safe. Personally, I had my doubts about opening the house any time soon, but until I had evidence to back up my misgivings, I stayed quiet.

"How did the mansion end up with the museum?" I asked. "I know the museum's trust runs a couple of historic homes. Does this happen a lot?"

Alistair shook his head. "This was definitely a strange one. Apparently, Sullivan set it up a very long time ago—when the museum was founded."

Teag gave him an incredulous look. "That was in 1773."

Alistair grinned. "I told you it was strange. Gideon Sullivan was a founding benefactor of the Lowcountry Museum. He arranged it so that the mansion would pass to the museum's protection when it was no longer lived in by one of his direct blood relatives. That last descendent was Elizabeth Sullivan, who died a few months ago at the age of ninety-seven."

As he talked, Teag, Alicia, and I turned in slow circles, taking in the impressive foyer. The woodwork alone was magnificent, not to mention the cantilevered grand stairway, parquet floor, and plaster ceilings with ornamental moldings.

High on each of the foyer's walls was an odd cross. Instead of just the plain 'T' of the regular Christian symbol, this had an extra, shorter crossbar, a style called a "patriarch cross." Every inch was carved with letters and sigils I couldn't make out from this distance. Teag spotted them as well, tapping me on the shoulder and pointing upward.

I nodded. "Plague crosses. Interesting—given all the witchy plants outside, I didn't figure Sullivan for a very religious guy."

"With as many outbreaks of Yellow Fever as Charleston had during his lifetime, maybe he believed in hedging his bets," Teag replied.

I paid close attention to the mansion's details, spotting a few modern upgrades, like electric lighting. No doubt the home had added an updated heating and cooling system as well as indoor plumbing over the years to make it comfortable for more recent residents. I'd been in enough historic homes to know that those modifications could be made so skillfully that they were nearly invisible.

Sullivan's sanctuary had an understated elegance which made me think the sea captain built the home to suit himself, not to impress anyone. Its location would have been considered remote at the time. Those who wanted to be seen and admired built their grand homes along the Ashley River or south of Broad Street. Edisto Island had been almost wilderness when Sullivan chose his location.

"Why here?" I asked. "He was born to Charleston society, raised in a wealthy family, and made his fortune. He could have built anywhere. This is almost a hermitage."

Alistair shrugged. "I don't know for sure what his reasons were, although having grown up at the top of the social heap, he knew what he was leaving. Maybe his interests changed after all that time at sea. Perhaps he didn't want to be bothered. After all, when he finally came home to stay, it was after an accident that put an end to his career."

I knew that part of the story, although the details were sparse in any of the sources I'd checked. Gideon Sullivan had escaped numerous close calls with pirates, sometimes thanks to the help of a friendly privateer.

But his luck ran out in a fatal battle that destroyed his ship, the *Resilient*, and while Sullivan had survived, his injuries meant that his sailing days were over. He came home to his mansion, and for fifteen years Sullivan never left the property. Rumors said a handful of very loyal, free servants and a nurse took care of him and the mansion, staying in his employ for decades. In his later years, Sullivan built a large, elaborate, fortress-like mausoleum on the far end of the property, where he was buried.

"Was the mausoleum part of the grant to the museum?" I asked.

Alistair shook his head. "No, oddly enough. The building, the land, and the road to get there were specifically carved out. His fortune provided an endowment that should keep the taxes paid and maintenance handled for a very long time."

Gideon Sullivan clearly didn't build the house to one-up his social rivals. Charleston has a lot of grand homes. I've toured most of them, and while they are picture-perfect, few of them feel homey. They're stiff, formal, and expensively decorated, but not comfortable. They're showpieces meant to announce and solidify the owner's social position with their location, size, and opulent extras. Even the personal rooms feel contrived, self-conscious, and sterile.

Everything about Sullivan's house celebrated life. Large windows and wide porches looked out on the sea he loved and brought light and air into the interior. Handmade Killim and Mashad rugs were even more beautiful, worn by age. Fireplaces with elaborate surrounds spoke of warmth and comfort. Most of the wood was old-growth cypress, the color of clover honey.

Some of the furnishings were old enough to have belonged to

Gideon, while much of the rest reflected the tastes of subsequent generations. I knew antiques, and it was clear that Sullivan had a good eye for quality and timeless design. Leather chairs invited guests to linger. The paintings and knickknacks reflected decades traveling abroad. Everything told me that Gideon Sullivan had gathered the best memories of his seafaring days to blunt the loss of his ship and his freedom. And every room had a plague cross somewhere in it.

Most of the artwork had a Caribbean or Central American feel—not surprising considering where his ship spent its time.

"There are a lot of pieces that look Dominican to me," Teag murmured. "Maybe also from Hispaniola?"

I nodded. "Some Cuban too. And he obviously liked Bermuda." Paintings of the British island's rainbow-hued buildings and pink sand beaches were a common thread as we walked through the well-appointed rooms.

"No hiding that he was a ship's captain," Teag commented, and I followed his gaze to the brass sextant, armillary, and compass on shelves around the library. A telescope on a stand stood beside one of the nearly floor-to-ceiling windows.

"And a book lover," Alicia added. The walls were completely covered with bookshelves filled with leather-bound volumes. A wide desk with drawers no doubt held maps. The chairs were overstuffed and perfect for reading, with ottomans and side tables to accommodate a quiet day. Decorative items on the shelves ranged from wood carvings to unusual shells to ceramic figures. Most were painted bright colors and struck me as the sort of thing bought from street hawkers rather than purchased in a store or gallery.

Despite all the generations that had lived here since Sullivan's time, the home still had a distinctly masculine feel with wood paneling, massive fireplace surrounds, and brass fixtures. Walls painted hues of deep blue and green were so much like a ship's interior that I wondered how desperately Sullivan missed the sea after his injury.

Leather high-backed chairs flanked a fireplace featuring hand-painted tiles from the islands beneath a heavy, hand-carved cypress surround. Old, delicate sweetgrass baskets and elegant Catawba pottery graced the mantle. Above the fireplace hung two very different oil paintings.

"I'm guessing that Gideon Sullivan is on the left," I said. The large painting was formally posed, showing a wealthy man in his thirties wearing a dark blue jacket with brass buttons over an ivory vest and a ruffled white shirt. The man's blond hair was caught back in a queue— a fashion rebellion against the powdered wigs of the era—and a tricorn hat with a jaunty cockade. Unlike the portraits of many men of his station and age, Sullivan did not look soft. High, sharp cheekbones, a square jaw, and a stubborn glint in his blue eyes suggested strength and character.

"Who's the other man?" Teag beat me to the question. "He looks like a gentleman pirate."

Alistair chuckled. "You are looking at the eighteenth-century equivalent of sending someone a selfie. The man is Ramon Montero, and he was a legendary privateer. He and Sullivan struck up an unlikely friendship over the years, having the opportunity to rescue each other on several occasions.

"Legend has it that Montero commissioned the painting as a joke and gave it to Sullivan, who returned the favor with one of his own. Supposedly, they embellished the paintings a bit before they gave them back again and then started the cycle all over."

Montero's painting showed a rakishly handsome man in his late twenties with fiery black eyes, tawny skin, a mane of wavy dark hair that fell shoulder length, and features that suggested a combination of Spanish and Caribbean heritage.

His fitted black waistcoat showed off broad shoulders and a muscular chest. Leather belts crisscrossed around his waist, holding daggers and a spyglass, while a wicked cutlass hung at his hip. High leather boots and a black cloak with a red satin lining completed the badass buccaneer look, and the knowing smirk on his full lips radiated cocky confidence.

"At some point I guess they just stopped trading them back and forth?" I asked.

Alistair shrugged. "I don't know. Given their long-standing joke, I wouldn't be surprised if they each had a copy made when Sullivan's sailing days were through. A reminder, perhaps, of better times."

The paintings held my attention, two men so different in circumstances united by the sea and an unlikely friendship. I loved when something humanized the past, making those long-ago people real and relatable.

"Are you picking up anything?" Teag looked from me to Alicia.

"There are ghosts, but I don't sense danger," Alicia replied. "They've been here a long time, and I think they see themselves as guardians, like the mansion's name said."

"Guardians of what?" Alistair asked.

Alicia gestured vaguely toward everything around us. "This house. Sullivan's history. They're protectors, and as long as they don't think someone is trying to cause harm, I don't think they'll hurt anyone."

Teag's gaze flicked to me.

I found myself drawn to a piece of scrimshaw on one of the bookshelves. Teag followed as I walked over, hanging back to spot me if I needed help. Intricate carvings decorated the yellowed conch shell, and their delicate lines were inked black to stand out.

The moment I touched the shell, I felt a connection to its owner.

Moments from a long-ago lifetime flashed in my mind's eye. I saw a large sailing ship and the endless ocean and felt a sense of belonging. Images of a woman and a young boy flashed and faded, replaced by a dark-haired man with a dangerous glint in his eyes. I saw sunny tropical islands and rainbow-hued bungalows, as well as black thunderclouds and lightning striking the open sea.

In the next breath, the house rose from mere blueprints to its current grandeur, like a time-lapse movie. Other faces flickered by in a rapid montage, and I watched the trees and plantings grow from saplings to maturity in a blink. A torrent of emotions swept over me as if I was absorbing a lifetime of memories in the space of a few breaths. I soared with elation and plunged into despair, then settled into a warm feeling that surprised me.

When I set the scrimshaw-like shell back on the shelf, the vision faded. Teag was right behind me with a bottle of water and a protein bar, which I accepted gratefully. Alistair and Alicia waited for me to regain my senses.

"This is going to sound strange," I said when I had recovered, "but I sense...contentment. Sullivan was happy here. At peace. He and the servants were an odd little found family." I concentrated, then frowned as I remembered a darker undercurrent.

"Something worried him, gave him nightmares. I'm picking up fear...and sacrifice." I looked up and shook myself out of my trance. "I know that doesn't make a lot of sense."

Alistair crossed his arms. "Sullivan survived a number of sea battles with pirates and nearly died in one. I imagine he had plenty of fodder for bad dreams."

Each room made me more intrigued by the man who had built this sanctuary for himself. *How did he occupy his time? Did he do more than read and star-gaze? Was he estranged from his family?*

Plenty of second sons from wealthy families didn't stand to inherit the family business or the bulk of the fortune. But they reveled in their lack of responsibility and the hedonism money could buy even in a place like the "holy city."

"What happened in his last battle?" I asked. "The accounts I found contradicted each other."

Teag wandered off to study a painting done in the folk-art style of the southern Caribbean, while Alicia seemed intrigued by a music box in the corner of the room.

"I'd love to know the facts myself because the story seems to have grown with the telling," Alistair said. "According to the legends, the *Resilient* was attacked by four pirate ships. The numbers were against them. Then out of the cannon smoke, Montero's sloop *Hidalgo* bore down like the Pale Horseman. When the smoke cleared, the pirate ships were burned to the waterline, and the *Hidalgo* and its captain were never seen again."

"What about Sullivan?" Teag asked.

"Again, the reports vary," Alistair said. "They all say that he was pinned when a mast broke away from cannon fire, but some reported a broken back, while others suggested burns from sails that had caught on fire. Whatever happened, it was enough to make him give up his ship and retire, although he was only in his late thirties."

From there, we headed toward the kitchen. It was a newer addition since it would have been in a separate building for fire safety in Sullivan's day. Care had been taken to have it match the older section of the house. We walked through a small private eating area, more of a breakfast room. That's when I realized there was no formal dining room, and I commented on the omission.

"No, there isn't," Alistair agreed. "The house wasn't built to entertain, and his descendants appear to have followed his penchant for keeping to themselves."

Without the grand dining and reception areas, the mansion's scale felt more intimate. We finished with the main floor and then walked through the upstairs rooms and servants' hallway, but neither Alicia nor I picked up anything malicious. Teag checked the fabrics in the home, but none of them had anything supernatural about them.

"Sullivan kept the same cluster of five or six servants with him for decades," Alistair added as we walked through what would have been their quarters. "They were all free men and women, notable at the time. Some were emancipated slaves, while others had completed prior indentures. He paid them fairly, treated them well, and they repaid him with loyalty and discretion."

I lingered in the master bedroom, with its massive mahogany four-poster British Colonial-style bed. I knew without needing to touch the bed that it was original to the house, dating from Sullivan's time. The matching wardrobe and side table would have cost a fortune even back then, and I suspected it was a personal indulgence.

Paintings of the sea adorned the walls, beautifully done works that showed both tranquility and violent storms. A large music box sat on the bedside table, made of burled wood. Pieces of scrimshaw and delicate shellwork adorned the room's mantle.

I tripped over the edge of the throw rug and caught myself with one hand on the mantle. My breath hitched as my touch magic connected with the powerful memories and the resonance of energy bound up in the scarred wood of the fireplace surround. I had an instant to wonder whether it had been salvaged from the doomed *Resilient* and to hear Teag shout my name before everything around me blurred.

I smelled the spray of sea air and felt the wind against my skin as the ship rolled with the waves beneath my feet. The creaking of the timbers and the snap of the sails filled me with satisfaction.

Around me the crew saw to their duties, shouting and bantering, intensifying the feeling of contentment. I sensed a deep yearning as well, something or someone missing, and anticipation so sharp as to be both pain and pleasure.

The skies darkened, waves rose, and the images shifted. Lightning flashed, and a strange blue glow limned the highest tips of the masts. Rain soaked the sails and the deck, and I struggled to keep hold of the ship's wheel, defying the storm.

Another scene shift, and this time, clouds of cannon fire hung in the air as the Resilient *blasted back at the pirate ships that dared to fire on her. The air smelled of gunpowder and ash. I spotted another ship, painted black and flying a privateer's flag, bearing down on the attackers through the fog.*

Images flashed strobe-fast, hard to process. I saw bursts of fire from the cannons, heard wood splinter and men scream as the sea rolled beneath us. Then there was a loud crack like thunder close enough to deafen, billowing shrouds of white hurtled toward me, and I felt something heavy and solid smash my body to the deck and keep me pinned and helpless in a growing pool of warm, red blood...

"Cassidy!" Teag sat on the floor beside me, gently patting my face. He dug out a bottle of water from his backpack and supported me with one arm so I could sit up to drink. After I'd collected my wits, I saw Alistair and Alicia standing off to one side, waiting for me to come back to myself.

"I'm okay," I croaked and swallowed down more water. "I think that the mantle was made from some of the *Resilient's* planking. I bumped into it and got an eyeful."

Teag handed me a small candy bar, which I wolfed down, chased by the last of the water.

It has taken me years to gain enough control of my psychometry to be able to navigate historic homes without serious incidents. Teag had witnessed some of my more spectacular reactions when the violent emotions connected to a place or item made me sick or knocked me out. Those had grown less frequent as I learned to recognize problem situations before I got in too deep and got better at controlling my gift.

"What did you see?" Alistair asked. He's not intimidated by my touch magic "swoons" since he's seen me do this more than a few times.

"A lot of short images from aboard ship," I said, trying to gauge whether I'd get a headache for my trouble this time. Sometimes I bounced back quickly, and on other occasions I couldn't ditch the low-grade throbbing for the rest of the day. "Good weather and happier times at first, and then I might have seen the battle that cost Sullivan his ship and his health. One thing came through clearly—he was truly in love with the sea."

Teag pulled me to my feet and asked with a raised eyebrow whether I was okay to finish the tour. I nodded, not wanting to pass up the opportunity. We had brought extra water and recovery snacks for just such a situation, but I was hoping I didn't get walloped again.

"If you feel up to it, let's keep going," Alistair said, leading the way.

Bedrooms are always the inner sanctum, and I hung back, lingering to appreciate the room and take in impressions of the man it belonged to. It made sense that for Sullivan, the room would call back to the sea that he treasured and the Caribbean he sailed. I loved finding clues to what the long-ago residents of a home had been like outside the public eye.

The four-poster mahogany bed dominated the room, generously sized and beautifully carved. It looked like a custom piece, and I recognized the style as being popular among the planter class living in the islands during the colonial period. From the dimensions of the bed and all of the chairs in the house, I suspected Sullivan was a tall man, as solidly muscular as his portrait suggested. Clearly, Sullivan liked things that were well-made and comfortable, not fussy. The custom-made bed would have been indulgently expensive even in his time, and the idea of a badass sea captain with a softer side intrigued me. I respected the authenticity in his choices and felt curious enough to want to learn more.

"I'm impressed that the generations who came after Gideon kept so many of the original furnishings in place," I remarked. Obviously chairs had been reupholstered, and the bedding and other soft goods had been replaced with modern reproductions. I knew it was unusual to find personal belongings so well-preserved.

"We haven't completed our inventory yet, but that does appear to be the case," Alistair remarked. "I suspect it was a condition of inheritance and inhabiting the mansion, although clearly some allowances had to be made."

"Is everything just the way Gideon left it?" Alicia asked as we returned to the first floor.

Alistair shook his head. "The outbuildings haven't survived, and that's a possible focus for the future. We think there was a stable, a barn for horses and livestock, like goats and chickens, the original kitchen, and some storage buildings. I'd love to be able to restore them someday."

The thought of eight or more generations of Sullivan's descendants remaining in the house intrigued me. Old houses were expensive to maintain, lacked some modern amenities, and weren't to everyone's taste. Those factors often lay behind the decision to gift a historic home to a museum or foundation as much or more than being dedicated to preservation.

"If the house remained with his descendants, then Sullivan must have had a family of his own," Teag said.

Alistair nodded. "Sullivan married Annabelle Morrison, and they had one son, Edward. She died in one of Charleston's many Yellow Fever outbreaks while Sullivan was out to sea, and Edward was sent to boarding school in Massachusetts. He remained in the northeast, and Sullivan went back to his ship. After Sullivan's death, Edward and his family came down and moved in."

I suspected that there was a whole lifetime of family drama packed into that short statement.

We finally returned to the front entrance. Alistair paused and reached into his messenger bag. He withdrew a rectangular package wrapped in old brown paper and yellowed string.

"Sullivan entrusted his estate with Richardson, Stokes, and Nelson, a law firm that's still in practice," he said. I'd heard the name—it was a pillar of the Charleston business community. "He specified that when the day came for the mansion to be transferred, this package was to be delivered." Alistair held it out to me.

I looked at the package in shock. "Me?"

Since we didn't know if the paper-wrapped object packed a psychic punch, Teag intervened and took it from Alistair. "Look at the address," Teag nudged.

In faded ink and spidery, old-fashioned lettering, the address read: *Trifles and Folly.*"

Holy shit. I looked up, and Alistair grinned. "That comes with being one of the oldest businesses in Charleston. I guess the shop's reputation has held for a long time."

Alistair didn't know the half of it because my business partner Sorren—an almost six-hundred-year-old vampire—had founded Trifles and Folly with one of my ancestors roughly three hundred and fifty years ago. Odds were good Sorren had known Gideon Sullivan personally or at least had crossed paths.

But why had Sullivan wanted to entrust something to the shop unless there was an occult connection? Alicia hadn't found malicious ghosts. Did this have something to do with the mansion's odd name and the wardings? There was more to this situation than we knew, and that made me nervous.

"Thank you," I said. "Just to be safe, I'd like to open that at the store where we can control the situation a little more." Meaning I wanted to have as many protections in place as possible before we tore off the paper and looked inside.

"I understand," Alistair replied. "But please—I'm dying to see what it is, and you know what they say—'pictures, or it didn't happen!'"

We promised him that we would take plenty of photos and keep him in the loop. I thanked him for showing us through the mansion, and Alicia repeated her impression that the ghosts seemed harmless, at least for now. Alistair said he'd be in touch, and we all headed home.

Once we had dropped off Alicia and thanked her again for her help, Teag turned to me. "What was your read on Sullivan?"

I've known Teag for a long time, and we've shared many late-night popcorn-wine-movie nights when his fiancé, Anthony, was out of town. Teag doesn't ask questions to hear himself talk. He had picked up on something and wanted to know if I'd noticed.

"All the things I told Alistair were true from the vibe I got. Sullivan seemed remarkably genuine and unpretentious. Whatever magic or supernatural threat had him worried enough for those wardings, once he was inside, he seemed happy and content." I gave Teag the side-eye as I drove, navigating my RAV4 through Charleston's barely-there traffic.

"How about the portrait 'joke'?"

I hadn't given it much thought at the time, trying to take in the whole room and "listening" with my psychometry for anything I might pick up from being near all those personal possessions. Now that I stopped to consider, trading huge oil portraits back and forth seemed rather elaborate for a prank—especially for two men who lived most of their lives on ships.

"You think Sullivan and Montero were more than friends?"

Teag rolled his eyes. "I don't think you even need gaydar to come to that conclusion. You've got two young, rich, good-looking men who didn't give a rat's ass for social convention. They chose to go to sea— an all-male setting notorious for defying norms and turning a blind eye on 'unconventional' relationships. They keep 'crossing paths' and saving each other. One of them gets injured, and the other mysteriously disappears?"

"That makes a lot of sense—more so than the official version," I replied. "But what they could get away with onboard or in far-away harbor towns wouldn't fly here in Charleston."

"Unless Sullivan became a recluse—and hid Montero in his sanctuary."

I had to admit Teag's scenario had a romantic, swashbuckling charm. He and Anthony had never needed to hide their relationship, even here in South Carolina, in part because Anthony's prominent family and wealth provided a degree of protection. Gideon and Ramon wouldn't have been truly safe even with their combined fortunes unless they took themselves out of the public eye.

"Let's open up the package and see what 'time capsule' Gideon's sent us," I replied, practically bouncing in my seat with excitement. "I can't wait to discover what was important enough to arrange for a special delivery two hundred years in the future."

CHAPTER THREE

THE TREMOR HIT AS WE WALKED INTO TRIFLES AND FOLLY, HARD
enough to rattle the dishes on display in the cabinets. It didn't last long,
but I saw from the expressions on Teag's and Maggie's faces that they
were as freaked out as I felt.

"Is everyone okay?" I asked. They nodded. A glance around the
store told me that nothing had fallen or broken—yet. If the quakes kept
getting stronger, we were in for trouble.

"Still up for opening the package?" Teag held up the mysterious
parcel Alistair had entrusted to us.

"Absolutely." Maybe when we figured this out, we'd solve the
tremor problem too.

"I'll handle the shop—but I want to know everything that
happens!" Maggie said when we gave her the quick recap about
Gideon and his mysterious package.

We headed to the break room. I set down a salt circle around the
table and then a smaller one on the tabletop, good for containing ghosts
and some kinds of dark magic. Then I added iron filings, plus a few
types of dried, protective plants, and sprinkled holy water. That
covered a lot of supernatural threats, but we didn't know what we were
dealing with here.

"Ready?" Teag asked. He retrieved more items from the office—a silver-coated metal net, protective scarves for both of us woven with Teag's magic, and a strip of his special cloth that would enable him to see what I saw when my psychometry gave me visions.

"Ready as I'll ever be. Do you have the sweet tea?" Reading an object can be draining—and dangerous. We've learned to have Southern sweet tea handy as well as snacks to help with the recovery—just in case.

"Already poured." Teag gestured toward two tall glasses on the counter that were sweating with condensation despite the air conditioning.

"Guess I'm out of excuses," I joked, although I knew Teag could hear the nervousness in my voice.

Teag brought out the package and laid it in the center of the circle. We sat next to each other, and I took a deep breath. Teag took one end of the strip of cloth, and I took the other in my left hand. Then I reached out with my right and let my palm hover just above the brown paper wrapping.

A tumult of emotions washed over me. Resignation and old grief—the dregs of a long life. Gideon Sullivan was dying. Beneath the sadness, I sensed the same satisfaction I'd felt at the mansion. Sullivan was ready to move on, and he was proud of the legacy he'd leave behind.

Thrumming beneath it all like a heartbeat was an echo of deep love and the yearning to remain together forever.

Teag had been right about Gideon and Ramon.

Now that I processed the strong feelings, I didn't sense any other magic or supernatural power. Just the need to tell his story—and sound a warning that a forgotten threat was ready to rise again.

"Wow." I came back to myself like waking up from a vivid dream and shook my head to clear it. Teag grabbed a glass of tea and pressed it into my hand. I drank it all in one gulp. I looked at him. "Did you see?"

"Yeah. Sounds like it's safe to unwrap. What was that part at the end about an old threat waking up?"

"No idea—but it sounds like something we need to know more about."

Teag carefully cut the string and gentled off the brittle brown wrapping paper. Inside was a thick journal with an embossed leather cover. He opened it to the first page. "I think this is Gideon's story," Teag said, peering closely at the careful, fluid script written in ink that had faded with the years.

"Those wardings at the mansion, the fortress-mausoleum, and now this. Do you think he and Montero encountered something supernatural?" I asked.

"Let's read it after dinner tonight and find out."

Teag's partner, Anthony, and my boyfriend Kell were both working late, so we had the whole evening free.

"I'd rather not open it up here," I said. "Not private enough." I had a hunch the book should be hidden, and I'd learned the hard way to trust my gut.

"Sounds like a plan," Teag agreed. "But right now, if you can spare me up front, I want to see if I can figure out who stole the djinn-bottle and where we can find the thief before he wishes us all into some crazy alternate universe."

I put the book in the safe, then went back to help with customers and give Maggie a break while Teag holed up on the computer. His magic lets him weave data into information, which makes him a hell of a hacker.

An hour later, after a sudden rush of shoppers headed out with their purchases, Teag called me. I found him glued to his computer screen.

"Take a look at this," he said as I drew up a chair.

I watched traffic cam footage that had been spliced together from several cameras, changing angles to reveal a spectacular five-car wreck. But when Teag had the loop repeat, I realized that the accident was all wrong.

The first car headed into one of the busiest intersections with another car following close behind. An SUV came barreling in from the right, way too fast to stop in time. Yet—miraculously—it veered at the last second to strike the second car, shoving it across a lane of traffic and tangling up several parked cars and other vehicles in its wake.

"That shouldn't have been possible," I murmured, watching as the loop started again.

"I know, right?" Teag agreed. "It's almost like someone made a desperate wish that got granted."

I stared at the smashed cars, screaming pedestrians, and mangled signage. "How many people got hurt?"

"People in the other cars and the driver of the SUV, as well as a few folks who were walking by at the wrong time," Teag reported. "Everyone's commenting on how 'lucky' that first car was. And—oddly enough, on how miraculous it was that the driver of the second car walked away without a scratch, although the car was totaled."

"It could just be luck."

He fixed me with a look. "The SUV shouldn't have moved like it did. It practically *hopped* to avoid that first car."

"Did you get license plates for the first two cars?" Since the first car wasn't part of the wreck, it had gone on its way as chaos exploded behind it. The SUV hit a minivan, and behind that was a sleek black sports car that looked familiar.

"Do you doubt me?" Teag teased with a grin as he handed over a page from a notepad with the numbers on it. "And yes, I ran the plates for the first several cars. The lucky one belongs to Donny Wilton. Thirty years old, multiple prior arrests for theft, spent two years in prison for burglary. He's had sticky fingers all his life. And it looks like he was part of a painting crew at a house on Clyde Kenner's street when the bottle was snatched."

"Let me guess—he quit right afterward?"

Teag nodded. "Yep. I called his employer and said I was Wilton's parole officer. The guy was happy to gripe to me about Wilton being a lousy employee. He told me everything he knew—which wasn't much. I got an address that matches what I got when I ran the plate."

"What about the car behind the one that got hit by the SUV?"

"That was a surprise. It belongs to Carter Etheridge," Teag said.

"Shit. He could have been tailing Wilton. Etheridge must have found out about the bottle somehow and decided to steal it from Wilton," I said.

Teag frowned, thinking. "Or…remember what Kenner said about there being a fancy car parked on his street that didn't belong? What if Etheridge knew about the bottle all along—and hired Wilton to steal it?"

I raised an eyebrow. "You think Wilton double-crossed Etheridge? That's a special kind of stupid."

"Only if you knew who—and what—Etheridge is," Teag replied. "Maybe the bottle convinced Wilton to do it and 'protected' him to get away."

I didn't like that scenario, but I had to admit that it made sense. "Only one way to find out. Want to go pay Wilton a visit?" Much as I didn't want to run out on Maggie again, we couldn't let Carter Etheridge and his witchy family get their hands on that spirit bottle.

"Yeah, the sooner, the better. And I don't think the bottle spirit is a djinn," Teag added. "Kenner said they picked up the bottle in Korea. It's more likely to be a Dokkaebi, which is a Korean goblin. That's probably a good thing, because Dokkaebi aren't said to be as powerful —or as crafty—as djinn."

"Before we go barging in, do you know how to trap the spirit if it gets loose?"

Teag grinned. "Dokkaebi have a bit of a drinking problem—and they like the juniper in gin. Legend says it tastes sweet to them and drugs them. I'm going to buy a bottle of gin—would you mind picking up a bottle basket from Mrs. Teller, please? I called her—she's expecting one of us to come for it, and she knows what it's for. I'll meet you back here, and then we can go looking for Wilton."

We explained what was going on to Maggie. There wasn't much of the day left, and we decided we'd just close early once Teag and I got back.

I headed for the City Market a few blocks away. The mostly open-air marketplace is a landmark and a big favorite with tourists. The mix of food, clothing, gifts, souvenirs, jewelry, art, soap, and more changes frequently, most of it created by local companies and artists.

At the entrance to each of the buildings, sweetgrass basket weavers showcased their wares and talked with passersby. All of them did beautiful work, but I was looking for one particular vendor who I knew would be in her usual spot. I called out a greeting to Mrs. Teller and her daughter, Niella.

"Cassidy! Lord, what have you and Teag gotten into now?"

Mrs. Ernestine Teller is one of the best sweetgrass weavers in South Carolina. Along with Niella, she's also one of the most revered Hoodoo root women in the Lowcountry. She's been Teag's mentor in Weaver magic for years.

"You know us," I replied. "Never a dull moment." She and Niella had helped us face down monsters before. I was hoping she could help us trap one now.

"Isn't that the truth! I wasn't surprised when Teag called—figured I'd be hearing from one of you any day," she replied. I must have looked at her oddly, because to my knowledge, visions aren't part of her gift.

"Oh, no child. Nothin' like that. My *other business* has been so busy, I'm fixin' to take a vacation when all this is over! Charms and protections are just about jumping off the shelves; people are so worried about the omens," Mrs. Teller went on. Niella kept a lookout, making sure no one interrupted our conversation or lingered to eavesdrop.

"People have noticed?"

Mrs. Teller gave me a narrowed look as if I'd just said the dumbest thing in the world. "Noticed? Sweet Jesus! They're beside themselves. If it's not the crows, it's those ghost bikes, or that wandering monk ghost, or a dozen other things that shouldn't be but are. They come to me already wearing a crucifix and saints' medallions, and they leave with gris-gris and mojo bags, Jack balls, and goofer dust. They are *scared*, and they should be—'cuz a storm is coming. I know you feel it."

"More than one storm, we think," I said in a low voice. "Teag said you had something for me?"

Mrs. Teller reached into the large woven straw bag at her feet and pulled out a woven sweetgrass sleeve to go over a fifth-sized bottle. "There's plenty of magic and protection woven into this." She handed it over, and I felt a tingle as soon as I touched it. "Still a good idea to mark up the bottle with sigils and have Teag wind some blessed woven threads through the wax you use to seal it."

She reached out for me and pressed a small bar of red wax into my other hand. "Use this. It's made from several different spell candles and a few other ingredients to help bind the spirit."

I slipped both into the shoulder tote I brought. "Thank you so much."

Mrs. Teller smiled warmly. "I put it on the store's tab. Tell Sorren he should stop by at the house sometime when he's awake."

I promised that I would, thanked her and Niella once more, and headed back toward Trifles and Folly.

Normally the walk between the City Market and the shop relaxes me. I love to see the hubbub of Charleston on a beautiful day, with locals and tourists filling the sidewalks, dining at umbrella-covered café tables, and chatting with friends over coffee. Today I felt jumpy, with all my senses on high alert.

"I need to talk to you." Carter Etheridge seemed to appear out of nowhere. He looked like he came from an upscale office, in dress slacks and a white shirt with the sleeves rolled up to the elbows. White-collar warlock. Whatever he wanted couldn't be good.

That's when I noticed that a couple of burly men now loitered at either end of the block, between me and the cross-streets.

"I have nothing to say to you." I moved to go around him. All-too-coincidentally, no one else was in this section of the block except for the bruisers at the intersections, something I suspected had to do with magic.

"I want Gideon Sullivan's grimoire."

He thought the book Alistair had given me was a grimoire? Interesting.

"Contact the estate's lawyers," I replied, annoyed as he shifted to block my path.

"I'm sure we can work something out," Etheridge said, with a smile that didn't reach his eyes and barely hid his teeth.

"We're done. Get out of my way." I suspected that Etheridge chose to waylay me in public because the wards and layers of protection around the shop wouldn't let him enter.

"I just want you to hear me out." He blocked my path once again. "All I want is the spell book. Give it to me, and I'll leave you alone."

I'd been primed for trouble all day and prepared accordingly. I gave my left hand a shake, where an old dog collar was looped around my wrist, jangling the tags. At the same time, I let the wooden wand tucked into the sleeve of my sweater drop into my right hand.

A dog's low, angry growl echoed from the brick-walled buildings around us. A ghostly Golden Retriever, my old dog Bo, manifested beside me, teeth bared and hackles raised.

"I said, get out of my way."

I gambled that Etheridge didn't want to have a magical shoot-out in broad daylight just off Market Square. Then again, he might. I didn't know his abilities—but he didn't know mine, either. His eyes flicked to the wand in my right hand, made from the handle of my grandmother's best spoon, filled with powerful emotional resonance to fuel my touch magic.

"We can work this out." He tried to sound accommodating and just managed insincere.

"I don't think so. Clear the path." I didn't think that a magical duel was of benefit to either of us, and I gambled that he didn't want to make more of a scene than we had already. I suspected that he'd put some kind of a minor spell on this stretch of the street that made passersby and drivers want to go around rather than come past us. We were in too busy of an area to have the sidewalk all to ourselves.

"Be reasonable," he said, in the tone of voice used by someone who is annoyed that it's not easier to take advantage.

I jangled Bo's dog tags, and he growled louder, teeth bared. From the way Etheridge eyed my spirit protector, I knew he could see the ghost.

"The teeth feel solid," I assured him. "Now let me pass."

"This isn't over," Etheridge muttered, although he got out of my way.

"It is for today." I gave him a wide berth, alert for tricks, keeping Bo's ghost between us and my wand in hand. The goons at the intersection eyed Bo warily and let me pass. I didn't turn my back until I reached the busy sidewalk on King Street. Bo vanished right before I stepped out of the side street, and the wand was easy enough to tuck back up my sleeve, easy to hide when most of the crowd is either snapping photos or talking on their phones.

"What's wrong?" Teag asked as soon as I walked back into the store. I saw that he and Maggie had already started to close up.

"Carter Etheridge demanded that I give him Gideon Sullivan's 'grimoire.'" I was still angry. "We had a little stand-off until Bo persuaded him to move."

"Who does that arrogant son of a bitch think he is?" Maggie demanded.

"Heir to one of the most powerful witch-families in Charleston, I imagine," Teag observed. "I've heard what Beck has to say about the Etheridges, and they're worse than the Pendlewoods."

"Yeah, well. He's not getting the book," I muttered.

"I hope Bo took a bite out of his butt," Maggie said.

That made me chuckle. "Bo was totally willing. You know what they say about dogs sensing bad people."

"Interesting that he assumes it's a grimoire," Teag mused. "What does he know that we don't?'"

"No idea—which scares me." I told them what Mrs. Teller said and her comment about a coming storm. "I really don't like the sound of that."

"Maybe Etheridge knows—or thinks he knows—about the storm, and he's trying to gain an advantage," Teag suggested. "That might explain his interest in the Dokkaebi."

"I doubt he'd tell us if we asked," I said in a dry tone. "So we're going to have to figure it out the hard way."

We closed up for the evening and walked Maggie to her car. I left Gideon's book in the safe at the shop, figuring Teag and I would stop back for it. Even though my car was warded, the store's protections are stronger, and now that I knew the Etheridges wanted the book, I wasn't about to leave it unprotected.

We took Teag's Volvo to the address he'd found for Wilton. His old Volvo wagon had been a victim of a vindictive witch. He'd replaced it with a well-used S80—much to Anthony's dismay, who'd wanted to buy him a new car. Understanding both sides of the argument, I chose to stay out of it. I brought the woven bottle sleeve, and Teag had a brand new fifth of gin. We'd wait to mark sigils on the bottle until the spirit was inside to keep from scaring it away.

"Maybe he did steal it just for the booze," Teag said when we pulled up near Wilton's apartment. "Looks pretty sketchy to me."

"We're not exactly unarmed." Neither of us needed to carry a gun to protect ourselves. I'd learned how to channel my touch magic defensively, and Teag used to do competitive mixed martial arts. He's got plenty of other tricks with his Weaver magic, and he's good with knives.

"Good point," he conceded.

Still, it didn't pay to be reckless. We scoped out what we could see around us and were ready for trouble when we got out of the car.

The stairwell smelled like piss and weed. I had my wand in hand, and Teag had a variety of unconventional protections ready to use with a second's notice. Four doors opened into the hallway at the top of the steps. The paint had a gray cast, or maybe that was due to one of the overhead fluorescent lights being at half-wattage. The odors of bacon grease and cooked cabbage filled the small space. It didn't look like anyone had bothered to mop the worn vinyl flooring in a long time.

We knocked at the door to Wilton's apartment.

No one answered.

None of his neighbors peeked into the hallway either. Teag made short work of the lock, and we stepped inside warily.

"Someone's been here—but I don't think it was Wilton," I noted. The place had been tossed—furniture overturned and cushions ripped apart. Wilton's bed was off its frame as if someone had searched beneath the mattress, and the empty dresser drawers had been thrown onto the floor.

"Wilton was already gone," Teag said. "There's no clothing, no electronics, few personal items. He was out of here before someone came looking."

"Whoever did this had magic," I said quietly. "Strong enough power that I can sense the residual energy. It feels…slimy, rotten. Whoever was searching for Wilton wasn't here to help him."

"Etheridge?"

"That would be my guess." The bad feelings settled heavily in my stomach like curdled milk.

The studio apartment left only the bathroom as a possible hiding place, and a quick check showed it was empty—and disgusting.

"Maybe Wilton figured his luck turned, and he could do better," I said.

"Or maybe he's got other reasons to run that have nothing to do with the spirit bottle," Teag replied. "Like double-crossing the witch who hired him." He stepped toward the galley kitchen and froze when something crunched under his feet.

I stayed close to the door in case any of the neighbors decided to get nosy. Teag moved around to the other side of the counter and swore under his breath.

"Shit. He drank it."

Teag bent down and then held up a broken bottle that matched the picture, still marked up with sigils. Only unlike in the photo, the wax seal at the top had been scraped off, and the cap was gone.

"Can one of those Dokkaebi's possess a person if he swallows their gin?"

Teag looked flummoxed. "I have no idea. Nothing in the lore mentioned *drinking* one."

We checked the small space, hoping to find a clue to where Wilton had gone, but all that turned up were overdue utility notices, spoiled milk in the fridge, and an overflowing trash bin that was going to stink real soon without a tenant to take care of it.

Not our problem. We had a goblin to stop.

Teag braved a glance at the garbage. Using a latex glove from the stash in his pocket, he gingerly fished out a couple of official-looking letters. "Eviction notices," he said. "Behind on his rent, and complaints about noise and that the place 'reeks of pot.'" He tossed the letters back into the bin.

"Could be another reason why he's gone. Maybe he doesn't realize he's got a lucky genie."

"Or maybe, despite what the old man told you, the spirit doesn't grant every wish. If it's malicious, maybe it only listens if there's a way it can screw you over by giving you what you think you want," Teag said.

"Cheery, aren't you?" I muttered. Then I got an idea. "I'm going to touch the doorknob and see if I can pick anything up from his emotions when he left."

"Good thing I've got hand sanitizer in the car," Teag snarked.

"Cover me." I grabbed the knob.

The images jerked and stuttered, making me wonder if Wilton was using. Everything looked just a bit unfocused, which supported my guess that he was buzzed or high. I pushed with my magic, looking for answers. Wilton was worried, running from something. I didn't pick up anything supernatural in the sensations, like a tag-along ghost or goblin. He was preoccupied, twitchy, and scared, and in the background was a small bungalow-style house, white with purple shutters.

Before I could think much about the house, the images came again, and I knew right away they were from a different person. Fury washed over me, along with the desire to punish someone who had defied an order, broken a deal. These impressions had none of Wilton's fear. Instead, cold relentlessness mingled with the certainty of power and privilege.

I came back to myself with a gasp, and Teag was right beside me with a hand on my shoulder to steady me.

"Get something useful?"

I dug into my bag for a bottle of water and took a few gulps. "I think so. Part of it was Wilton—and I'm sure the other part was

Etheridge. Let's get out of here. I'll tell you on the way back to the shop."

We locked the door behind us, careful to wipe down anywhere we might have left behind fingerprints, and cautiously made our way back to Teag's car.

"Wilton's scared," I told him, pausing to take another drink. "I'm positive now that Etheridge hired him to steal the bottle, and Wilton took off with it—but I couldn't tell whether that was his idea or the Dokkaebi's. I'm also pretty sure he's on something, aside from drinking the genie-gin. I wonder if he was with it enough to even realize that it was unusual for him to have not been hit by that SUV."

Teag glanced at me, surprised. "Shit. That might explain why he isn't wishing for the moon. He might not have made the connection between his wishes and what happens."

"Which means he's about as dangerous as a nuclear bomb walking around primed and ready to blow." All he needed to do was make the wrong kind of wish.

"You said you got images from Etheridge too?"

I nodded. "It must have been the residual of his magic I picked up —which was effin' creepy. It felt...polluted. Etheridge is furious that Wilton ran, and he's looking forward to making him pay." A shiver ran through me at the ruthlessness I sensed, the cold focus on getting what he wanted.

"I'll get Seth to help me do some hacking and see if Ben can use his private eye skills to turn up anything, now that we at least have a photo, a license, and an address. We'll find him," Teag assured me. The friends he mentioned were just as skilled as Teag in accessing hidden and protected information. I knew they could find almost anything.

The question was—could they find Wilton fast enough to keep him and the Dokkaebi away from Etheridge and from wishing away reality as we knew it?

CHAPTER FOUR

TEAG AND I KNEW THAT WE COULDN'T DO JUSTICE TO GIDEON'S memoir during the workday, even without our extra trip to try to find Wilton. I already felt guilty about having Maggie cover for us so often, so meeting up that evening after all the excitement of the afternoon was—hopefully—over—seemed like the perfect solution.

We stopped by the store to get the book from the safe. The wardings at my house were just as strong as those around the shop, and we could be more comfortable digging into the book's details.

Knowing Etheridge was out there, we didn't take chances. I had my wand and the walking stick that had once belonged to Sorren's maker. Both let me channel my touch magic into a defense—one as a blast of force and the other as a stream of fire. Teag had his martial arts knives as well as a curled metal whip that gave him more range. I put the book into a cross-body messenger bag and grabbed a sweatshirt from the hook on the wall, pulling it on over the bag and zipping it shut.

If anyone tried to take the book, they'd have to fight for it.

"Ready?" Teag asked.

I nodded. "Ready as I'm going to get."

We had parked right in front of the store. The wardings on the building extended a few inches beyond the shop's front windows but not all the way across the sidewalk. According to Rowan, it was more difficult to put a permanent warding on public land than on property owned by an individual.

All we had to do was make it three feet to the car. Usually, I wouldn't think twice—Charleston's crime rate is pretty low. But now that we knew we had a powerful witch out to grab Gideon's book, three feet felt like a sprint across the DMZ.

Teag used his key fob to unlock the Volvo and moved to stand between me and the sidewalk, covering me as I locked up. Despite the streetlights, the area in front of the store seemed darker than usual. Intuition told me bad things were coming.

A low growl drew my attention as I stepped forward to stand beside Teag. The shadows shifted around the car, but the motion was all wrong—certainly nothing human. What I could make out in the dim light had arms and legs that were too long and jointed backward.

Sharp nails scratched against concrete. The creature unfolded, standing up to its full height, and now we could see it in the street-light's glow.

The body might have once been human, but now it was unnaturally elongated, changed into something monstrous. The creature looked as if the skin had been stripped from its body, revealing sinew and muscle like a moving anatomical figure. It threw back its head and howled, revealing a maw of razor-sharp teeth.

"Rawhead," Teag murmured. "Bloody Bones." I recognized both names from the lore but never thought I'd see one.

I shook the dog collar on my left wrist, and Bo's ghost appeared. Bo's hackles raised, and he lowered his head. He took one look at the Rawhead and growled protectively.

That drew the Rawhead's attention, and it fixed its lidless eyes on Teag and me, then opened its maw again, exposing sharp, pointed teeth.

"If we can draw him away from your car, I can blast him without torching your Volvo."

Teag took a half-step forward, and the Rawhead shifted to track him. "Let me see what I can do."

I drew Alard's walking stick and waited for my chance.

The *zip-zing* of Teag's metal whip cut through the silence, and the Rawhead shrieked in pain as the sharp edges cut into its exposed muscle. Teag moved another half step to the left, and the monster mirrored him, gradually putting more distance between itself and the car.

I glanced around, certain that we weren't alone. Etheridge seemed the type to send a monster to do his dirty work and then stand back and watch the show. I couldn't see him, but intuition told me he was out there somewhere.

Bo seemed to sense what we were doing, because he lunged at the Rawhead, coming at the creature from the side closest to the car, forcing it farther away.

That created the opening I needed. I focused my touch magic on the old walking stick, calling up the resonance of memories—mine and Alard's—and drawing on them for power. I felt the magic rise up from deep inside, then surge through my arm, hand, and finally into the walking stick. A torrent of fire burst from the tip, streaking across the space between me and the Rawhead and enveloping the creature in flames.

The Rawhead screamed, and the smell of burned meat filled the air. Teag snapped his metal whip again and again as Bo's ghost dodged back and forth, trapping the monster in the fire.

Finally, the Rawhead collapsed into a pile of ash. The fight had been fast, and I expected the cops to show up at any moment. Bo returned to my side, tail wagging, grinning like only a Golden Retriever can.

"Good boy," I murmured as he vanished.

"Come on," Teag said, jerking the driver's door open. I didn't bother going around and climbed over the console to the other side, with Teag crowding in behind me. He was barely seated before we were moving. Neither of us wanted to stick around to see if Etheridge had other tricks handy.

In the distance, I heard sirens. Teag automatically altered his course to take a less direct route to my house in case anyone had spotted us.

"What do you think they'll make of the ashes?" I asked, now that my heart had stopped hammering.

"Illegal trash fire? There'll be fewer questions than if we left a monster body behind, that's for sure." Teag had a white-knuckled grip on the wheel, and I could tell from his tone that he was shaken.

"We're safe," I said, needing to reassure both of us. "Etheridge must want Gideon's book pretty badly to come after us on a public street." Even though the shops around us were closed, anyone could have driven past. Then again, I wondered if he had used a distraction spell like when he'd cleared the street and sidewalk for our last "conversation."

"Sorren's not going to take it well," Teag replied.

"Of course, we can't prove it was Etheridge," I pointed out. "I'm pretty damn sure he's behind it, but we didn't actually see him. Rawheads don't make a habit of wandering around downtown, but there's no *proof* that Etheridge arranged it."

Teag swore under his breath. "So he'll get away with it."

"Maybe. Maybe not." My call to Sorren went straight to voicemail, so I left a detailed message and figured he'd get back to me as soon as he could.

Teag and I were both antsy when we parked at the curb outside my house. We looked both ways and didn't see anything, but another Rawhead could have hidden itself in the shadows.

"We'll make a run for it," Teag said, getting his weapons ready.

I nodded. "Together."

We both got out on the passenger side and ran for the door. Teag covered me while I unlocked it, and we crowded through into the walled garden. He used his key fob to lock the car from a distance. Everything inside the walls was protected by the same kind of wardings we had at the shop, so I didn't think any Rawheads could be lying in wait.

That didn't mean I was willing to take a chance. We hurried up the steps onto the porch, and I got the house door open, then both of us breathed sighs of relief when we were safely inside. Baxter, my little

Maltese, danced around our feet, glad to see us. I scooped him into my arms for a hug before setting him back down to run to Teag.

"Do you think he can summon another Rawhead?" I asked.

Teag shrugged. "No idea. I don't know how hard it was or how much power it took. But if he could have, I'd think there would have been one waiting here. So maybe we're okay for now."

I had to consciously relax my jaw and shoulders, then my stomach rumbled. "If we're not in mortal danger, maybe we should make dinner."

Teag managed a grin. "I'm in favor of that. Monsters can wait."

We headed for the kitchen and washed up. "How are the wedding plans going?" I asked Teag as we moved around each other in my kitchen. We've cooked enough meals together that he knew where everything was. Tonight we were making spaghetti with meatballs, garlic bread, and a bagged salad because that was easy, and we wanted to get to reading Gideon's book as quickly as possible. Baxter sat off to one side, waiting for anything to fall on the floor like a furry little Roomba.

"Nerve-wracking," Teag replied. "I keep hinting about running off to Vegas. I want to *be* married to Anthony, but the process of *getting* married is going to make me crazy."

I chuckled. "Family complications?" I couldn't imagine Anthony Benton quibbling over the menu or decorations, although his South-of-Broad family might.

Teag sighed. "Sort of. The Bentons have all gotten married at St. Philips Church for a couple of hundred years. His family has been longtime, major donors. But he and I can't get married there. They're one of the churches that split from their denomination over marriage equality."

He grimaced. "So we agreed that we'd like to be married at Father Anne's church for many reasons—including that we'd be welcome."

"What's the issue with his family? If the church won't allow you to be married there, it's out of your hands." I watched the pasta to make sure it didn't boil over.

"You'd think it would be simple, but it isn't. We could get married somewhere totally modern and secular, like a hotel ballroom or a park. Maybe the courthouse or a justice of the peace. Or do a destination wedding and just go somewhere else entirely. We both nixed the idea of a historic location because it's Charleston, and they're all...problematic." Teag looked far more distracted than I had expected.

I hadn't realized the wedding hit a snag, or I wouldn't have brought it up. Teag and I had been through a lot together, and we often confided in each other. Since he hadn't mentioned the issue before, either it had just happened, or it weighed so heavily that he hadn't been sure how to discuss it.

Charleston was a beautiful city built on rivers of blood. Its wealth came at the expense of generations of enslaved people. I understood Teag and Anthony's aversion to using any place tainted by that history as a backdrop for a wedding, but that ruled out most of the likely venues.

"Anthony's parents are being very good about not turning this into a huge social event," Teag went on. "They agreed early on that we could do a small wedding for immediate family and friends, and then they could throw the reception of the century if they wanted and invite all their business and social connections."

"Then what's the problem?" I asked. Something had him upset, which was strange because I'd seen Teag face down vengeful ghosts and vicious werewolves with aplomb.

"It's a big deal for a Benton wedding not to be at St. Philips. It's a bigger deal for the Bentons to pull their endowment over it."

"Holy shit!"

He nodded. Endowments weren't part of Teag's and my background, but they were serious commitments for Anthony's family. The Bentons had deep Charleston roots, both socially and on account of Benton Connor Hawthorn, the family law firm which had been settling messy issues for more than one hundred and fifty years.

"We didn't ask them to do it," Teag hastened to add. "But Anthony's parents said that if their son wasn't welcome because of who he loved, then they, their membership, and their money would go elsewhere."

"That's great of his parents to back him up like that, but how come I haven't seen it splashed all over the *Post and Courier*?" Charleston's newspaper still had a "Social" page, and the Bentons often showed up in photos of business events and charity galas.

"They haven't announced it yet, because we hadn't set a date. But now that we have…"

"The shit is going to hit the fan."

Teag nodded. "Yeah. And that sucks because we just want to get married. This guarantees there'll be a media circus."

Anthony's folks were good people, and I respected their stance about St. Philips. But my heart went out to Teag and Anthony, who were caught in a situation that they couldn't avoid and couldn't control. Unfortunately for them, eloping was out of the question.

"Hey, if you need me to smuggle you two out in my RAV4, you know how to find me," I joked.

"I wish." Teag rolled his eyes, but I'd made him smile, which was what mattered.

I heard a yip and looked down at Baxter, who bounced around my feet like a caffeinated bunny, trying to convince me to feed him dinner early.

"Not time yet," I said and bent down to pick him up so we could see eye-to-eye. Baxter was a total badass, with the heart of a warrior in the body of a guinea pig.

"The garlic bread is ready, so at the risk of you accusing me of being on Bax's side…" Teag teased.

"Bax paid you off, didn't he?" I looked at Baxter, but his little black eyes just blinked back at me, the picture of innocence. Yeah, right.

"Totally," Teag admitted. "You've caught me. I'm on the take to your dog."

"Well, he is cute," I joked. "He has a way with people."

Teag plated the food while I fed Baxter, and my stomach growled. "I hope all that tastes as good as it smells because I'm starved."

We sat at the table and kept the conversation light. Nothing about magic, sea captains, or weddings. It felt good to take a breath before we dove into Gideon's life story.

Once we ate and cleaned up, we poured some Malbec and headed into the living room. "Anything from Sorren yet?" Teag asked. I checked my phone.

"Since he didn't pick up, I figure he and Donnelly are dealing with something big, and he'll get back to me when he can." I shrugged. Yes, my vampire business partner uses a cell phone, computer, and the internet. Sorren is quick to point out that immortals who can't adapt as times change don't stick around long.

"Just curious to see what he makes of Etheridge's involvement," Teag replied. "What about dead Dante?"

I rolled my eyes. "That's not really his name, you know."

"He's your ghostly ancestor. And he was a privateer too, right? Revolutionary War era or just before? Maybe he ran across Sullivan—or Montero."

"I imagine Simon will hear from Dante if there's a connection," I answered. Simon was my cousin, a gifted psychic medium who lived in Myrtle Beach with his partner, Vic. Simon had channeled Dante's ghost on more than one occasion.

I carried our wine glasses, and Teag brought the bottle. We were ready for adventure, and I couldn't wait to find out where Gideon's memories were going to take us. Baxter followed us and stood on his hind legs at the edge of the couch, begging to be picked up. He settled in happily between Teag and me, and I picked up Gideon's book.

"Read me a story," he said with a grin.

I stared at the old book, still scarcely believing that it had been bequeathed, all those years ago, to my shop. Leaving it to the museum, I could understand. But to Trifles and Folly? That had to be because Gideon knew that something supernatural from his sea days remained dangerous, and he trusted us to stop it.

The book was heavy in my hands, not just from its size, but from the weight of the emotions I could sense bound up with the paper and leather. Too many feelings to name, bright and dark, and everything in between. I wondered if just touching the book would trigger another vision. It hadn't—for now. I didn't think that luck would hold.

Night had fallen while we were eating dinner. A knock came at the door—the one on the porch, not the sidewalk entrance. Very few people are permitted past the wardings. Baxter ran to the foyer, yipping like a wild thing, then suddenly sat and went quiet with a happy little smile and an adorable head tilt.

Vampire glamour has an amazing effect on dogs.

I opened the door, and Sorren stepped inside. He looks like he's in his late twenties, but he's closer to six centuries. His blond hair had a fresh cut in a trendy style that drew attention to his gray eyes, the color of a storm at sea. He looked utterly normal in a burgundy T-shirt and jeans; before he was turned he'd been the best jewel thief in Antwerp. Sorren glanced around and greeted Teag with a nod, then looked us both over, clearly triaging for injuries.

"You're all right?"

I could hear the worry in his voice. "We destroyed the Rawhead. But I can't believe it turned up by accident. And we know Etheridge is chasing Donny Wilton, the guy who stole the Dokkaebi bottle," I said. "I guess you can't just…rough him up a little?"

Sorren gave a wry smile. "Unfortunately, not without bringing a witch war down on our heads. That's drama we definitely don't need. But I can apply…pressure…elsewhere."

"Somewhere painful?" Teag asked with a dark, hopeful expression.

"In a manner of speaking," Sorren replied, clearly amused. "Etheridge has enemies within his family, and there are others among the covens of Charleston that would like to see his dynasty come to an end. I can offer them resources to complicate his life and distract him. Perhaps without time on his hands, he will have less time for mischief."

"That would be good," I said. "He's becoming a real pain in the ass."

"I wish I could just make him go away," Sorren said. "But even I am not powerful enough to stand against all the covens of Charleston if they turned against me, and we need their help for the Alliance to do its work. But I will do everything I can to keep you safe from him, and if it comes to it—I'll handle Carter Etheridge myself."

"Any idea why he's so hot for that spirit bottle?" I asked.

Sorren grimaced. "Mostly rumors. There's word on the street that although Carter inherited the leadership role in the family, his magic may not be as strong as others who are farther down the pecking order. That would make him vulnerable to a challenge—unless he could gain or steal more power."

"From the Dokkaebi or Gideon's 'grimoire,'" I supplied. "As motivation goes, that makes sense."

Sorren smiled. "Enough about the Etheridges. I'm curious about Gideon Sullivan's book. Am I too late for the reading?"

"You're right on time. Is Donnelly with you?"

Sorren shook his head. "Archibald stayed up north to wrap up some loose ends. He'll be here in a few days. We'll have to go back to New York—there's a hell of a mess to work through—but given what's going on here, I needed to be in Charleston."

His concern warmed my heart and loosened some of the tension in my shoulders. Sorren had promised us his protection when we agreed to work with the Alliance. Although I knew he had stores and teams all over the world, he had never failed to keep his word. I believed that he viewed us all as family and did his very best to keep us as safe as possible.

"We're glad you're here," I replied. "Come, have a seat. We won't get through the book in one sitting, but I'm itching to get started."

Sorren sat in one of the wing chairs, and Baxter settled happily at his feet.

Comfortably ensconced in my corner of the sofa, I started to read aloud from Gideon Sullivan's memoir. "I am Gideon Sullivan, second son of Josiah and Marianne Sullivan, brother of Joshua. Captain of the *Resilient*. Builder of Custos Sanctum. Married to Annabelle Tanner until her death in 1787. Father to Edward. And husband to Ramon Montero, captain of the *Hidalgo*, by matelotage, in the year of our Lord 1790.

"I leave this record so that when we are gone, an understanding will remain of what we did to stop the darkness, how we came to choose that path, and why we must convey this burden to a successor so that all we did and the price we paid is not in vain.

"My family made its wealth shipping goods from the Caribbean and Bermuda to the port of Charleston. Joshua was destined to inherit the family business. I was destined for the sea—not just by vocation, but because of the energy that sang in my blood, in tune with the waves and the swells. I knew the sea like a master from the first I laid eyes on it, could tell its currents and storms through an uncanny bond. I know not the source of that bond, but something so fierce and wild I cannot call evil.

"I took command of the *Resilient* in 1782, at the age of thirty-one, after having already spent more than half of my life aboard ships. She was a brigantine, fast in the wind and sure in a storm. She remained under my command until we both were too broken to remain at sea."

I looked up to find Teag staring at the book with rapt attention. Sorren had a look of concentration, and I wondered what memories the reading stirred.

"Did you know Gideon Sullivan?" I asked Sorren. "Did Dante?" Dante was my long-ago privateer ancestor, and he had worked closely with Sorren not long after the American Revolution.

Sorren roused from his thoughts and shook his head. "I knew of him—heard of the family, certainly. I didn't know him personally, but I don't recall him spending much time in Charleston."

"What about Montero?" Teag asked. "Did he and Dante get along?"

"I don't recall ever having heard that they didn't," Sorren replied. "If Montero and Sullivan didn't serve the Pendlewoods or the Etheridges, then Dante wouldn't have had a quarrel with them. But it's worth asking Simon to have a chat with Dante's ghost. Maybe Dante will remember something important."

"I'm surprised at Gideon's candor," I said. "He just lays it all out, doesn't he?"

Teag nodded. "My hunch about Montero was right. Once they left the sea and the Caribbean ports that didn't police social conventions, the only way they could have been together was in seclusion."

Even Sullivan's wealth and position might not have saved them from consequences had their relationship become known. Charleston, in his day, turned a blind eye to the horrors of slavery but would have been outraged over two men in love.

"What's matelotage?" I'd gained a fairly unusual vocabulary working with antiques, but that word stumped me.

"Think of it as a pirate civil union," Teag answered. "Actually fairly common. It was an agreement between two sailors that the survivor would inherit the dead partner's possessions. I've seen historians quibble over whether all of the pairings were romantic, but many definitely were."

"Such things were not as rare as certain people would have you believe," Sorren said. "That becomes clear when you've lived for a few centuries. Some historians left out those details to protect vulnerable individuals, while others either could not see things as they were, or chose to erase them from memory."

"Now I want to know how Sullivan and Montero got together," I said. "There has to be a good story there."

"Guess we'll just have to read the rest of the book," Teag said with a grin.

"Sullivan had magic," I pointed out.

"Maremancy," Teag replied. "Sea magic."

"Like Dante," Sorren added. "He was also a water witch."

"Handy in a family that owns merchant ships," I noted.

Teag raised an eyebrow. "Gideon probably wasn't the only one in the family with that ability, but he might have been unusual in admitting it to himself. Being a witch didn't go over well in polite society either."

"I want to know what he meant about needing to 'stop the darkness' and passing the 'burden' on to a successor." I paused to sip my wine and tuck my legs crisscross beneath me. "I'm going to skip around a bit because it looks like he goes into details about the ship or some of their voyages that might be important for history's sake but aren't what we need right now."

"Plenty of time to go back and study it later. Let's go for a good story for the first pass," Teag agreed.

I propped the book on a pillow in my lap and began to read again.

"I had been married for seven years when I became captain of the *Resilient,* which required even more time away from home than before. Annabelle and I had an arranged marriage, brokered by ambitious parents on both sides. She was a kind soul and an excellent mother, and she bore one son who lived—Edward. We were compatible and happier than many couples, I suppose.

"Yet when the chance to command a ship of my own arose, I went without a second thought. Annabelle could not join me, even had custom and motherhood allowed it, since the movement of a ship at sea made her violently ill. And I was never more alive than when the wind billowed the sails and the prow sliced into the waves.

"The longer I sailed, the more the sea spoke to me. My bond became stronger. I could not call a storm or banish one—such power belongs only to the Almighty—but I could and did reckon the course of a storm unerringly to sail around it. More than once, I willed the waves to let us pass so that while we were storm-tossed, we were not swamped or overturned. If my crew noticed anything unusual, they did not speak of it for me to hear.

"They are seasoned men, all of them, and know the danger of the unfettered sea. Every one of them wears charms and has rituals and superstitions to protect them, in addition to prayer. What am I but one more amulet, someone who is 'lucky' with the ocean? I make no spectacle of calling upon my bond, just the silent imposition of my will. They accept me, and I am as good a captain as I know to be, feeling them to be more my family—God help me—than my flesh and blood.

"Even so, the sea offers perils aplenty. Wild winds and sudden storms, treacherous shoals, and always the threat of pirates. We had cannons aboard and knew how to use them, and that together with my bond afforded us some protection. Yet I feared what might happen if we were to encounter more pirate vessels than we could handle on our own. Nightmares plagued me of such a battle, in which the *Resilient* sank into the depths, taking the crew and me with it.

"Nor am I the only one with a strange connection. More than once on the Bermuda run, we have spotted a square-rigged ship glowing blue upon the horizon. Not a trick of the moon; of that I am certain. I knew in my heart when I saw the ship that unholy magic shielded it. So close to Bermuda, I am certain it belongs to the Pendlewoods, a family known for dark power and darker deeds. We steered a course clear of it, minding our business, and went on our way, but I can't help but wonder what made the ship thus, and why."

"Can't say I'm surprised the Pendlewoods showed up," Teag commented, finishing the last of his wine. He refilled my glass and his own. "Wonder if Beck knows anything he can add to the story?"

Beckford Pendlewood was the rightful heir to his family's fortune, but he had renounced the power he inherited and refused to be bound to a demon to perpetuate their wealth. Doing so had averted a catastrophe that might have leveled the Eastern Seaboard, but it made Beck a target for retaliation among his relatives and their many enemies.

Which was why Beck and his boyfriend Logan were now under the protection of the St. Expeditus Society, in what Teag referred to as the "supernatural witness protection program." In exchange for safety, Beck had become an asset, willingly using his knowledge about the occult to help us fight those dangerous paranormal threats.

"Worth a shot to ask," I replied. "Since he's on the outs with his family, it's not like he can call and ask someone, but maybe there's something in the files we scavenged from his cousins' offices."

"The Pendlewoods and the Etheridges ran very powerful shipping empires back in the day," Sorren said. "If you had seen the kinds of things both families were willing to do for occult power and riches, you'd understand how remarkable Beckford is for turning away from his legacy." He looked to me. "Please go on with the reading. I think we'll find clues to the cause of the omens in the memoir. I don't think it's a coincidence that the book comes to us at exactly the same moment that the harbingers appear."

Curled up on my couch with a glass of wine, it would be easy to forget that Gideon's book was history and not exciting fiction. Only someone as twisted as Etheridge would assume it was a spell book. I took another sip and picked up the volume once more.

"We have all heard rumors about the Pendlewood witches. Some tales, no doubt, have grown with the telling, but on the whole, I believe the stories. A vivid dream warned me away from having dealings with them, though they pay well for carrying cargo. Not well enough to lose my life, as has befallen a number of ships that agreed to their terms.

"Those ships did not fall prey to the normal dangers of the sea, though they are many. Witnesses claimed to see the Pendlewood cargo ships struck by blue lightning, or torn asunder by fearsome beasts from the depths, or sucked down into maelstroms that opened just for them and closed as quickly. I fear that the witnesses speak the truth, and I have no desire to visit danger on my crew and damnation on my soul for transporting their accursed relics.

"I do not fear magic itself; I am neither superstitious nor religious. But as with any power, I fear how men of ill intent may wield it, and I pray that I resist temptation to use what little ability I have for harm."

"Guess he wasn't a fan of Beck's family," Teag snarked.

"Beck isn't even a fan of his family. Kinda how he ended up in hiding, remember?" I replied. "But now I *have* to call and see if he ever heard stories about Gideon. If Beck was able to retrieve anything from the family homes, maybe there's something about ancestors of his who were Gideon's contemporaries."

"You think there's a connection between the Pendlewoods and this 'darkness' Gideon mentioned?" Teag set his glass aside and leaned forward like a kid eager to hear another chapter.

"It's possible. That glowing ship on the horizon didn't sound like a good thing," I said. "Gideon doesn't seem like a guy who scared easily, even about supernatural stuff. Which worries me about his warning."

"I remain most concerned about the 'darkness' he mentions," Sorren said. "With the strange omens and odd weather brewing, I fear it might be the 'storm' you mentioned in your text, the one Mrs. Teller warned you about."

Teag checked the time. "How about reading a little more before I need to go meet Anthony?" He grinned. "And it's not fair to read ahead without us."

"How about tomorrow night I make a big pot of Frogmore stew, everyone can bring potluck side dishes, and we get you and Anthony, Maggie, Sorren, and Kell together so we can all hear the story?" I suggested. "We might even get Simon, Beck, Travis Dominick, and some other folks on a video call." We would probably be going over Gideon's book again and again, looking for important tidbits we overlooked.

"Sounds good," Teag agreed. "I'll make cornbread and bring bourbon."

Maggie usually opted for dessert, and Kell would bring munchies and wine. We did these kind of gatherings often enough that everyone knew what to do.

"No need to set a plate for me, but I'll bring wine," Sorren said with a wry smile. He didn't need to kill to feed, choosing criminals and troublemakers for his meals. They found themselves unusually tired and with a few hours lost from their memories when they woke, and Sorren got the nourishment he needed to survive. In a pinch, he could live off the blood of livestock, but I got the feeling it was a poor substitute.

"All right," I said, glancing down at the book once more. I frowned and flipped a few pages from where we left off. "Some of this looks like details about his cargo runs—which might be useful later." I found a good starting point and started to read.

"One of the blessings and curses of being aboard ship is that the outside world fades away. We can be gone weeks or months depending upon our commitments, and only the gossip in portside taverns tells us what's going on elsewhere.

"We heard talk of another Yellow Fever plague in Charleston when we came into port in Havana, and my heart froze, worried about Annabelle and Edward. How wonderful it would be if we could talk across great distances as if we were in the same room—but that is a fantasy. Carrier pigeons cannot find ships at sea and neither can letters.

I was desperate for news but could only learn generalities which made my fears worse, not better.

"My heart sank when we reached Freeport, and I found a letter waiting for me at the inn where it has long been my custom to stay when ashore. Of course I had left an itinerary with Annabelle of our commitments and the ports we would be sailing between, but too many variables made it impossible to predict exact dates of arrival. I suspect a duplicate letter was sent to Hamilton, Port-au-Prince, and our other destinations.

"I found a private place to read the letter, fearing the worst. The letter was from Annabelle's father, telling me that this recent scourge of fever had claimed her life. Edward, thank God, survived. He has gone to live with his grandparents in Boston, who assure me they will enroll him in the best boarding school and see to his education. They are well-to-do, and I know Edward will want for nothing, but I regret that I cannot be with him to navigate this great loss and sorrow.

"I immediately penned letters to both Edward and Annabelle's father expressing my grief, my thanks that Edward will be well taken care of, and my condolences. These I sent by packet ship, with the hope they would arrive as quickly as possible.

"Edward is a fine, smart boy, and we had talked of sending him north to school in another year, so I tell myself he will thrive. Still, I cannot help but feel guilty for not having been present, although perhaps I might also have succumbed. Charleston is a seafaring town, as is Boston, and those who marry sailors are well-warned about the realities, but those cautions matter little in the face of deep loss.

"I wrote one more letter, instructing my banker to make provision for Edward's schooling and any costs for Annabelle's burial and to give a handsome sum to support the plague church that saw to her final disposition.

"I am usually a temperate man, as sailing men go, but that night I took a bottle of the innkeeper's best rum to my room and drank enough to blot out my grief."

I closed the book. Teag and I just stared at each other, blinking back tears. The raw emotion in Gideon's writing hurt my heart. From the expression on Sorren's face, I felt sure he remembered the events of the Yellow Fever epidemics first-hand and that they were even worse than Gideon described.

"He was so conflicted," Teag said, staring at the book in my hands. "He truly loved the sea, but he wanted to do right by his wife and son, even if it wasn't a love match."

"It's an oddly modern problem," I replied. "I've known a lot of folks who travel a lot for business and feel the same kind of conflict."

"Long separations were not uncommon back then," Sorren said. "The ability to travel great distances quickly is recent. Men would take passage to the colonies, and it could be years before they could send for their families. It caused hardship and grief, but when a thing is not possible, it takes away guilt over the 'choice' of it."

Teag picked up his wine glass and the now-empty bottle and carried them to the kitchen. I followed with my glass in hand, as did Sorren. Baxter trailed after us, probably thinking we were going for snacks.

"Sorry, Bax," I told him. "No more food."

Teag bent down to skritch Bax behind the ears. "I'll come back with Anthony, and we'll bring treats," he promised.

"I'll join you after supper," Sorren said, carding his fingers through Bax's fur. Bax looked at him, utterly besotted, and wagged his tail.

"Tomorrow, I'm going to look into Sullivan's descendants," Teag said when he straightened. "I'm curious to see what became of them and what they made of their inheritance. I'd also love to see if there are other historical accounts that mention Sullivan, either by contemporaries or scholars. I've got a hunch I'll find something interesting."

"Some of the old families in Charleston have been on the Alliance's watch list for a very long time," Sorren said. "The Sullivans aren't among them. Many of his family went to sea through the years, both Gideon's descendants and cousins from other branches, and their shipping empire went on for a long time. If they weren't exactly allies, they also certainly weren't enemies."

"I want to get Beck in on this and see if the St. Expeditus folks have anything in that archive of theirs," I replied. "And sooner or later,

I want to see what Dante has to say about all this." My ancestor's ghost had strong opinions, and he had helped to save our asses several times.

Teag hugged me and then headed home. Sorren also took his leave, reminding me to call at any hour if I needed his help. I locked the door behind them, put our stemless wine glasses in the dishwasher, and headed back to the couch with Baxter on my heels. We'd barely gotten comfortable again before my phone rang. I recognized Simon's ringtone right away.

"Cassidy—what's going on? Dante won't leave me alone," Simon said. "He keeps saying 'the sea witch rises' and won't shut up."

"We need to talk."

CHAPTER FIVE

SIMON LISTENED AS I TOLD HIM ABOUT VISITING THE OLD MANSION AND receiving the memoir that Gideon Sullivan had addressed to my shop nearly two hundred years ago.

"Teag, Sorren, and I got through the first bit, but there's a lot more to read. If he thought it was important enough to arrange for it to reach us long after his death, then there's something here we need to know. I think it's got to do with the 'darkness' he talks about stopping— because he was afraid it would come back," I told Simon as Baxter curled up on my lap. "And—can't forget this part—there's a dark witch from a legacy family who is after the book because he thinks it's a grimoire."

"That's a pretty remarkable story—even for you," Simon replied. Simon's my cousin, and we grew up helping each other figure our respective psychic gifts.

He and his partner, homicide detective Vic D'Amato, keep busy hunting down supernatural killers in Myrtle Beach. The combination of Simon's abilities as a psychic medium and Vic's insights as a detective close a lot of cases. But until recently, Simon didn't realize the kind of potentially world-ending threats that Teag, Sorren, and our other friends and I went up against.

"I guess there's a first time for everything." I absently petted Bax and scratched his ears.

"Dante's been hanging out with us lately. He's a strong presence, and he doesn't want to move on," Simon explained. "It's been a while since he had a medium who would work with him—or who was comfortable channeling him. Channeling a spirit is tricky because I still need to remain in control—just in case the ghost doesn't want to leave."

I shuddered, remembering visions I'd had from cursed or danger-ously haunted objects that wouldn't let me go. I'd had to fight my way free, and sometimes in my nightmares, things turned out differently. My touch magic wasn't the same as Simon's visions or his ability to channel spirits, but the dangers were familiar.

"Dante tries to hang on?"

"No, no," Simon hurried to correct me. "He's always been a perfect gentleman. But many ghosts—especially those that have been around for a while—have begun to fade or fragment. They've started to lose their sense of self, their memories. Dante hasn't. He not only knows who he is and remembers who he was, but he's also still got his water magic. When we team up, we're pretty formidable."

No kidding. I'd seen his partnership with Dante in action. "For-midable" didn't begin to cover it.

"I'm not complaining. Dante's gotten us out of a lot of jams," Simon added. "I like the guy. I think he was lonely...all that sentience and not too many people over the years to play with. My point is— ghosts and other entities can persist. Dante's one of the good ones. But it holds true for the bad ones as well."

"Gideon's 'darkness'?"

"Yeah. Or what Dante calls a 'sea witch.'"

"Dante has water magic. So did Gideon. Is that the same as being a 'sea witch'?"

"I don't think so," Simon replied, and I wondered if he was pausing to listen to Dante's spirit. "Dante says he knew of Gideon Sullivan when they were alive. He thought well of him because Sullivan stayed away from trading in the sort of occult relics Dante and his crew risked their lives to get out of circulation."

"Wasn't he curious? I'm surprised Dante didn't try to meet Gideon. Maybe even team up." Just from what we'd read so far of Gideon's memoirs, I thought they might have hit it off.

Simon chuckled. "Both of them spent most of their lives at sea. Makes it hard to meet for coffee."

"I guess that's true. The term Gideon uses, 'matelotage'—was that real? Was Dante familiar with it?"

"Oh, Dante was familiar with it. He and Coltt were bound by a matelotage until Coltt's death."

"Wait—then how is he our ancestor if he was married to Coltt?" I noticed that Sorren had left out this particular detail when we had talked earlier and wondered if he figured it was Dante's story to tell.

"Dante and Coltt grew up together, best friends their whole lives. When the raiders destroyed their village, he and Coltt were the only two survivors. You've heard his story about his water magic raging in a storm and enabling them to kill the raiders and steal the ship—which is how they became privateers," Simon replied.

"They sailed together for years, and along the way, their relationship evolved from friends to business partners to lovers. They made it official with matelotage, which was respected onboard ship and in the harbor towns in the Caribbean. Back in Charleston...not so much." The bitterness in Simon's tone didn't surprise me, given some of the attitudes he and his fiancé Vic ran into, even now.

"Coltt died of malaria several years after they stopped sailing," Simon recounted. "Dante was forty and had no heart for returning to the sea without Coltt. Around that time, Evann—the proprietor of Trifles and Folly, the guy our many-times-great uncle was named for— was getting too old to run the store. His daughter, Olivia, was friends with Dante and Coltt and enjoyed talking with them when they stopped in to see Sorren, even though she was fifteen years younger. She had resisted offers from suitors because she wanted to carry on the family business."

"So after Coltt died, she and Dante married? I guess Dante was bi?" Not unlike Gideon Sullivan's first marriage.

"They cared about each other. It wasn't just for convenience and propriety," Simon said assuredly. "I've heard Dante speak of her with great fondness and admiration, although I believe Coltt was the love of his life. He and Olivia had three children. Dante also changed his surname to match her family name, rather than the other way around, because of his rather…checkered past."

"So the magic that runs in the family…from Olivia's father Evann, down the line to our recent Uncle Evan, to us…Dante's water magic is a part of that?" Somehow, I had just assumed my predecessors with the shop had all been psychometrics. I was going to have to think about everything I'd just learned. Maybe when we weren't in the middle of saving the world, Simon, Dante, and I could have a more thorough conversation.

"Sorren could give you more details," Simon replied. "Mediums apparently weren't common in our bloodline because Dante was ecstatic to find a descendant who could talk to him—me."

"Has Dante said anything else about the threat Gideon seems to think might come back now that his bloodline has died out?"

"Hang onto that thought," he said. "Because there's a reason the bloodline matters. Old, strong magic is bound to blood. If Gideon thought the threat was great enough, it's possible that he used some sort of magic to lock down the danger and—intentionally or not—forge a connection to his descendants that lasted until now."

"That's possible?" I'd seen a lot of strange things, but nothing quite like that.

"It's not common. It would take strong magic, total commitment, an iron will, and very possibly, life energy."

"Meaning it killed Gideon to work the spell?" I'd only just started to get to know the man from the memoirs, but the thought of him sacrificing himself hurt my heart.

"That's very likely."

"So we're going to need to figure out what he did and how it worked, so we can either stop the threat or put the protections back in place." I didn't want to think about what that might require.

"Guess we won't know for sure until we have the whole story, but it wouldn't surprise me," Simon replied.

"Here we go again." I was torn between terror and excitement, which happens a little too often lately. "Hey, before you go, any tips on trapping a Dokkaebi?"

Simon sighed. "You really know how to have a good time, don't you? Go ahead and tell me what you already know, and if I can add anything or find out new info, I'll fill in the blanks."

I explained about the stolen spirit bottle and the lore Teag and Mrs. Teller had already found. "We just want to put the genie back in the bottle, so to speak, before Wilton starts wishing big."

"You might tempt the goblin with *sikhye*, which is a Korean sweet rice punch," Simon suggested when I finished. "Kinda like offering a Southern spirit sweet tea. If you can get soju—a popular liquor in South Korea—you could use it instead of gin, if the gin doesn't do the trick. Everyone loves a taste of home."

"Not sure if I can find it, but I'll look." I tried to remember if there was a Korean grocery store in Charleston. "If Wilton drank the gin that was in the bottle, could the goblin possess him?"

"I guess that's always possible with a spirit, but it's not common for goblins," Simon replied. If it happened, my suggestion would be to knock Wilton out, get the goblin drunk, and then lure him from the rice punch to the soju and into the gin bottle. Maybe tuck a soft rice cookie into the gin as a special treat."

"I figured you'd know!"

He laughed. "Just lucky about the goblin—I did some research lately for another hunter who had a problem with a different creature that's closely related to your Dokkaebi. Good luck! And about the other stuff, I'll get started on the research," Simon promised. "I want to figure out what—or who—the sea witch might be and what the lore says. Maybe I can get Dante to be a little less cryptic. And find out about binding spells."

"Thank you." Knowing Simon was helping made me feel better.

"I've got some friends I can pull into this to maybe speed things up. We'll probably need all the help we can get." He paused. "I've seen clips on the news about the odd things going on in Charleston. And we're tracking the huge storm. None of that is natural—something big is going on, and I'm afraid you're smack in the middle of it. Do you need Vic and me to come down and help?"

I appreciated the offer—and if things got desperate, I might take him up on it. But Simon had a shop to run, and if a major storm socked the coast, Vic would be needed with the police department.

"Thanks, but hold off for now. You've got plenty of responsibilities in Myrtle Beach. Sorren's back in Charleston," I told him. "And Archibald Donnelly will be here soon." Archibald Donnelly was a powerful necromancer. He runs a secret archive that can come unstuck in space and time to provide a haven for explorers stranded outside their eras and a holding place for the most dangerous magical items.

"Just remember, Cassidy—we've got your back," Simon assured me. "We've got resources. I'll talk to Travis Dominick and see what he can rustle up at that secret Vatican library. We'll figure this out."

"Thank you," I replied, feeling much better than I had when we started talking. "I'll keep you updated."

"And I'll let you know what we find. Hang in there."

The call ended, and I flopped back into the couch pillows, still lazily petting Baxter's ears. I didn't know what kind of hot mess Gideon Sullivan had dropped on our doorstep, but it was likely to be epic. I was grateful to have help, but that didn't mean stopping the danger would be easy.

Kell's ringtone pulled me out of my thoughts. "Hey there. How's your stakeout going?" I asked.

"Hey yourself. I took a chance that you'd still be awake. The stakeout is going the way most of them go…lots of nothing and then suddenly something."

Kell Winston, my boyfriend, runs a video production company, but his real passion is ghost hunting. He also runs SPOOK, the Southern Paranormal Outreach and Outlook Klub, and they investigate hauntings to document the spectral activity. If they happen upon something dangerous, Kell calls me, and we figure out how best to handle it.

"It would be a lot more fun if you were here," he added.

"You want me spending the night in a plague church? Ask Teag about the reaction I had to a museum exhibition on 'plagues and pestilence' a few years ago." Although my control over my gift had improved, I was asking for trouble going into a place that had extremely strong emotional resonance. The powerful feelings trapped in relics and artifacts could put me on my ass and make me sick from the second-hand trauma.

"I know it wouldn't be a good idea, but I still miss you," he said. "And if this pans out, it might be your kind of thing. We picked this location because the monk ghost is back."

"I've heard. That can't be good." Pawley's Island has its Gray Man as a harbinger of deadly storms. Charleston has several guardian spirits that warn of danger. One of them is the spirit of Brother Johan, a monk who died caring for victims of Yellow Fever. Given Charleston's subtropical climate, Yellow Fever epidemics resulted in a high death toll until medicine created effective treatments.

No one back then knew that the fever spread by mosquitos, so strict quarantine measures were used to stem the infection. Thousands died but parishioners balked at holding the rites for plague dead in the same churches where they would gather days later for weddings, baptisms, and worship.

Saint Sebastian's Church was built to hold funerals for those who died in the epidemic without endangering other congregations. Saint Sebastian's had no members or regular services. It was staffed by monks who cared for the sick, said Last Rites for the dying, and were often the only attendees at their memorial services.

"People have been reporting sightings of Brother Johan all along the harbor coast," Kell said. "Usually that squares up with hurricane warnings—like that big storm everyone's talking about. The monk's been much more active than usual, so I don't think it's just the storm."

"When did the sightings start?"

"The first recent sighting was two months ago," Kell replied.

"Which is also unusual because the monk doesn't hang around for long periods when there's a disaster. He shows up hours or days in advance and then disappears until the next time."

"Unless he's predicting a different kind of danger." I wondered when Gideon's final descendant had died. Could the monk ghost know that with that death, a level of protection began to weaken?

"So far, he seems to be right about the threat level," Kell added. "The governor is calling for a voluntary evacuation because of the storm. I'm glad we did the investigation at the church tonight—things are going to start shutting down fast if that storm heads inland."

"I'm not sure this is the normal kind of storm."

"Shit. You've got another *situation*, don't you?"

I heard worry and frustration in Kell's tone. He knows the truth about what we do, and he's usually supportive. After all, he and his crew take plenty of risks themselves, going into abandoned buildings and trying to document ghostly activity. Kell knows better than most people that ghosts are real, and some of them are vengeful. That doesn't stop him from worrying about me when I'm the one taking the risks.

"Yeah—but I'm not quite sure what's going on yet. There's some kind of danger from the sea that's been bound for a long time and might be trying to get loose."

"Are we talking a threat to Charleston? The East Coast? Or the whole world this time?"

"Don't know. I'll tell you when we figure it out." I paused. "Are there plague crosses in the church?"

"All over the place. No surprise, considering. Why?"

I pulled up the photos I had taken at the mansion and texted them to him. "Do any of them look like these? The inscription on these crosses isn't the usual Saint Zacharias blessing."

"I didn't look that closely at the inscriptions, but I will now," Kell said. "Do you think it's significant? Desperate people are likely to say a lot of different prayers."

"Maybe. But I've got a hunch it matters." Something I've learned dealing with the supernatural is that usually, *everything* matters. Especially if magic is involved.

Kell sighed. "Okay. Just don't leave me out of the loop. I don't have all the fancy tricks you and your friends do, but I've got a shotgun loaded with salt rounds, and I'm not afraid to use it."

Kell had proven more than once that he had my back. Most of my friends have some sort of magic, which gives them a definite advantage. Kell has a give-em-hell attitude and a stubborn streak a mile wide, and most of the time, it's enough. The way I figured, it took more courage to go into a fight knowing you were outgunned and still stand your ground. Just another way he'd won my heart.

"You'll be here tomorrow night when we read more of Gideon's book, remember? Not leaving you out of anything," I promised.

Kell had all but moved in about six months ago. We'd been going out for a while, and he was unofficially spending more nights here than not. He mostly kept his apartment as an office for his video business and he still slept there sometimes if a big project was on deadline. We had agreed from the start to take things slow. It seemed to be working out.

"Good. I've got to admit I'm intrigued. Just…be careful, Cassidy. Don't rush in until you know what you're up against. Have you pulled in Sorren?"

Kell had been around for some heart-stopping near-misses. I couldn't fault him for being cautious.

"Yes, Sorren's back in town. Donnelly will be here soon. I promise to be careful. You too." After all, I wasn't the one spending the night in a haunted plague church.

"Promise. Love you," he murmured.

"Love you right back." When the call ended, I couldn't help feeling sad that Kell was somewhere else besides here.

"It's just you and me, Bax," I sighed. Baxter had flipped onto his back, presenting himself for a belly rub. His little pink tongue poked between his teeth, and his eyes were closed in total puppy bliss.

Baxter adores Kell. He gets twice the attention whenever Kell's here and more than double the treats. Still, I can tell that Bax likes not having a rival. He's a little possessive like that.

I was lucky that Kell understood so much about what we did and why we did it. The shop was a legacy, but keeping the world safe from supernatural threats was more of a calling. Now that I knew what was going on in the shadows and had both magic and a team of allies, I couldn't walk away. I knew it was dangerous. But someone had to do it.

Whether I was the best pick was definitely up for debate. But that "fickle finger of fate" my grandmother used to talk about had pointed at me, so here we were, planning to go up against something scary and horrible, all in a day's work.

"Come on," I said to Baxter. "Let's get some sleep. Might as well rest while we can."

THE NEXT DAY I called Teag to let him know I'd be late and headed for the St. Expeditus Society.

I kept checking my rearview mirror, expecting Carter Etheridge in his black BMW to follow me. When he didn't, I actually felt more nervous. Etheridge was going off-script. I figured that he'd keep showing up, harassing me, thinking I'd give in. Now, I had no idea what his next move would be, which put me on high alert.

My SUV is warded. Not as heavily as the house or the shop, but enough to hold off anything short of major magic, the kind likely to attract attention. Just to be sure none of the cars were trying to follow me, I took the long way, intentionally choosing a route that doubled back on itself. When the other drivers didn't stick with me, I wondered if I'd gotten lucky today. Maybe Etheridge was off causing problems for someone else for a change.

The St. Expeditus compound is far enough from the city to feel rural. Old live oak trees spread their limbs across the road, dripping with Spanish moss, and high weeds rose on the other side of the storm ditches. Soon I had left houses and shops behind, and empty land stretched in both directions.

I usually felt more relaxed out in the country. Now, I kept looking over my shoulder, tense and ready for an attack.

A large dark shape bounded from a stand of trees near the road as soon as I passed.

"What the hell is that?" I gripped the wheel tight. I couldn't afford to take my eyes off the road ahead of me for long, but I couldn't figure out what was chasing me from just a glance.

The creature resembled a huge black dog that got taken apart and put back together all wrong. Its powerful body rippled with muscles, long legs covering the space between us far too quickly. Dark hair bristled in a ridge along its hunched back, and its blocky, lantern-jawed head seemed too big for the body. Black lips pulled back to expose sharp fangs, and glowing red eyes made me certain my pursuer wouldn't be winning any dog shows.

Barghest, maybe. I thought, trying to identify the creature. *Maybe a grim. Hellhound?*

I remembered that "objects in mirror are closer than they appear" when those eerie glowing eyes loomed large.

Shit. He's gaining on me.

I sped up. So did the creature, narrowing the gap between us. It leapt at my bumper, claws scraping. I floored the pedal, jerking forward and nearly losing control. Training took over, and I kept the car from going off the road, but slowing down let the monster get closer.

This time, I heard metal tear as sharp claws ripped into the back hatch.

The compound's driveway was in sight, if I could get there before my pursuer ripped my SUV apart. I had no intention of leading a monster to my friends, but I also knew they would have the means to stop the barghest. I didn't dare try to use my wand or the walking stick while I drove, and parking long enough to fight would be suicide.

Father Anne had told me that the St. Expeditus property was protected by powerful wardings. I'd be putting them to the test.

I took the turn fast enough that I feared for a moment I'd either skid or rock onto two wheels, while barely keeping ahead of the creature. Now that it had locked onto me, it wouldn't give up its prey without a fight.

A quarter of the way down the drive, I felt a frisson of energy and knew I'd crossed some kind of magical boundary.

The barghest was right behind me. A Michael Bay-worthy flash of white light lasted only a second, and the creature came to a sudden stop as the air around it took on a strange sparkle. I saw the monster throwing itself against invisible walls, trying to get loose.

I pulled off as soon as the road widened. My hands shook and my stomach knotted with tension. I forced myself to breathe, and after a few moments, I felt steady enough to drive up to the main lot.

Father Anne met me when I parked. "I see you made it here, safe and sound." After a once-over to make sure I was unharmed, her gaze traveled down the drive to where the barghest raged in its invisible cage.

I walked around to look at the back of my RAV4, unable to hide a shiver at the damage. Four parallel grooves ripped into the metal of the hatch, a single swipe of the creature's claws. If it had managed to get onto the roof, getting into the passenger compartment would have been like using a can opener. I really wanted to throw up.

"Relax. You're safe," Father Anne assured me.

"Where did the barghest come from?" I sounded as freaked out as I felt.

Her expression darkened. "That's what I'd like to know."

"It's got to be Carter Etheridge." I told her about the Rawhead outside Trifles and Folly. "He's watching somehow, because there's no other way for him to know I was coming here."

"How is killing you going to get Gideon's book for him?" she asked as we began to walk toward the main building.

"Maybe the creatures were meant to intimidate, not kill. Etheridge flexing his muscles, making sure I realize what he can do. If that's the case—he obviously hasn't been paying attention." Much as facing down the two monsters had scared me, we had fought much more powerful and terrifying beings—and won. "How did the wardings know to trap the barghest?"

"Magic is as much about intention as it is about power," Father Anne replied. "The spells are subtle and complex, layered over the years—not much different from the ones protecting your house and the shop. In this case, they sense the intent to cause harm, and trap the intruder, then trigger a 'manual review,' so to speak."

"What are you going to do with the barghest?"

Father Anne sighed. "Either destroy it or send it back to its owner. Don't worry—we'll take care of the problem."

"Etheridge is going to be madder than a wet hen that we keep breaking his monsters," I replied, although a petty part of me kinda liked the idea.

"Yeah, well. He'll get over it." With her updated pompadour haircut, pierced eyebrow, and colorful tats, she was a memorable figure, especially when she wore her black shirt with the clerical collar. Father Anne was the rector at St. Hildegard's Episcopal Church—the priest Teag and Anthony wanted to officiate at their wedding ceremony. She was also a member of a secret society of clergy who were dedicated to stopping the things that went bump in the night.

"We skipped saying hello. It's good to see you," she said and folded me into a hug that squashed the air out of my lungs. I'm tall and reasonably fit, but Father Anne is taller. At least she saved my pride and didn't lift me off my feet.

"Good to see you too," I croaked. We'd fought back-to-back more times than I could remember, and I trusted Anne with my life.

"It's been a while."

"Probably since the last world-destroying potential cataclysm," I said with a conspiratorial grin as we walked toward the Society's main building.

"So...two weeks?" she quipped.

The Society has very old roots in the city. They're part of a larger network of badass priests who use their skills to protect the people who don't know that monsters and magic are real. Here in Charleston, the Society has a large estate, and the cops leave them alone. They also run a supernatural version of the Witness Protection Program, which is why I was visiting.

"Cassidy! Great to see you again!"

Beckford Pendlewood sauntered toward me, dressed in jeans, a T-shirt, and knock-off boat shoes without socks. His chestnut hair was collar length, and it suited him, framing a handsome face with intelligent brown eyes. Quite a change from the desperate young man who had claimed sanctuary wearing designer clothes and a haircut that probably cost more than my car payment. He drew me into a hug as the brown-haired man a few paces behind him chuckled in fond amusement. That was Logan Miller, Beck's partner.

"If you're here, that means the world is screwed, right?" Beck said.

"Pretty much," I admitted.

"I told you he was a smart guy," Father Anne chimed in, grinning at me.

Beck rolled his eyes. "Let me guess. It has something to do with my accursed ancestors."

"Got it in one," I replied.

"I was afraid of that. What do you need?"

Beck came from a family of dark witches. I admired the courage it took for him to break free and renounce his inheritance, but it came at a high price. He was safe, protected by the Society, but he might never be able to leave. Logan had fallen in love with him and chose to share Beck's exile.

Father Anne led us to the dining room, where we claimed a table in a corner, out of the way and quiet. The retreat campus was home to the priests and scholars who were part of the Society, as well as those claiming sanctuary. The food was very good, the library was arcane and awesome, and while the accommodations weren't luxurious, they were clean and comfortable. Spells and wardings protected the area and kept out unfriendly entities.

"How much do you know about Pendlewood history in the late 1700s?" I asked Beck. "Especially their feud with the Etheridges?"

He frowned. "That's rather specific. My father sent me off to boarding school to keep me away from the family, so I was gone by the time I was twelve. That cut down on being able to eavesdrop on adult conversations, although I still picked up a few things, and I've read a lot since we've been going through the boxes from Bermuda. The family has always been focused on expanding its fortune by trading in magical relics and occult objects."

I nodded. "Yep. And we think something that happened back then might be about to cause problems now. Do you remember hearing about Gideon Sullivan?"

Beck, Logan, and Father Anne listened intently as I recounted what we knew so far from Gideon's memoir. Beck's gaze flicked to meet mine when I mentioned the glowing ship on the horizon and Gideon's cautionary mentions of the Pendlewoods.

"That sounds exactly like something my family would have done, but I don't know any details," Beck said after he thought for a moment. Logan stayed close enough to bump shoulders, a reassuring presence. I suspected that talking about his family—after his cousins tried to kill him—was upsetting for Beck, but unfortunately he was our best lead.

"When your father shipped the things from the Bermuda house back to the States, were there any family histories? Because I have a feeling there's a connection between this 'darkness' Gideon talked about and some magic done by a Pendlewood or Etheridge, or perhaps a cursed object that they shipped."

"You're probably right," Beck said, rubbing the back of his neck with one hand while he held tight to Logan with the other. "If there were problems, my family was usually on the sidelines manipulating the situation."

He glanced at Father Anne. "After the whole demon box problem, the Society helped me track down and acquire as many of those shipping containers from the Bermuda homestead as we could find."

"Do you know where they are stored?"

"I imagine that some ended up with my cousins, but I think we got most of them. We haven't cataloged everything yet."

"It wouldn't take as long to go looking for something specific as it would to inventory everything," Logan spoke up. He looked hopefully from Father Anne to Beck. "If we're looking for family histories or journals from that era, that eliminates a lot of stuff we don't have to worry about. I can help."

"I'm sorry to ask—I know you've got obligations helping with research and the archive—but I think trouble's coming, and anything we can find out about the original situation is likely to be a big help," I said.

Beck nodded, sitting up straighter in his chair as Father Anne passed a pen and notepad to him. "What are we looking for?"

"It would help a lot to know what the Pendlewoods and Etheridges were up to in the last half of the 1700s, especially if it had a Bermuda or ocean connection," I said. "Any feuds they might have had, or cut-throat competition in the magical object trade. Anything about crossing paths with Gideon Sullivan or Ramon Montero or their ships—*Resilient* and *Hidalgo*. Or about supernatural creatures or phenomena in that stretch of ocean between Bermuda and the coast."

I gave them an apologetic smile. "I know that's pretty broad, but it's all I've got right now. As we get through more of Gideon's book, I might have specifics." I looked to Father Anne. "And if you've got any pointers about finding a rogue genie and trapping him, I'm all ears."

Beck took a deep breath. "That's enough to get started. Logan's right—we can eliminate a lot of items right away, and with several people helping, it shouldn't be too hard to skim what we find for the right time and place."

"We'll get on it right away," Father Anne promised. "And keep you posted on what we find."

"Thank you." I felt a weight lift from my shoulders. We still didn't know exactly what sort of threat we faced, but I felt certain that anything Beck and the others could find out about his family's activities would help us narrow down the possibilities.

We chatted for a while after that about everything and nothing—but specifically not any ghost-related topics. I knew I needed to get back to the shop and let them finish their work.

"I know you two can't leave the compound, but a bunch of us are getting together to read more of Gideon's book tonight. You're welcome to video conference with us. That's what Simon and Travis are doing."

"Count us in." Beck grinned. "It's been a long while since I've had story time."

~

I DROVE BACK to Trifles and Folly thinking about everything we had discussed. It wouldn't surprise me if Beck and Father Anne had new information by this evening. They had amazing research skills, and now they'd be laser-focused on finding what we needed. I relied on Simon as a historian, Teag's hacker skills to dig out hidden information, and I trusted Travis Dominick to ferret out buried tips from a secret Vatican library.

We had gathered a good team over the years, friends who became found family. I needed to believe that together we'd figure it out. That didn't stop the worry from scratching at my brain because we didn't know where or when the threat would strike or what, exactly, we were trying to protect against. Without that information, our odds of succeeding were slim.

Gideon sent the memoir to Trifles and Folly. That makes it our best clue. He didn't leave us a puzzle—he gave us a map. We just need to figure out the destination.

Gideon's story came from his heart, which meant it held a window to his emotions. That was like reading a book already highlighted to show the key parts. As I listened to Gideon's words, I also needed to sense his feelings so he could guide me through this map of his to know what was most important.

When he entrusted the book to Trifles and Folly, he chose us for a reason. Each proprietor of the store inherited in part because of their magic, even if the talents weren't all the same from one generation to the next.

Sorren had been involved with the store from the beginning. As an immortal, he had unique knowledge and abilities. If Gideon knew about the store's hidden role in safeguarding Charleston and the world, maybe Sorren's role was known to him too, even if Sorren hadn't known Gideon personally.

Was Gideon trusting that when the time came Sorren and the shop's proprietor would pull a team together that could handle the threat—a threat that Gideon sacrificed his life to keep at bay?

Late afternoon stretched the shadows. I took an alternate route back to the city, which ran close to the river. After I passed several restored old plantations, my course wended through a stretch of marshland before it would eventually emerge into gas stations and condos on the outskirts of town.

When I picked this way, I'd forgotten how long the stretch through the marsh was or how dark it got beneath the trees in the twilight.

And when ghouls started to climb out of the swamp, dragging their waterlogged corpses onto the guardrail, I realized I had also forgotten how many unfortunates lay unburied and unmourned beneath the cypress-black waters.

If I survived, I intended to have Rowan search every inch of my Toyota for a magical low-jack. I needed to find out how Etheridge knew where I was going and make it stop.

I could call for help, but the ghouls would be on me before Father Anne and her crew could get here. The road was an isthmus with swamp on either side, and ghouls were hauling themselves out of their watery graves both in front of and behind my car.

I was on my own.

I sped up, aiming right for the staggering creatures that blocked my path. Ghouls are smarter than zombies, but they didn't seem to register the danger of tons of steel hurtling towards them.

I am so getting bull bars put on my next car.

Ramming a Nephilim that was trying to kill me wrecked my last car. It looked like I'd be shopping for new wheels after I scraped ghoul guts off my RAV.

I braced for impact, forcing the car to go even faster so that I stood a chance of knocking the ghouls out of the way and not just driving over them. Their wasted corpses weren't like the muscular fallen angel who smashed my windshield and crumpled my hood before. I felt the car hit, and then they were gone, and I was free—

I forgot how fucking fast ghouls can be.

They raced after me, dropping to all fours but moving more like spiders than animals. They scaled trees and jumped at my car, landing on the roof and hood until I swerved crazily to throw them clear. Evasive maneuvers weren't easy on a two-lane road, and I'd be in even worse trouble if I went over the side into the swamp. If they swarmed me, I wasn't sure I could break free.

There were too many of them, and outrunning the ghouls wasn't working. So I opened the sunroof, grabbed Alard's walking stick, and hoped it was true that the gods smiled on idiots.

I didn't dare slow down, but focusing my concentration on the walking stick while still keeping the car on the road posed a new challenge. I did my best to angle the walking stick toward the ghouls in my way, divided my focus as best I could, and *pulled* with my touch magic.

A torrent of fire blasted the ghouls that blocked the road, hot enough to burn even though they still dripped black water from the dumping ground for their corpses. The smoke smelled of rotted meat and burned hair, thick enough to make me gag. My eyes watered, and my throat burned.

I felt a jolt as more ghouls threw themselves at the back of the SUV, and I tried to angle the stick for another blast of flames without setting my car on fire. My aim mostly succeeded, and the ghouls behind me fell away.

I felt lightheaded from the power drain, high on adrenaline from fear. One final blast cleared the road in front of me. I floored it, relieved and surprised when none of the ghouls followed. When I checked my mirrors, I saw them all burning, leaving nothing but blackened piles of charred bone.

What the police would make of that, I had no clue.

I didn't start shaking until the danger was over and didn't dare stop until the cindered ghouls were miles behind me. Only then did I pull into a busy convenience store parking lot to call for backup.

"Cassidy? What's wrong?" Father Anne knew right away that this wasn't a social call.

"I got ambushed by ghouls on the river road." I hated how my voice trembled. "I'm okay. I got away. But I left a bunch of greasy, grimy ghoul guts on the asphalt that might freak the mundanes."

Father Anne chuckled, and I knew she appreciated my grim humor. "So you need a 'clean up on aisle nine'? You got it. I'll send people. Thanks for letting me know." She paused. "And Cassidy? I'm really glad you got away. Please, don't take chances."

I promised that I'd be careful, and ended the call, but it still took several more minutes before I was ready to drive the rest of the way to the shop.

I got lucky this time. That wasn't something I intended to count on.

Speaking of luck, we had a Dokkaebi to catch.

CHAPTER SIX

"DID I MISS MUCH?" I ASKED WHEN I GOT TO THE STORE NOT LONG before closing time.

Maggie looked up and Teag pulled me into a tight hug.

"Father Anne called. Glad to see you in one piece," he said, relief clear in his eyes.

Maggie sniffed back tears and patted me on the shoulder.

"Happy to be here," I replied. My fear had morphed into anger. I refused to let Carter Etheridge make me afraid to set foot outside my home. And I'd be damned if I'd let him intimidate me into failing the trust Gideon Sullivan had placed in Trifles and Folly.

"Did you eat? There are cookies from Honeysuckle Café in the break room," Teag said, pulling me out of my musings. He knows me far too well, and I felt certain he could guess the turn my thoughts had taken. "And I think I got a location on Wilton."

"We had a busy day, but nothing we couldn't handle." Maggie finished off one of the cookies. She's a whirlwind, a retired teacher who came looking for a part-time job working with my Uncle Evan and ended up signing on to help save the world. Today her silver bob had magenta tips that matched her broomstick skirt. Maggie's got a business school mind paired with Woodstock fashion sense. She knows what we really do, and it hasn't scared her away yet, even though she doesn't have any magic.

"Couple of tour buses dropped their people off on King Street," Teag translated. "It was a madhouse, but we sold enough to make this a very good month."

I took pride in the shop doing well and turning a profit. Sorren was wealthy enough to cover a shortfall, and he made sure we drew hazard pay above the salaries we earned from the store. But Trifles and Folly had been in my family for more than three hundred years, and so running it like a regular business—covering our expenses and paychecks and turning a profit—mattered a lot to me. Teag and Maggie made that possible, in addition to being two of my best friends.

I took advantage of a lull in the traffic to fill them in on the details of being stalked by the barghest and ghouls since I figured Father Anne had just hit the highlights. I felt certain both had been sent by Carter Etheridge. I also caught them up on my time at the compound with Beck, Logan, and Father Anne.

"Seth Tanner and I built off Wilton's license plate to see what we could find out about his jobs, family, prior apartments—anything that might give us an idea where he'd go to ground if he thought someone was after him," Teag said. "We also turned up some other examples of 'remarkable luck' that might have been the bottle spirit keeping Wilton out of Etheridge's clutches."

I raised an eyebrow. "Clutches? That sounds so…mustache-twirling."

Teag shrugged. "Kinda fits, doesn't it? Etheridge is like this weird cross between Pharma Bro and Snidely Whiplash—with magic. Ruthless, but with an odd dramatic flair."

Despite everything, Teag's description made me chuckle, and I saw satisfaction in his eyes that he had gotten me to laugh. "Yeah, it does."

"I'm waiting to hear back from Seth," Teag continued. "When we put our findings together, we should have a short list of Wilton's usual bolt holes and habits."

Teag's Weaver magic makes him one hell of a hacker. Seth is a computer security whiz who also hunts the bad things that go bump in the night. He's part of our network of friends and allies and had recently paid us a visit.

I told Teag about my call with Simon. "He says we need to knock Wilton out to summon and trap the Dokkaebi."

"Damn—and I left my tranquilizer rifle at home." Teag smirked. "I think I can magic him so he goes to sleep—no saying wishes aloud, and no thinking them, either."

"I like that better than trying to roofie him," I confessed. "And you don't own a tranquilizer rifle."

"No, but Chuck does," he replied. Chuck Pettis was an ex-military demon hunter with an impressive arsenal and plenty of experimental "toys."

The way things were shaping up, I figured we might be pulling him in to help.

"I'm working on some woven pieces that hold spells to put Wilton into a sound, dreamless sleep," Teag added.

"No amazingly lucky news bulletins while I was gone?"

"Hard to say. There were a few odd coincidences that might have been Wilton, but I haven't been able to confirm." Teag shrugged. "Maggie's keeping an eye on the local channels. There were a couple more tremors—minor but still worrisome. The crows are gathering in Whitepoint Garden and freaking people out. So the signs of the apocalypse haven't gone away."

"If he stole the bottle, then he has to know Etheridge is looking for him," I replied. "I'm thinking Wilton is laying low. And if the Dokkaebi is protecting him from Etheridge, we need to figure out how to keep it from seeing us as a threat too."

"Yeah, I thought about that. Let's hope the spirit can sense intentions." He shot me a tired look. "Don't worry, Cassidy—we'll find him and the Dokkaebi too."

"I tracked down a Korean grocery store, so I can pick up the things we need on the way home."

Teag quirked an eyebrow. "Are you sure that's safe? What about Etheridge?"

"I'll be staying in the downtown area during business hours—nice and visible," I said, hoping I was right. "I don't want to risk having a hot lead on Wilton and needing to stop for supplies on the way."

"Just be careful," he warned.

"I promise. After all, we're going to be reading Gideon's book tonight. I want to know what's in it that Carter Etheridge is so determined to steal. He called it a 'grimoire' and mentioned spells, but so far, there hasn't been anything like that, even in the parts I scanned and skipped over."

"Maybe he's wrong," Teag replied.

"Maybe. Or he knows something we don't." I wadded up the paper from my cookie. "I can't wait to see what your research comes up with —and you can share with the crowd at dinner tonight."

"I made pecan pies and pralines for this evening," Maggie said and tossed her empties in the trash. "They're in the fridge, so I can come over early and help you get things ready. And after I talked to Mrs. Teller, I mixed up a bucket full of protection for the sidewalk in front. Holy water, salt, colloidal silver, and red brick dust, then used a broom to sweep it between the door and the curb. It won't hold off everything, but it should help some."

"Thank you," I said. "I'm in favor of all the protection we can get. Can you please give me that 'recipe'? I'd like to do the same for the sidewalk at my house."

"Already emailed you," Maggie replied with a wink.

"I brought my cornbread too. Didn't want to leave it for Anthony to bring in case he runs late," Teag added.

"Yum! First, we feast. Then we talk about stopping the end of the world—again." If we were staring down another potential apocalypse, at least we'd go out with full bellies, great company, and good food.

I constantly checked my mirrors when I went looking for the Korean grocery store. Nothing emerged from the shadows or crawled out of hiding places, but I wasn't ready to let down my guard. I had no way of knowing how much summoning the barghest and the ghouls had cost Etheridge or whether he'd had help. If we were lucky, he had depleted his energy and would need to rest up before making another strike.

I wasn't sure that luck was on our side lately.

The small shop sat tucked between a barber and a mobile phone center in a busy plaza that looked like it was both a relic from the 1970s and a gathering place for the community. Clusters of people chatted, sat together on benches, and leaned against the pillars that supported the roof overhang, some smoking cigarettes, others enjoying ice cream cones.

The sign for Park's Grocery repeated the name in Korean characters, and since several of the signs in the window were only in Korean, I figured the place was legit enough to draw customers who knew the real deal.

The aroma of gochujang and bulgogi sauce filled the air and made my stomach rumble. I saw a small take-out counter and figured that was where the tempting scents were coming from. Colorfully packaged items lined the shelves, most of which I could only guess at since none of the packaging was in English. I fought the urge to explore, remembering I had guests coming for dinner.

I must have looked lost. An elderly woman came up beside me, and I startled, since I was focused on finding the items on my list.

"Can I help you?"

I wondered how often they had people wander in without a clue. "I'm looking for a couple of things, and I have no idea where to find them," I admitted. "I need *sikhye*, soju, and rice cakes. Can you please point me in the right direction?"

Her eyes narrowed, and she gave me a hard once over. Maybe what I'd asked for was well-known goblin fodder, and she was wondering what the hell I was up to. She seemed to make up her mind and beckoned me to follow.

She led me past tanks of fish and bins of unfamiliar fruits and vegetables. I promised myself I'd come back when the danger was over to try the take-out food and stock up on ingredients for new recipes.

"Here," she said, handing me two green bottles. "Sweet soju will work best," she added, moving on before I could ask any questions. Two yellow cans quickly followed, with what I gathered from the picture on the front was rice punch. We stopped at the bakery, and my guide spoke in rapid Korean to the woman behind the counter, who handed over a small bag with three little round, pastel-colored balls inside.

We wound back through the store to the register, and I put the items I was carrying on the counter. She gave me another measured look, then reached underneath and withdrew a bracelet made of red string threaded through a gold metal cylinder embossed with Korean characters.

"Take this," she said, pushing it into my hand. "It brings protection. You will need it."

"Thank you." I wondered if she was psychic or if she just figured I'd need good luck if I was buying a Dokkaebi summoning kit. She rang me up, and I paid her, slipping the bracelet on while she put the other items into a paper bag.

I felt a tingle of energy when her fingers brushed mine as she handed over the package. She murmured something in Korean and then met my eyes with a very direct stare. "Wishes can deceive. Be careful."

"I will," I promised. I thought about asking questions, but someone called to her, and the woman headed away with a wave of her hand in my direction.

I couldn't shake feeling spooked. Before I headed to my car, I loitered in the grocery store's doorway, checking the parking lot. Etheridge's BMW would have stuck out among the Hyundais and Fords, and I breathed a sigh of relief when I didn't see it.

As soon as I came close to the SUV, I knew the wardings had been disturbed. They held—whoever had been here either wasn't strong enough to break the protections or hadn't wanted to risk making a scene. It would be too much of a coincidence for the trespasser to be after the spare change in my console.

I heard a rustle of clothing and noticed a petite woman in a loose white dress who had been hidden behind the passenger compartment of my SUV. She moved toward the front of the car, and instinct made me step back toward the protection of the shop. The stranger's face was turned away from me, so all I could see was her long, dark hair.

She didn't seem to be paying attention, and I wondered if she was sick or high. Just as I was about to ask if she needed help, her image shuddered like a video glitch, and all of a sudden, she was crawling across the hood of the SUV, one hand outstretched with fingers bent like claws.

That's when I saw her corpse-pale face and the blackened, empty eye sockets.

I snapped Bo's collar, and he appeared, putting himself between me and the creature. A shake of my arm let my wand drop into my hand from beneath my sleeve, but a blast of energy didn't do anything to the apparition.

She dove at me, and I raised my right arm as a shield.

The ghost hissed, blackened lips pulled back over rotted teeth, and recoiled. I realized the red bracelet was wound around that wrist.

The old woman from the shop came running toward us, shouting in Korean. She waved a large kitchen knife in one hand and hurled dried beans at the ghost with the other hand. With a loud cry, the shop woman threw the knife, and it stuck fast in a telephone pole. The ghost vanished.

I should have jumped in the car and peeled rubber, but I kept looking at the old woman. She stood with her hands on her hips and gave a satisfied nod.

"What was that?" I managed.

"*Gaekgwi* are bad trouble," she replied as if what had just happened was completely normal. She walked over to the pole and reclaimed her knife, then headed back to the store. A younger woman came outside and began arguing with her in Korean, in a tone that sounded more worried than angry. My protector shooed the other woman back into the shop before returning her attention to me.

"*Gaekgwi* wander," she said. "They did not die well, or no one remembers them. Makes them angry." She tipped her head, looking at me. "Why you?"

"I don't know." We were already pursuing a Korean goblin. *Could the Dokkaebi recruit help?*

"You have a goblin problem. Now, ghost problem." She frowned and approached my car, then murmured something and held out her hand, drawing back quickly. "Witch problem too. You are unlucky."

"Thank you for saving me."

She pressed a half-empty bag of dried beans into my hand. "Take this. The witch might send her back."

Had Etheridge compelled a nearby restless spirit to attack me? I heard the purr of a sports car's engine and caught a glimpse of a low-slung, black car speed past. *Etheridge.*

"Thank you," I repeated.

She gave a curt nod and pointed to the wristband she had given me. "Never take it off. I will put the ghost to rest. Now, go."

I figured I had worn out my welcome, or she didn't want my "bad luck" rubbing off. I thanked her again and drove away. She stood outside the door to the grocery store like a sentry, holding the knife, and watched me leave.

I called Teag and filled him in.

"You want me to meet you and be your escort?" he offered.

"I don't think that'll be necessary, but stay on the line with me in case I'm wrong," I replied. "I'm still a little freaked out. Lucky for me, that lady at the grocery store was a total badass. But I don't know how she guessed I had 'goblin trouble.'"

"A Dokkaebi is unusual for us, but it could be familiar to someone from Korea," Teag said. "After all, what would someone think if you went into a store looking for wooden stakes and silver bullets?"

"Good point." At the next traffic light, I took a picture of the bracelet and texted it to him. "Can you look up the markings on this, please? She said it was important for me to wear it, and the ghost didn't like it at all."

Teag was quiet for several moments while I drove.

"Got it," Teag said. "The symbols match a line from a common Korean prayer for protection. Who knows? Maybe the Dokkaebi will pay more attention since it basically says 'go away' in his own language."

"Interesting. Anything else?" I didn't want to be alone after the day I'd had.

"Give me a minute to chase a hunch," he said. After a while, he was back.

"The ghost who attacked you might have been Choi Sung-min," he said. "She lived in an apartment nearby and was killed in a mugging gone wrong about six months ago. That would fit the criteria to become a *Gaekgwi*—wandering spirit."

"Why me?"

"My guess? Etheridge tailed you and used the ghost as a weapon because she was handy. Sounds like the lady from the grocery store knew how to banish the ghost, so no one else gets hurt—and Sung-min gets peace."

We chatted while I finished the rest of the drive. Teag and Maggie were nearly done closing the shop for the day.

A helpful distraction spell keeps the parking space closest to my door open most of the time. I only had to cross the sidewalk to get within the house wardings, but the encounter with the Rawhead put me on high alert. I kept my wand in hand as I grabbed my purse and the bag and had my key out so I could slip inside as quickly as possible.

Farther down the block, two men tried to look casual while having no reason to hang around in a residential neighborhood where they didn't belong. I doubted they were random burglars and figured they'd been ordered to keep an eye on me and make sure I didn't forget that Etheridge wasn't giving up.

Once the door shut behind me, I realized how fast my heart was beating. Etheridge's attempts to get the book had failed so far, but it would be a mistake to underestimate him. Whatever spell he was after, he wanted it badly enough to keep trying. I texted Sorren about the new stalkers, hoping he'd take care of them.

Baxter greeted me with a happy dance, tail wagging. I fussed over him while I filled his dish and then washed up and started to pull everything together for company. Then I read through the instructions Maggie had sent me for protecting the sidewalk and mixed up the ingredients, trying not to think about how weird it was that I had them all on hand.

I went back outside and fixed my two stalkers with the stink eye as

I swept the mixture over the sidewalk to the curb. They didn't try to come closer, and after the day I'd had, that was wise on their part because I was done being messed with. I felt better with the new layer of protection in place and decided to add it to my daily ritual until our problem with Etheridge was over.

I had started chili that morning in my slow cooker as an extra entree, and the aroma permeated the house. That left the stove free so I could make the Frogmore stew. Despite the name, the dish has nothing to do with frogs. It's named after a tiny town, and the seafood boil is a classic Lowcountry recipe.

Teag and Maggie arrived and put the food they brought on the table, then grabbed aprons from the pantry. They've been here enough to know where everything is.

"Put us to work," Maggie said. "What do you need?"

"I've got a bag of potatoes to quarter, andouille sausage to slice, plus the corn to cut," I rattled off. I was letting my big stockpot fill while I gathered the seasonings, took the fresh shrimp out of the fridge, and set the hot sauce on the table. I also grabbed several cans of beer to add to the pot for extra flavor.

Teag and Maggie got busy cutting things up while I let the water heat. I added the spices and beer and then tossed the other ingredients into the pot along with the shrimp once the water was hot.

Right on time, everyone else started to arrive. Kell slipped up behind me, put his arms around me, and kissed me on the back of the neck. "Everything smells great," he whispered into my ear. "And you taste good too." I shivered. He's several inches taller than me, with light brown hair, blue eyes, and at this time of year, a great summer tan.

"Can you please lay out bowls, silverware, and plates on the kitchen table?" I asked after turning to kiss him on the lips and return the hug.

Father Anne arrived next, and since we had the cooking taken care of, she headed into the living room to arrange chairs for all of us to gather after dinner. Anthony ran late, but I figured he stopped to change before coming from the office since he had switched his suit for khakis and a polo shirt—as dressed down as he usually got. Sorren planned to arrive after we finished eating.

By the time the food was cooked, the counter had filled up with a serve-yourself buffet that included coleslaw, potato salad, Teag's cornbread, and Maggie's sweets. Everyone filled their plates and took their food into the dining room, where pitchers of sweet tea were waiting.

Teag set up the video conference so Travis, Simon, Beck, and Logan could join us for dinner conversation before we dove into Gideon's memoir. Despite the serious work to be done later, talk around the table was lighthearted and full of friendly teasing. I felt some of the day's tension slip away listening to the laughter and the chatter. Being surrounded by friends and allies made me feel safe and loved.

After we cleared the table and put the leftovers away, we all carried our desserts and after-dinner drinks into the living room. Teag brought the laptop and set it up where Simon and the others could see and hear everyone. Sorren arrived just after sunset with several bottles of very good wine.

I settled onto the couch with Kell beside me. Teag and Anthony sat on the loveseat, which left the wing chairs for Maggie and Father Anne, while Sorren brought a chair in from the kitchen. Then I picked up Gideon's book, feeling like a teacher at story time. The now-familiar mix of emotions that shot through me from touching the journal made me even more curious to see what new adventures lay ahead for Gideon and Ramon. Everyone quieted, and I started to read aloud.

"Our journey, these last few weeks, has tried our souls. 'Tis the season for storms, and they are upon us nearly every day. Some pass quickly, while others challenge us even with my gift to blunt the worst of the waves.

"Twice, we have glimpsed St. Elmo's fire upon the masts. The sailors take that as a good omen, but I am not so sure. This stretch of sea is treacherous and has seen more than its share of wrecks, even with seasoned crews. I will not sleep until we are through the worst of it.

"Tonight we caught sight of another glowing ship. It was a brigantine, glowing blue on the horizon, fully rigged. While I struggled to temper the waves and my crew fought the winds, the glowing ship appeared to pass unhindered through the storm. I have seen ghost ships, and this looked far too solid to be one of those. By what sorcery it remains immune to the forces of nature, I know not, but I am certain the Pendlewoods have a hand in it.

"As if the storms were not enough, the pirates have grown bolder. Twice we skirmished with smaller boats that were ill-prepared to face our guns, and we drove them back.

"Today our luck turned. Three fast sloops, each with twelve guns apiece, came at us out of the fog. We were outgunned and outmaneuvered. My ability works better to calm rough seas than to pitch still water, so I had little to offer except to exhort our riggers to fill our sails and give the blackguards a run for it.

"I feared we would lose this time, and I saw that dread on the faces of my crew. We had already taken damage, and we would not be able to outrun all three of them.

"The winds shifted, and another sloop emerged from the fog, guns blazing. I thought that we were finished, then I realized the new ship fired on the pirates, not on us, and flew the flag of a privateer.

"Surely its captain was a madman, with the way the sloop maneuvered, as if it commanded the winds to suit its whim. With the pirates in disarray, I pondered whether to flee while our enemy was distracted or stay and fight. I did not care for the idea of abandoning the ship that saved us, and the crew seemed of like mind with how quickly they changed tack to come about and attack.

"The black sloop's fearless commander thought nothing of sailing straight for one pirate ship and then another as if he meant to ram them —a game of nerves he won every time as the brigands got out of his way, sometimes with barely enough room to clear. The madman fired a broadside for good measure as he forced the ships to make way.

"As quickly as it started, the battle was over, with one of the pirate ships sunk and the other two damaged and fleeing fast as the winds would take them.

"Amid the maneuvering and cannon fire, I glimpsed the name of the privateer ship—*Hidalgo*. I feared they flew a false flag and might turn on us now that the competitors were gone, but they did not. Across the distance between our ships, I could see the *Hidalgo's* captain, and he gave me a cocky salute before the winds rose, suddenly changing direction, and bore our rescuer away."

I had gotten so caught up in Gideon's tale that I nearly forgot my reading had an audience. When I looked up, they were all listening intently, shaking themselves out of their concentration.

"Pretty amazing stuff," Kell said. "I'm impressed by Gideon—but the *Hidalgo's* captain was a total badass."

"It seems a bit of a stretch to think the winds favored the *Hidalgo* so consistently without some help," Father Anne observed.

I nodded. "Gideon was able to influence the waves and water—at least to a degree. It sounds like Montero—the other captain—could control the wind." That would make Gideon and Ramon a formidable team at sea. I itched to read ahead and find out more.

"Given his family's success with shipping, that sort of magic doesn't surprise me," Sorren said. "The power might manifest defensively even if the wielder didn't acknowledge it—meaning his family could have benefitted from the magic without realizing they were causing the outcomes. Convenient if you don't want to face up to being a witch."

"Gideon didn't seem to have any qualms about acknowledging his abilities," I said. "Then again, he wasn't trying to fit in with the Charleston social set."

"Gideon Sullivan was a major patron of the St. Expeditus Society," Father Anne said. "That raises all kinds of questions that I'd love to learn the answers to."

"There was a plaque to him in the plague church as well," Kell spoke up. "I didn't question it because Cassidy said his wife died from Yellow Fever. But do you think it might be more than that?"

"Did you get pictures of the plague crosses?" I asked.

Kell pulled out his phone. "Right here. I'll send them to you."

I looked to Simon and Father Anne. "I remembered seeing plague crosses at Sullivan's mansion. I thought they looked different from the ones we've seen come through the shop. Alistair took some photos for me. It might be nothing—but it could mean something. If I send the pictures, can you please take a look and see what you think?"

"Sure," they agreed. "We'll let you know what we find."

"We've only just started going through the containers from Bermuda," Beck added. "But I think I've found some manifests that might be from the right era, which could give us an idea of what kind of cargo the ships Gideon might have encountered were carrying."

"Anything you can find out is good," I replied. "Because right now, we don't know exactly what we're looking for. But I think we'll know it when we see it."

"It's still early," Teag said. "Why not read some more from the book?"

Everyone nodded. Teag refilled my glass, and I opened Gideon's book once more and began to read aloud.

"The next month was quiet. I needed that, as it was the anniversary of Annabelle's death, and I found myself more melancholy than usual. She was a fine companion, a good person, and I cared about her even if we were never in love.

"I had gone ashore in Hamilton, hoping that taking in the familiar sights would lift my mood. The city reminds me a great deal of Charleston, and I feel less homesick when I walk along the streets of rainbow-hued buildings and beautiful wrought iron railings.

"The change of scenery helped, but not enough. I found myself at the Royal Mile, a pub favored by seagoing men looking for good food, fine rum, and civil conversation instead of brawling and wenching. I took a seat at my favorite table and ordered my usual bangers and mash along with a glass of rum.

"When he walked in, the crowd went silent, and I caught my breath. The black-clad stranger wore a long coat over a full shirt, fitted pants, and high leather boots. No one could miss the sword that hung at the man's side or the flintlock pistol shoved into his belt.

"His raven-black hair and dark stubble gave him a roguish look, though it did not detract from a strong jaw, high cheekbones, and eyes dark as a starless night. He was as tan as a Spaniard, not unusual among those who spent their days at sea. It looked good on him, and I wondered if he was of mixed blood, as is common in the islands.

"I did not expect to find those obsidian eyes fixed on me.

"The crowd parted without a word as he strode across the room, closing behind him with knowing nods and whispered words. He moved with a predator's grace, fluid and powerful. That dark gaze transfixed me, and my heart pounded, though I am yet unsure, even in hindsight, whether in trepidation or something completely different.

"He greeted me and asked if I was the captain of the *Resilient*, and I nodded. His accent suggested Cuba or Hispaniola. Then he took the seat across from me, a bold move. He smelled of leather, cherry tobacco, and bay rum. Up close, I could see that his outfit was made of good cloth, well-cut and finished, though without adornment.

"I asked who he was when I found my voice, taken aback by his brashness as well as his beauty.

"I will never forget his answer. 'Ramon Montero. the privateer who saved your ass.' So this was our savior, the reckless captain who had driven off the pirates. I hoped by all that's holy that I did not betray how his arrival flustered me. I had known since I came of age that I found the male form more pleasing than the female. Certainly, I had done my duty to my wife and taken pleasure from it, but I leaned more toward masculine company.

"Given Charleston's sensibilities and my father's stern religion, I had never acted on those thoughts back home, fearing scandal or ruin should I be caught out. At sea, such things are reckoned differently. Long voyages in close quarters meant taking companionship where it could be found. I did not permit hedonism or debauchery aboard my ship, but I saw no sin in two men finding comfort where they could. Many among my crew were partnered, and some had made matelotage vows. I reckoned it was their business and not mine and ignored the envy I sometimes felt on solitary nights.

"On occasion, in island ports away from the taverns where my crew congregated, I had sought solace in hurried touches and fumbled couplings. Those encounters had confirmed my desires, but they lacked the most satisfying thing that my Annabelle had been able to give me —friendship and a trustworthy companion.

"All that flashed through my brain in the blink of an eye as I regarded Montero. My body made its interest clear in a way I could not ignore, and I was glad for the table that hid my reaction from view.

"I thanked him, hoping my voice did not betray me.

"After all these years, I still remember the slow smile that spread across Montero's face. He said he had heard of me and wanted to know if I 'measured up' to the stories.

"The wicked gleam in his eye and the change of his tone suggested a more salacious meaning. My heart thudded as I feared my secret might be caught out. I wasn't sure which would be more terrifying— for him to be mocking me or to somehow, impossibly, return my interest.

"To steer the conversation into somewhat safer territory, I asked by whose letter of marque he sailed. Pride colored his features as he assured me the 'John Company' issued his letter.

"I knew he meant the British East India Company, a reputable—if ruthless—force in the Caribbean. Given his fearlessness and his crew's mastery of their ship, I did not doubt that Montero turned a handsome profit for himself and the company.

"A strange recklessness came over me, and I offered to buy his drinks in gratitude for saving my ship. I did not want him to leave.

"He smiled, and even now I remember the speculation in his gaze and the dimples that were to be my ruin as he accepted my offer.

"We talked for hours. I feared that we might have nothing in common except for the details of sailing, but I found Montero to be educated and well-read, and our discussion ranged from books to the theater to favorite coves in the West Indies. Time flew, and before I knew it, the tavern had emptied, and the barkeep told us to call it a night.

"To my surprise, Montero rose and made a courtly bow. He thanked me for my company and told me that he felt sure we would meet again. His rakish smile haunted my dreams for weeks.

"I watched him leave, and I knew in that moment that something connected us far more than a battle or the sea itself. I felt certain that we were to be something to one another, but what, I did not know.

"For the first time in a very long while, I felt hope stir."

I read for another hour and a half, still finding no spell reference that would make this a grimoire. Then I looked up with a sly grin. "What do you think?"

Teag smirked. "Is it hot in here, or is it me?"

"Day-um," Maggie said. "You didn't tell me this was pirate porn."

"Dante says that Gideon's description is accurate for the time and place," Simon spoke up. "Dante visited the Royal Mile often. He said to tell you that it's not a bad thing that he doesn't recall Montero or his ship. It means that Montero was never a problem or got in their way. Dante's crew left the other privateers alone."

I exchanged a look and a shrug with Teag. *So far, Gideon's story seemed to be checking out.*

A glance at my phone reminded me that it was getting late, and tonight was a weeknight. I turned to Kell. "Before we finish up, can you tell us how your investigation went at the plague church?"

"Sure," he replied. "We decided to investigate St. Sebastian's Church because of the appearances of the monk ghost on The Battery and increased paranormal activity inside the church itself."

"Harbingers," Father Anne said. "Warnings that something bad is coming."

Kell nodded. "Usually, we try to document the activity when we go to a location. In this case, we didn't need to confirm that the reports were real—we wanted to find out what they meant. We took Alicia Peters with us, hoping that the spirits would talk to her and that we could record the encounter."

"What happened?" Simon asked.

"Let me show you."

Kell sent the video to Teag to screen-share it on the laptop, making it visible for Simon, Beck, Travis, and Logan as well as the others in the room.

"Saint Sebastian's is maintained as a museum," Kell narrated. "It never functioned as a regular parish church because it was built as a place to hold the funerals for the people who died in the plagues that hit Charleston—mostly Yellow Fever and Malaria. Just to put it in perspective, there were seven Yellow Fever epidemics just between 1792 and 1800, and more later."

"Wow," Logan murmured.

I knew that statistic, but it always floored me to hear it repeated. I couldn't imagine what it had been like to have lived through that or to see so many friends and family members die.

"There's a story that one of the monks—Brother Johan—had prayed to heaven every day to stop the plague, to no avail," Kell continued. "Finally, he offered to sell his soul to Hell. The plagues ended and didn't begin again for seventy years. But Johan was damned to remain bound on earth as a harbinger of looming disaster."

"Theologically questionable, but it makes a good story," Father Anne said.

Kell's video showed the inside of the old church. Saint Sebastian's was plain in comparison to many other churches in Charleston—a city with so many places of worship its nickname is the "Holy City." The walls were white, adorned only with a series of large plague crosses, each one easily three or four feet long, some made of metal and others of wood.

A plague cross looked like a regular Christian cross but with an additional, shorter crossbeam above the main one. Prayers to one of the plague saints and protective symbols were usually carved into the cross. The amulets were thought to ward off disease and dated back at least to the Black Death in the 1400s.

"You're right, Cassidy," Simon said. "Those crosses look different. I doubt that's an accident."

"SPOOK had already done observations down at Whitepoint Gardens and elsewhere along The Battery," Kell went on. "We didn't capture Brother Johan on tape, but we did get high EMF readings and some interesting EVP."

Ghosts were a manifestation of energy. While they were difficult to photograph, the energy readings provided valuable information about their strength and usually lingered even after the visible appearance faded. EMF measured the energy, while EVP recorded sound.

"We found similar readings at Saint Sebastian's to the EMF we gathered along the sea wall," Kell said, and the video showed a monitor with an array of red lights. "Very strong energy—you can see that the meter's pegging the red zone."

"You think the same spirit is haunting the church?" Beck asked.

Kell shook his head. "Not exactly. There were more ghosts inside the church, while Johan is the only one who shows up at The Battery. He might be trapped by his deal or bound by the need to protect the city. A number of spirits haunt Saint Sebastian. Some are repeaters—flickers of fading energy stuck in a loop that shows them doing the same thing over and over. Others might be monks who died of the fever carrying out their work and felt connected to the mission, so they stayed."

I'd had plenty of run-ins with ghosts. Some were truly trapped and wanted to be set free to move on. Others chose to remain behind for a purpose—usually revenge or protection. A few didn't realize they were dead and just needed a nudge in the right direction. Charleston is known for being one of the most haunted cities in the country. Ghost tours are big business, and being haunted is a selling point for restaurants and hotels.

"So here's the best EVP clip," Kell said. "We sharpened it, but we didn't distort it or change anything."

A strange bass voice spoke a few words. The first time it played, I only caught one word—"deep." Kell played the clip a couple of times, and as I grew used to the echoey voice, I thought I heard a bit more, but I still wasn't sure.

"Could you get anything out of that?" Anthony asked. "It's muddled."

Kell nodded. "When we ran it through some audio sharpening software, this is what we got." He clicked on another clip.

"Witch of the deep," the sepulchral voice said. "Witch of the deep."

A chill slithered down my spine, and I remembered Gideon's warnings about the darkness, a threat he had sacrificed himself to avoid.

"How about Alicia?" Simon asked.

"That's coming up," Kell replied. In the video, we saw one of his SPOOK team set out a folding chair so Alicia could sit down. I knew from working with her and Simon that channeling a spirit takes a lot out of a medium, an energy drain that can be dangerous. Alicia closed her eyes and breathed deeply for a few cycles before speaking.

"I wish to speak with Brother Johan, the protector," she said, eyes closed, concentration clear in her features.

The tape picked up the quieter voices of Kell and his team, and it looked to me like shadows moved around the walls where there shouldn't have been motion.

"We were getting a really strong EMF," Kell narrated. "It got cold, and we felt a breeze when there hadn't been any before."

I noticed the salt barrier that Kell and his team had laid on the floor around their equipment. Salt repelled spirits. It wouldn't stop their technology from recording what it saw and heard, but it would keep the ghosts from trashing their stuff if things went bad. Alicia needed to be approachable, so her chair was outside the salt circle—a necessary risk.

"Brother Johan? Why have you returned?" Alicia sounded small in the big, empty church. Unlike a regular sanctuary, Saint Sebastian's had no pews and only a basic apse and altar. The monks who said the funeral mass and buried the bodies were most often the only ones in attendance since family and friends feared infection.

I knew when Johan answered her because I could see the change come over Alicia. Her bearing shifted, and something in her expression looked different. Alicia wasn't completely herself, something my hind-brain recognized and responded to with primal fear.

"I remain." The voice coming from Alicia had changed its timbre, deeper and more masculine.

"Why do you stay?" Kell's voice carried from off-screen in the video.

"I made a pact."

"With whom?" Kell asked.

"Whoever would listen."

That sent another chill through me since it sounded like a deliberate non-answer. Sentient ghosts retained the ability to lie, or even more dangerously—withhold information.

"Why have you reappeared after being quiet for so long?" Kell asked from behind the camera.

"The protectors have grown weak."

"Protectors from the fever?" Kell probed.

"From the darkness. The Witch of the Deep."

"Can you protect us?" Kell's question hung between them for a moment.

"Not the same."

Alicia was tiring. Kell must have noticed it as well. "Brother Johan, it's time for you to go."

"Restore protection or remove the witch."

"Thank you for your efforts. Now please, let her go."

Alicia trembled, then slumped in her chair. She would have fallen if one of Kell's team members hadn't caught her. They pressed a bottle of water and a protein bar into her hands and waited while she regained her strength.

Kell ended the playback. "We got more EMF and some EVP but nothing as clear…and I think it was plague-related, not connected to Johan's mission."

"I took a quick look at those photos," Simon spoke up. "I want to study them more closely, but I see a couple of things right up front. Most traditional plague crosses call on Saint Sebastian or Saint Roche. The crosses in the pictures call to Saint Elmo—the patron saint for protection against sea monsters. There are some markings that I want to check, but I think they refer to a very old term for monsters —'leviathan.'"

"Seriously?" Anthony echoed. "Okay, I accepted vampires and werewolves, but you're telling me the Loch Ness monster is real too?"

I felt for him. Anthony loved Teag with everything he had, but he was still new to accepting the supernatural. Teag and I suspected that Anthony's highly accurate intuition might have more to do with latent magic than luck, but he wasn't ready to accept that—yet.

Simon laughed. "We're not talking Godzilla," he said. "At least, I don't think so."

"When I was a boy, before I was sent away, my father told a story about a presence that haunted the waters of the Caribbean," Beck said. "I thought it was just a faerie tale, but all this has me thinking there might be more to it."

We all turned to look at Beck on the laptop. "He said that there were ancient spirits tied to land and water. The old cultures knew this and respected it, but nowadays people had forgotten those beliefs. Sometimes the spirits were guardians, and other times they were malicious. He said they caused wild storms, maelstroms, and shipwrecks."

"That's not a lot to go on," Teag said.

"It's a start." Simon looked thoughtful, and I had a feeling he'd be hitting the books as soon as our video call ended. "There are a number of entities that might fit that story. At least that narrows the search."

"Glad it helped—because as a bedtime story, it sucked. Gave me nightmares every time," Beck muttered.

I knew everyone would rather stay up and brainstorm possibilities, but we all had jobs waiting in the morning. Simon, Travis, Beck, and Logan logged off after wishing everyone a good night.

Sorren turned to me. "I've taken care of the 'stalkers' you told me about, but Etheridge may be headstrong enough to send more. I paid a visit to his office after sundown. Ruffled a few feathers, I'm sure. He wasn't there, but his people knew *what* I was, if not *who* I was. I made it clear that Charleston was *protected* and that I took Carter's hostilities as a personal affront—for which there would be repercussions."

His lips quirked in a faint smile. "Message received. I can't guarantee that Carter will change his ways, but his entire organization is now on notice that the Alliance is involved and—what's the phrase? 'Taking names and kicking ass?'"

"Thank you," I said, leaning against Kell as the day caught up with me. "I appreciate it."

Sorren shrugged. "Carter Etheridge is not immortal, but his thinking is mired in the past, and he will understand the threat for what it is. So will those in his organization, and they may weigh the odds of their long-term survival against their loyalty to one reckless man."

Sorren checked outside, then motioned for the others to exit, keeping watch so that they got to their cars safely. Everyone else except Kell and Sorren went home with the leftovers of their choice, which still meant I had plenty of food for the rest of the week. Baxter climbed onto the couch, figuring we'd be back, maybe with treats.

"Stay alert," Sorren warned. "Carter Etheridge isn't going to give up easily. Don't go anywhere alone until we can deal with him. If his father were still alive, I'd have already spoken to him, and he'd have at least cautioned Carter to not be so blatant. Buell Etheridge was old school, and he observed the decorum of the supernatural community—at least when it served him," Sorren added with an expression of distaste.

"Carter's more of a smash-and-grab sort of guy. He doesn't respect anything but force. He knows that you have powerful friends—and it's not stopping him, so just threatening him isn't going to make him change. There are others in his family who might be more willing to see reason, but they don't have enough influence as long as Carter's in charge." There was a note of frustration in Sorren's voice. "Be careful —and I will see what can be done."

I thanked him again and then locked up. It had been a busy day, and now that the adrenaline was fading, I was tired.

"Did you have a good evening?" Kell stepped up close behind me. He pulled me into his arms, and I rested my head on his shoulder.

"It's always good to be with friends," I said, warm from dinner and the wine. "And Gideon's story is turning out to be a lot more than someone's dusty memoirs. I didn't expect him to be so…candid."

Logically I knew that people from long ago were just like us—that they loved and lusted and made impulsive choices based more on heart than head. Still, I couldn't help feeling surprised at Gideon's account of meeting Ramon and how completely modern it sounded.

"Makes me wonder where the story goes from here. We might not have gotten to the juicy parts yet." Kell waggled his eyebrows lecherously.

"This might make up for some of the dry-as-dust textbooks I've read. Sexy history would probably attract a lot more students," I joked.

"Much as I'd love to keep going with Gideon's life story, it's after midnight, and I've got a very long editing session tomorrow," Kell said. "I'd rather spend the rest of the evening with you."

I stretched up to kiss him. "Invitation accepted."

CHAPTER SEVEN

WE WERE SLAMMED AT THE STORE THE NEXT DAY, WHICH WAS GOOD for sales, and less so for sleuthing. Everyone had commitments that night, which meant we couldn't get together in person, but we agreed to connect by video call at ten. They all wanted to hear me read more of Gideon's book, the oddest type of bedtime story.

The creepy stalker dudes down the block from my house were gone when Teag drove me home and waited while I sluiced the front walk with a fresh batch of the protection mixture. He assured me he was using the same mix at his home with Anthony. I felt exhausted by the time I went inside, but having Baxter hopping around my feet perked me up. A text message from Kell let me know his video editing was taking a lot longer than usual, and he was probably going to sleep at his place so he could work into the wee hours. He wouldn't be on the video call but wanted an update if we found out anything important.

"Guess it's just you and me for dinner, Bax," I said as I put kibble into his dish. The fridge was full of leftovers from the night before, so I wasn't going to starve. I made myself a plate, microwaved it, and turned on the TV news while I ate.

I couldn't wait to dive into Gideon's story. My intuition said that we had a deadline, reinforced by the omens, which were getting worse.

News chatter focused on the "monster" storm in the Caribbean that looked likely to hit the coast hard within a few days. Charleston's tremors had grown more frequent, and experts worried about a fault line between here and Bermuda that had been dormant for years and suddenly showed signs of activity.

The governor made an evacuation order—voluntary so far, but that would become mandatory if the storm moved closer. I knew we wouldn't be leaving no matter what the orders said. We had a job to do, and most of us had extra abilities to help us survive. Teag and I knew that Kell and Anthony—and Maggie—wouldn't leave without us, so we'd need to provide for their safety. My house was the best bet for a sanctuary. It had withstood hurricanes for a hundred years. Unfortunately, I had no idea whether it was strong enough to outlast an earthquake. I hoped I didn't have to find out.

I got comfortable with Baxter next to me and opened the memoir to where we had left off, looking for the best place to start while I was waiting for the others to come on the video call.

I skimmed several pages as Gideon talked about the difficulties on a voyage due to bad weather and illness among the crew. He wrote at length about the repairs his ship needed after another run-in with pirates and how he used the time in port to set up business for the rest of the season.

Gideon's personality and voice came through in every line, and despite the centuries between us, I felt like I was getting to know him in a very real way. I loved how he tossed in little asides about the weather or the birds, described a particularly good meal or a beautiful sunset, or spoke of sighting dolphins or watching shooting stars with a sense of awe.

His entries made it clear that he knew each member of his crew and was concerned when any took sick or were injured, mentioning them by name and noting how things turned out. It didn't surprise me that his crew would return that loyalty, even so far as overlooking their captain's witchy skills.

Then again, as Gideon had pointed out, social conventions aboard ship veered from the hidebound rules of Charleston or London. If life partnerships between two men could be taken in stride, then perhaps it wasn't a stretch for the crew to accept a captain who could magic the sea, particularly if his abilities increased their safety.

When I was focusing on Gideon's words, I tried to tamp down my touch magic to avoid distraction. Now, I opened myself to that connection. I trusted Gideon not to have sent something with a resonance that would hurt me since he had clearly expected a psychic to receive his book.

Joy. Loneliness. Wonder. Fear. Curiosity. Competence. A shifting kaleidoscope of emotions were clear and strong even across centuries. *Love. Loss. Friendship. Loyalty. Anger. Peace.* I didn't try to examine the feelings; I just let them wash over me, suspecting that if I needed to, I could pin each one to specific pages or passages. A lifetime's worth of sensations, unfiltered and unashamed.

I came back to myself with a gasp. Usually when I read the resonance of an object, I saw vivid images, like I had at Gideon's home. In that way, it was more like seeing a ghost doomed to repeat a key moment from their past, or a snippet from a video on a permanent loop. Oddly, Gideon's book varied in its emotional wallop by section, as I'd experienced the other night when I had a ring-side view of the action.

The pages I skimmed that told of everyday concerns didn't try to project images or pull me in. I'd rarely run into an object that affected me in more than one way. Most of the time, I only got a single key image or impression. The complexity of the link with Gideon's book intrigued me, and I felt a mix of anticipation and trepidation over what might rise from the next section of pages.

Baxter lifted his head to give me a curious look and then went back to sleep. Gideon Sullivan was an intense guy, and it would take me a while to sort out my impressions. I felt closer to him than ever before and went back to skimming the book to get to another key section.

I knew I'd found the right spot when Montero's name caught my eye. Not wanting to trigger an incident or get ahead of the group, I marked the page and closed the cover, waiting for the right time to start the video call.

∽

ONCE EVERYONE HAD GATHERED ONLINE, and we exchanged greetings and quick updates, I opened the book and started to read.

"We've had a good run these last few months—calm seas, fair winds, and clear sailing. Business has been better than usual, and a full cargo hold means the crew gets paid on time, often with a little extra if things go our way.

"I stood on deck last night, watching the stars. A clear sky allowed the constellations to shine bright. Despite the night's peacefulness, my restless mind rambled, keeping me from sleep.

"Letters from Edward and Annabelle's father caught up to me at my Hamilton address. He's doing well in his studies and excels at sports. The headmaster speaks well of Edward, and he seems healthy and happy. His grandfather owns a counting house, and I don't doubt that so long as Edward shows aptitude, he will find a place there when he is old enough. It's honest work and will let him provide for a family, but my soul shrinks from the thought of it.

"My heart has always yearned for the sea. Here in the salt air, with the flap of the sails and the constant rolling of the waves, I am at home and know as much peace as might be possible. Someday the hardships of this life will undo me, and I know not what will become of me then.

"Twice now, Ramon Montero has crossed my path since the battle with the pirates. Once was in another skirmish, where our two ships handily chased off the attackers without incidence. The second was in a harbor bar in Port-Au-Prince, where we passed a pleasant evening over dinner and brandy.

"A wise captain keeps his own counsel aboard ship, and while I trust my second-in-command with my life, there are things better suited to discussion with a friend than with a colleague. I did not realize how much I missed having a friend like that until my conversation with Montero. He is as easy to talk to as Annabelle used to be, with the benefit that Montero knows and loves the sea as I do, something Annabelle and I did not share."

I paused, a little overwhelmed at how much of himself Gideon revealed in his journal. It was hard to believe he had written this more than two hundred years ago.

"Wow," Teag said, leaning against Anthony. "I expected an adventure story—didn't know we were going to get a romance with it!"

"This would make a great movie," I agreed. "And we haven't even gotten to the saving the world part yet."

"Don't keep us hanging," Maggie begged. "Keep reading!"

I lifted the book again.

"We came back to Hamilton after a hurricane sorely tried the *Resilient's* mettle. We prevailed, but the ship took enough damage that I thought it wise to return to port for repairs before another storm caught us unprepared. It will mean being late delivering some cargo, but better to be behind schedule than to land at the bottom of the ocean.

"I keep a house in Hamilton since business brings me here often, and I find myself avoiding Charleston of late. The property is modest, nothing like the grand house in Charleston. Then again, it is plenty for my needs. The home is made of limestone covered with stucco, painted a sunny yellow. Best of all, it sits high enough to have a good view of the ocean and catch the breeze while being far enough inland to be relatively safe from storms.

"There are only three rooms—an office, a sitting area, and a bedroom—plus a separate kitchen behind. An island woman cooks for me when I am in residence; else, I would starve since I can set a fire in the fireplace but have never managed to prepare anything worth eating. I have a comfortable reading chair sufficient for quiet nights and a broad porch where I can sit when the mood strikes. My one indulgence has been a mahogany four-poster bed I purchased in Barbados. It welcomes me home whenever I stray.

"For the most part, I am content with my own company, but some nights are darker than others. After being onboard a ship with more than one hundred men for weeks at a time, solitude is a precious gift and a rare curse. It soothes and bedevils in equal measure. Annabelle used to tease that I got stuck in my head too much. That was true, and she alone knew how to jolly me out of melancholy thoughts.

"At sea, work keeps my mind clear and tires the body so that sleep is long and mostly dreamless. On shore, I have few distractions, just my books and my daily walk. Every few days I go to the pub for an evening, but once I arrive my contrary mind tries to convince me to go back home. I do not do well at loose ends."

I paused to finish my drink and rested my left hand on the book. The world swirled around me as a vision came over me so fast I barely registered dropping the glass in my hand. Voices called to me, too far away to make out the words. Then the resonance of the book drew me in, and I saw Gideon's story through his eyes.

A knock at the door startled me since I did not expect company. To my surprise, and I confess, excitement, Ramon Montero stood on my porch in the moonlight, and I wondered if he was real or my imagining.

"Gideon." Just the way he said my name, I knew something was wrong. I looked again and saw dark stains on his white shirt. He leaned against the railing, making me wonder if he could stand unsupported.

"Ramon. What happened?"

"Help me." That was all he said before his eyes rolled back, and he slumped to the floor like a dead man.

I feared the worst as I dragged him inside. Before I shut the door, I looked one way and the other in case whoever had done this to him followed him here. I saw no one, which made me all the more curious as to how Ramon had been overpowered. It seemed impossible that a privateer could survive as long as he had without excellent fighting skills, so I assumed he'd been ambushed and outnumbered.

There would be time enough to hear his story if I could stop the bleeding.

I grabbed towels and pulled the kettle from the hearth. Ramon hadn't moved from where I left him sprawled in the entranceway, a bad sign that worried me. Even in the candlelight, he looked pale, and his breathing was too shallow for my liking.

A bruise darkened one cheekbone, blood dripped from his split lip, and I saw the beginnings of a black eye. Several suspicious welts would blossom into colors by morning. He'd been beaten.

"You got yourself into a bit of trouble, didn't you," I said aloud,

knowing he wouldn't respond. Anger stirred in my belly. I doubted Ramon had lost to a single opponent, and I hated the bully packs that roamed the waterfront looking for trouble.

I stripped away his ruined shirt and caught my breath when I saw the damage. He'd been slashed across the chest, deep enough that it would scar no matter how I treated the wound. Another slice bled from his side just above his hip bone, probably not damaging to his insides, but sufficient for pain and blood loss.

Despite how carefully I handled him, Ramon moaned without waking.

"Stay with me," I urged as I cast his bloody shirt aside and dipped a towel into a basin of water. I wrung it out and went to work cleaning the wounds, daubing gently while I cursed his attackers under my breath.

It struck me odd that Ramon, wounded and desperate, had come to me of all people. Did he have no one else he trusted? That saddened me, although a hidden spark glowed brighter at the thought. I was honest enough to acknowledge my desire for the privateer. I suspected he might return my interest, but until tonight had no real confirmation.

Turning up half dead on my doorstep wasn't exactly a declaration of love, but it would do.

I hummed as I carefully washed away the blood, more to calm my thoughts than for amusement's sake. Time and again, I rinsed out the towel until I had cleaned him up and cleansed the wounds.

I reached for a jug of rum and poured a thin trickle over the torn flesh.

Ramon cursed in Spanish and jackknifed at the pain. He looked around wildly, and I scrambled back, in no hurry to be punched for my efforts.

"You're safe," I promised. "Seguridad." I knew a little Spanish, a necessity in the islands.

His dark eyes found my face, and all the fight left him. "Gideon. Thank God."

I laid my hands on his bare shoulders and forced myself not to stare at his naked chest. I had been alone far too long, and Ramon presented a nearly irresistible temptation.

Ignoring those thoughts, I gently pushed him to lie down. "I'm not done. You're still bleeding. Need to bandage you."

I tore strips from his ruined shirt and wrapped his chest and side, winding the bandages as tightly as I dared to hold the edges of the wounds together. I said a silent prayer to a God I wasn't sure existed that infection didn't set in.

"Thank you." The deep rumble of his voice that captivated me was now weak enough to be concerning.

"You're welcome. Should I get my musket? Are the people who did this likely to come bursting into my house?"

He shook his head, eyes still shut, so I knew he was in pain. "No. I got away. They didn't follow. Had nowhere else to go."

How he knew where to find me was a conversation for another time. I was glad he had come to me, and the thought of him injured, friendless, and alone hurt my chest.

"Let me get you onto the couch. Then I have rum for the pain."

Ramon was not a small man. I couldn't carry him, but I helped him up and supported him as he hobbled to the sitting room. He fell more than sat, and I lifted his ankles and pivoted him so he could lie down.

I left him for a moment, returning with a pillow and blanket, then went to the sideboard and poured us both glasses of rum. I put a hand behind his shoulders to lift him up enough to drink. That he allowed it gave me an understanding of his condition.

"In the morning, I'll have my cook fetch the makings for a poultice to draw out any poison in the wounds," I told him. "Until then, sleep. I'll keep watch."

He murmured his thanks and quickly fell into deep slumber. I stared at him, watching his chest rise and fall, and wondered how in the name of the fates I would survive having the man who haunted my dreams so close at hand.

When I came around, Baxter was licking my face, and my friends on the video call were calling my name, sounding panicked.

"I'm...okay," I managed, and sat up, still gripping the book. I was glad my glass had been empty because it lay on its side on the throw rug. "Give me a second—I'll tell you all about what I saw."

I picked up my fallen glass and went out to the kitchen, snagging a can of soda from the fridge and gulping it down. I headed back to the living room, feeling a little chagrined even though I knew my friends understood about visions. Simon and Trent knew what it was like, first-hand since they had them too.

"Sorry about that," I said, settling on the couch with Baxter and the book again.

"We were just worried," Teag said. "I was about to head over there if you hadn't come around when you did."

"Thank you," I replied, knowing how lucky I was to have so many wonderful friends in my life. I gave them the condensed version of what I had seen. "It was pretty intense—I suspect that's how I got sucked in," I said at the end.

"I can't imagine reliving that from Gideon's perspective," Anthony added. "Do you think he intended all along for someone else to read his story, or was he writing for himself at first?"

"Maybe we'll find out," Simon mused. "I don't think Gideon had an idea of the big picture yet, or the role he ended up playing."

I eyed the book. "I think there's more to the vision. I'm willing to see what the book wants to show me—just stick close, please. I promise I'll tell you everything when I come back out."

"We've got your back," Teag assured me. I took a deep breath and laid my hand on the book once more.

I had hoped to prevent Ramon's wounds from going bad, but luck was not on our side. The cuts festered, despite every poultice and potion I could find. I dosed him with an extract said to lessen malaria's effects and tea steeped from willow bark, but the fever still raged.

Pale with sickness, lips red and eyes sunken, he seemed a shadow of the brash man I had seen leaping from rails to rigging, giving the devil his due. Delirious, he ranted in Spanish and English, switching between the two mid-sentence, sometimes word by word. I couldn't pretend to catch most of it.

I removed the rags of his tattered, bloodied clothing, doing my best to remain clinical and not notice the strong body beneath them. I forced my thoughts away and focused on saving his life. I suspected he shared my attraction, but all was for naught if he didn't survive.

Cold water was a rarity in Bermuda in any season. I drew a bath and covered him to his chin, repeating as often as the heat from his body warmed the water past usefulness. During the long hours of the night, I spoke to him constantly of everything and nothing because I could not bear the silence.

I told him about Annabelle and Edward and spoke aloud for the first time that while I mourned her as a friend, I did not grieve her as a husband. I rambled, recounting tales from my childhood and curiosities from past voyages. Knowing that Ramon liked books, I spun stories from what I remembered of what I'd read, filling in the gaps with my own fancies when memory failed. When all else failed, I sang and hoped he was not particular about music.

Never had a night seemed so long, not even when I had suffered a bout of malaria the doctors feared would claim me. Then, I had been lost in delirium. Now, I felt the passage of each minute.

Just before dawn, the fever broke. I hauled Ramon from the tub and collapsed next to him on the floor, utterly spent. But he was breathing, and his skin no longer burned from inside. I had no way of knowing whether the fever had harmed his mind or his heart, but I would take this win and deal with the rest later.

We both slept, completely exhausted. I came back to myself before he woke and manhandled him onto my couch. I found him a pair of my drawers and did my best to drip more willow bark tea and extract down his throat and made him as comfortable as possible.

I felt weak from hunger and parched with thirst and made myself eat and drink, although I tasted nothing and feared I might not keep down what I consumed. Then I went to my bed and pulled off the pillow and blanket, carrying them into the parlor so I could sleep beside the couch, in case Ramon stirred or woke in a terror.

My dreams were dark. More than once I woke shuddering from remembered fears. Often, my mind set out twists of fate that might have been but for the grace of fate. My imagination supplied the horrors, none worse than hauling Ramon's lifeless body from the water and finding no breath or heartbeat.

I knew then what I doubted I would ever publicly confess. I cared deeply for Ramon, and I desired him. The truth of it chilled my marrow, but I could not deny its reality. I held hope that he returned the senti-ment, but for now, until he was more than a step away from death's door, the point remained moot. Yet, for the first time in a very long while, a spark flickered in my heart, and I felt more alive than I ever recalled.

Ramon slept for two days, and when he woke, the fever was gone. I had cared for him with the intimacy of a nurse, but neither of us felt shame. Once he regained his strength, Ramon told me about the cutpurses who jumped him outside a tavern. He had fought them off—four to one—but nearly at the cost of his life. He thanked me for taking care of him, but how could I have done anything else?

He stayed with me for another week until we both had obligations that would take us back to sea. To my amazement and great joy, Ramon returned my feelings, and we began what would become the central relationship of the rest of our lives.

But still, we were captains of two ships, with crews and customers reliant on us. Back to the sea we went, but for the first time, I did not feel the joy the ocean had always brought me. Always before, I had found peace and solace in the waves and the wind. Now, I felt as if I were missing a piece of myself, something that nothing could fill except Ramon.

We had agreed to meet in two months in Havana, and I could not restrain myself from counting down the days like a lovesick teenager. I lost myself in the details of my business and the day-to-day routine of running the ship, far more involved than I had been for years. It helped me pass the time and kept me reasonably sane.

Ramon and I had not only acknowledged our love for each other; we had shared our other deepest secret—our magic. I could bend the waves to my will while Ramon called to the winds. That explained our success when we fought pirates together since we controlled the elements by which ships plied the ocean.

But recently the sea had become more dangerous, and our abilities might not be able to protect our crews much longer. The Bermuda run had always been hazardous—pirates and wild storms claimed ships and lives all too often. Lately, the toll had risen sharply, and we believed that something supernatural lay behind it.

I came out of the vision easier this time, they all listened carefully as I recapped what I saw.

"Maybe we should take a break here and let you catch your breath," Teag said. "We can pick up where we left off tomorrow."

"Let me get a good night's sleep," I said, grateful for the break. "I'm just afraid there'll be something I sense in a vision that I'd miss otherwise. But we can decide that when we get back together."

Everyone on the call wished me well, promised to get back to me on the pieces of the puzzle they were working on, and said goodnight. Sorren was the last to log off.

"Cassidy, if you're up for it, I think it would be good for you to join Archibald and me at the Briggs Society tonight to discuss the situation. I'm sorry to ask it of you after your visions, but I have the feeling that time isn't on our side."

The effects of the vision were already fading. I hadn't planned on going out, but it was only around midnight—not late by my standards. "Yeah. That works."

"Good. I'll be by to pick you up in fifteen minutes." The video call ended, leaving me staring at the screen as I adjusted to the sudden change of plans. Bax gave me a highly disapproving side-eye as if he understood that cuddling would be interrupted.

"Sorry, Bax," I said as I set Gideon's book aside. I had changed out of my business casual workday clothes when I got home and figured that after the day I'd had, jeans and a T-shirt would be just fine for an impromptu get-together at a place that didn't really exist.

CHAPTER EIGHT

SORREN SHOWED UP RIGHT ON TIME IN A SLEEK BLACK AUDI R8; immortality is great for building wealth, and Sorren allowed himself few other indulgences. The car was fast and maneuverable—helpful in a pinch—and if circumstances required running without lights, Sorren's heightened senses would compensate.

I slipped into the passenger side, appreciating the luxury. "Thanks for the lift," I said. "Did Etheridge send any new goons, or did you scare them off for good?" Come to think of it, I hadn't seen them when I came out.

He shot me a crafty smile. "They were middling witches, but still dangerous if they had gotten the drop on you. I compelled them to return to their master with a message and reminded Etheridge that you and your friends are under my protection. I also reminded him of what happened to his ancestor who overstepped."

Sorren's tone had gone cold, and his smile revealed the tips of his fangs. Most of the time he easily passes for human. But my business partner hadn't been mortal for a long time, and in moments like this, my hindbrain remembers just what a scary mofo he can be when his people are threatened.

"Thank you," I said.

"He's being exceptionally reckless," Sorren replied. "That means he believes the stakes are worth the risk. He wants control of the witch of the deep, and he's convinced himself that Gideon's book holds the key."

"It's a memoir, not a grimoire," I replied.

Sorren shrugged. "A man like Carter Etheridge could never imagine exposing his life and thoughts like that—so he can't fathom that anyone else would do so without a hidden agenda. I owe you and the 'fellowship' an apology," Sorren added. "I should have been here and realized what was happening before it got this far. Unfortunately, between the Huntsman problem in New England and the paranormal trafficking network we've uncovered in the Midwest, there's a lot going on that Archibald and I can't fully hand off to others."

The idea that our situation wasn't the only potentially world-ending one going on at any given time gave me the heebie-jeebies.

"Dante has been bugging Simon over the sea witch problem," I said. "He seems to be taking it personally for a guy who's been dead for nearly two hundred years."

Sorren chuckled. "Dante had a serious soul. Not that he couldn't be funny and lively—he and Coltt loved to pull pranks on each other in their younger days. But he had a sharp mind and a talent for seeing to the heart of a problem."

His voice grew wistful. I didn't envy him his long existence if it meant outliving so many friends and loved ones.

"Dante and Coltt grew up in a fishing village. They never intended to become privateers, but they knew how to sail, and they realized that if someone didn't stop the raiders and the occult smugglers the raiders traded with, more villages would suffer like theirs did," Sorren went on. "They were so young when they first came to Evann. We watched them grow up and grow together."

"That…their relationship…wasn't a problem?"

Sorren shook his head. "They were discreet about it around city folk. Onboard their ship, and in harbor towns in the islands, the rules were not the same as those for 'proper' society. I came from Europe and a very different time. I have seen opinions and laws change on so many things. Immortality provides perspective on what is and isn't important—and which 'truths' are merely the whim or prejudice of an age. Evann knew history and understood those things as well. We were happy that after all their loss, they had each other."

I couldn't wrap my mind around personally seeing six centuries unfold. But I knew from what I'd studied that so many things that were once thought to be absolutes turned out to be a lot less black and white and much more nuanced. I was glad Dante and Coltt had found acceptance and safety with Sorren and Evann.

"Dante's magic grew more powerful the more he used it and studied. We knew that there were other privateers determined to take the Pendlewoods and the Etheridges down a peg and welcomed the help. If I heard of Montero at the time, I don't remember now," Sorren went on.

"Why did Dante and Coltt decide to stop being privateers and take over the shop?"

Sorren was quiet for a moment; I figured that pulling something from old memories probably took some searching, given the centuries that had passed.

"They reached the age where they knew the sea would claim one or both of them if they kept sailing, right about the time that Evann's health began to decline. He had stopped doing any of the fighting long before, serving as the researcher for our little team of allies. His close association with me extended his lifespan—as it has for all of the shop's proprietors, as it will for you and Teag. Consider it a perk or a hazard of the job."

He'd told me about the added lifespan before, but it tended to slip my mind. That "benefit" didn't make me bulletproof—it just meant that if I didn't die fighting evil sons of bitches, I could look forward to a longer-than-usual retirement.

"Evann's mind remained sharp to the end," Sorren went on, affection clear in his voice. "He worried about his daughter, Olivia, running the store on her own. Not because he doubted her capabilities—Olivia was a lot like you. But it was even more difficult back then for a woman to make her way alone in the world than it is now. And as you know, what we do brings its own dangers. He didn't want to leave her unprotected."

Sorren's lips quirked in a sad smile. "By then, Dante had lost Coltt to malaria. He was inconsolable, and I feared we might lose him too. Olivia helped him through his grief over Coltt, and Dante eased her pain when Evann died. Eventually, I believe they helped each other find peace—and their friendship became something more."

"Did Olivia fancy Dante before Coltt's death?" Not that it mattered, but the details intrigued me. I had heard Dante's version via Simon, but I was curious to find out Sorren's perspective.

Sorren was quick to answer. "Dante, Coltt, and Olivia were fast friends from the time they met. Olivia had put off suitors, and I don't think she ever planned to take a husband. Unmarried women with means were afforded some extra privileges back then, although there were additional difficulties, as well."

"And marrying Olivia would have deflected any suspicion the society mavens might have had about Dante and Coltt's relationship?" I asked.

"He protected her freedom, and she silenced the rumors. The large age gap was common back then. Quashing gossip might have been a benefit, but I believe they did what they wanted to do, and the devil take the hindmost."

I thought of Gideon and Ramon, their beautiful secret, and the dangerous deception required for them to stay together. Teag and Anthony could be open about their relationship, officially marry and go on with their lives. I celebrated for them, even as my heart ached for those who came before.

Since the Briggs Society rarely showed up in the same place twice, I wasn't sure where we were going. Sorren pulled into a curbside spot in one of the older historic neighborhoods, but the two white "single houses" beside us were definitely not our destination.

"Wait for it," he said. Between one breath and the next, a two-story, brick Georgian building appeared between the two homes, looking as if it had always been there.

I'd asked but never gotten a good answer on how the Briggs comes and goes, where it is when it's not here, and why no one seems to notice when it shows up. The answer is obviously "because it's effing magic," but I still itched for a more detailed explanation that I would probably never get.

We walked up to the door, and I saw the bronze plaque—*The Briggs Society. Explorers welcome. Ring bell.*

Before we could do so, the door opened, and a man in a formal butler's uniform opened the door. "Good evening. You are expected. Please follow me."

"Hello, Higgins. Good to see you," Sorren said.

"Always a pleasure, sir," Higgins replied, "and if I may say so, pleased to have you back with us again as well, Ms. Kincaide."

I knew that asking him to call me Cassidy was a lost cause.

"Thank you. It's nice to be back," I answered.

It had been a while since I'd been here, although I'd seen Donnelly on several occasions. The decor was the height of Victorian style, filled with treasures and mementos from around the world and every culture and time period.

The foyer was a rotunda with an overhead dome ringed with windows that, during the day, probably flooded the area with light. In the center, instead of a table with a floral arrangement, stood a taxidermied Percheron horse in full steel barding.

"This way, if you please." Higgins directed. Higgins might play the role of the perfect British butler, but I had seen him in a fight, and he could kick ass like a ninja. Donnelly was a powerful necromancer and close to immortal in his own right. I wasn't sure if the Society had any other live-in members, but Donnelly and Higgins together could take on most threats and come out on top all by themselves.

Even though I had been here before, I couldn't help swiveling my head to look around. The rotunda was ringed by portraits of famous explorers who had disappeared without a trace. Glass cases held treasures like the bound volume of Virginia Dare's memoir, art thought to have been destroyed in wars which was actually cursed by dark magic, as well as relics and occult objects too dangerous to allow out of the Briggs' reach.

The Society's interior spoke of age and wealth. Dark wood paneling covered the walls and trimmed the doors and windows. Parquet floors inlaid with elaborate protective sigils graced the hallway and foyer, adorned in places with priceless Killim rugs and ancient Aubussons. Bright brass fittings shone in the gaslight fixtures, hinges, and doorknobs. The ceilings were easily thirteen feet tall, maybe more, so while the doors and windows were proportional, they were also huge and imposing.

The masterpiece paintings, sculpture, tapestries, and relics here hadn't been appropriated—they'd been secured in the "super max" of vaults. I wondered where Donnelly had stored the Nephilim paintings I'd helped him acquire after the artworks' subjects proved capable of stepping out of the frame and causing havoc.

Higgins opened one of the hallway doors and moved to the side for us to enter. Inside, seated in wing chairs on either side of an elaborate fireplace with a roaring fire, was Archibald Donnelly and another man who looked uncannily familiar.

"Sorren! Cassidy! Come in, come in." Tall and raw-boned, florid-faced, with a mane of white hair and mutton-chop sideburns, Archibald Donnelly looked every bit the Victorian adventurer.

"May I present Captain Benjamin Briggs," he said, gesturing to the other man. Briggs had dark hair and a full beard, and I had figured him to be in his forties before I met his gaze and realized he was younger by a decade. His plain black suit, coupled with a pensive expression, gave him an austere presence.

"You were captain of the *Mary Celeste*," I said as I remembered. "One of the most famous lost ships in history."

"I thought that he might be able to shed some light on your current problem," Donnelly said. "Come in, have a seat. Higgins will bring refreshments."

Sorren and I each claimed chairs, while Higgins poured us measures of Scotch, then retreated to stand inside the closed doors, more bodyguard than manservant.

"Tell us about Gideon Sullivan," Donnelly said after we'd had a chance to taste the exquisite liquor. I couldn't imagine how long it had aged, but it was certainly the best I'd ever had.

They listened without interruption as I told them everything we had learned. "We think that Gideon and Ramon defeated some kind of entity and bound it at great cost to themselves," I said. "That binding used blood magic tied to Gideon's descendants. The last of his direct line just died, so the bond is breaking. We don't know what's heading our way."

"It sounds like a sea witch," Briggs said. "A witch of the deep."

"That's what the monk ghost said at the plague church. The ghost is a harbinger of destruction, and he's back," I replied. "Who is the sea witch?"

Briggs shook his head. "Not a 'who,' a 'what.' And there are many of them, so it all depends on *where* they bound the witch."

"Can you explain?" I didn't feel bad about being confused since Sorren and Donnelly looked equally bewildered.

Briggs managed a wan smile. Grief still haunted his gaze, and I remembered that he had lost his entire family and his crew in the incident that left his sailing ship adrift and abandoned, becoming one of history's most famous unsolved mysteries.

"They are elemental spirits of the oceans. Genius loci. The spirit of a place," Briggs said. "We think of those spirits as being on land, but they are everywhere, including the vast mountains and deep caves beneath the sea. The elementals are as old as the world. Some of them choose to ignore humans. Others decide to be helpful. But some are territorial. They resent us crossing 'their' water. And they strike back."

"Is that what you encountered?" I asked.

Briggs nodded. "I believe so. One like it. As I said—there are many. And I have had a very long time to think about it and do the research."

I knew from prior encounters that the Briggs Society gave sanctuary to explorers who had been taken by magic or unusual phenomena. They went looking for them across time and space and provided a safe haven where they could recover among others who understood their situation.

This was the first time I had met one of the Briggs's members and wondered whether those within the society's walls did not age. "Why don't we hear about the effects of the sea witches—elementals now?" I asked.

"Same issues—different words," Sorren replied. "We call things 'freak storms' or attribute problems to broken equipment or 'magnetic fluctuations.' Remember the Bermuda Triangle panic a while back? Once in a while people notice, and then lose interest. Most of the time, people will come up with all kinds of explanations to make something supernatural make sense."

"If Gideon and Ramon were able to bind one of the sea witches, then whatever magic they did is wearing off. How do we recharge it?" I looked to Donnelly. "You're a necromancer. Can you find their ghosts and get an answer?"

Donnelly shook his head. "I've made several attempts since Sorren told me about the situation. Wherever Sullivan and Montero's spirits have gone, I can't reach them."

"There are stories about sea witches and how people tried to stop them," Briggs spoke up. "Jonah, for example, threw himself overboard and was in the 'belly of the monster.' I think it's actually a story of someone who sacrificed himself—or was forced to be a sacrifice—to appease a sea witch. Once he was in the water, the storm stopped and the ship was saved. Only in his case the sea witch let him live, and he washed up three days later."

That made a lot more sense than the version I'd learned in Sunday school.

"Scylla and Charybdis, too," Donnelly added. "Sirens. The kraken. There are tales from all over the world of inhuman entities hunting sailors and going out of their way to wreck ships. All the iron and steel in modern ships might make the spirits uncomfortable nowadays, or maybe it's just too much work to defeat the technology. Even so, ships still go missing every year, some with no explanation."

"Has anyone else bound one?" I hadn't gotten to that part of Gideon's book yet, but surely they weren't the only ones to figure out how.

"People have tried," Sorren said. "Sailors are known for being superstitious—with good reason. They've seen things the folks back on land wouldn't believe. They carry charms and wear amulets and saints' medallions, and get symbols tattooed into their skin. Ships have sigils carved into the bow, get blessed by holy men, and had figureheads installed on the prows for protection. Being at sea is dangerous business, even in peacetime."

"Did any of those precautions help?" I'd heard about shipwrecks all my life—just part of the history in the Carolinas. I'd always been intrigued by anything about the Titanic. But I'd never spent a lot of time thinking about the people on those lost ships, aside from historical curiosity. I certainly never expected to meet one of them.

Donnelly shrugged. "Probably. Some ships go down because of completely non-supernatural reasons, weather included. But ships cross a lot of territory. Most of the elementals don't care or aren't hostile—thank the fates. And the ones that are malicious aren't equal in strength. Those protections probably could ward off a weaker genius loci. But for the stronger ones…obviously they're not enough."

In my imagination I pictured the earth with its huge seas and all the many different kinds of ships crisscrossing every day. I'd always thought it took real courage to be out in the middle of the ocean in good weather or bad, and much as I'd enjoyed going on a few cruises, I'd never envied the crew.

Knowing now that—in addition to bad weather and pirates—the seas and probably the big lakes were haunted by powerful ancient spirits, I was in for a whole new round of nightmares.

"We will find out whatever we can from the Society's archives," Donnelly promised. "I suspect you've asked Travis Dominick to see what he can discover in the Sinistram's library?"

I nodded. "Beck and Father Anne are combing through the St. Expeditus resources. Chuck Pettis and his uncle said they'd put some feelers out to their old ex-C.H.A.R.O.N. contacts as well. I called in all my experts on this." I knew it was an acronym, but I could never remember what they stood for. Those in the know just used the initials as the proper name.

"I'll do the same," Sorren offered. "I've got the feeling that if the elemental that they bound gets loose, it's going to affect more than just some ships at sea. I suspect the consequences would hit land too."

"The storm that's got people evacuating, and the tremors…they're both originating in the stretch of ocean between the South Carolina coast and Bermuda—one of Gideon's main trade routes. Do you think it's related?" Even as I asked the question, I knew it to be true.

If Gideon and Ramon had worked magic powerful enough to bind the elemental—no doubt at great cost—they wouldn't have risked all of that if the alternatives weren't dire. And unless we could figure out how to reinforce their spell, we'd find out just how bad those other possibilities could be.

"I think that's very likely," Briggs said. "It's too much of a coincidence."

"By the way, the sea witch isn't our only problem," I added with a glance at Donnelly. "There's some kind of wish-spirit loose, and the Etheridges are playing hardball to get their hands on Gideon's mansion and his memoir." They listened as I caught them up on both problems.

"Some families keep turning up like bad pennies," Donnelly said with a sigh. "We finally got rid of the Pendlewoods. I'd have thought the Etheridges might have been smart enough to take a hint, but apparently not."

"We've been one step behind the gin goblin this whole time," I fretted. "Right now, the spirit is loose and beholden to a thief who double-crossed Carter Etheridge. If the Etheridges find the thief and the bottle-spirit before we do, we'll be in for even more trouble."

I told them what Teag and I had uncovered so far, as well as the vision at Wilton's apartment and Etheridge's attack-by-proxy with the monsters. "Sorren chased off a couple of goons who were lurking outside my house. Etheridge is taking 'obsessed' to a whole new level."

"The spirit won't go willingly to a warlock family," Donnelly said. "If it was a captive in the bottle—it would be a slave to their wishes. A battle royal between the two wouldn't be healthy for anyone."

"Unfortunately, the Etheridges have stepped up their game. When

Beck refused to lead the Pendlewood clan, and the rest of his cousins went to prison, it left a power vacuum," Sorren said. "I've had a word with Carter's underlings, but he's managed to evade a face-to-face meeting with me so far. That will make it all the more unpleasant when I find him. He has forgotten the rules." The chill in his voice made Sorren's meaning plain.

"This whole bloody mess is like lopping snakes off the hydra's head. Cut one, and more grow back in its place," Donnelly muttered. "The Pendlewoods kept the Etheridges in check. Without them, the Etheridges expand their reach to fill the gap. Lately, we've started to see connections popping up among groups that used to work independently, and that means trouble."

"Does this have something to do with the Huntsman problem you've been dealing with up north?" I asked.

Sorren and Donnelly exchanged a glance, and Sorren nodded. "We think so. And it probably has tendrils that connect with those witch disciples that Seth Tanner and Evan Malone are chasing. Remember the site we shut down on the Darke Web that was trafficking shifters and people with supernatural abilities? Turns out they weren't the only ones."

"As if that wasn't bad enough, the dark covens and creatures used to avoid each other now, they've decided to collaborate, and it's a bloody mess," Donnelly said.

"Sounds like the Mob in its heyday," I replied. "Different families had their territories, but on big, lucrative projects, they worked together —and it made them rich and powerful. For a while."

"Now imagine organized crime families with magic and longer-than-usual lifespans," Sorren added. "The Alliance is trying to dig out the roots and cut away the branches, but it's slow going. This sort of thing has happened before, but not for a long while, and not with modern technology."

"How long ago?" I never get enough time to ask Sorren all the questions my history-loving heart wants answered.

"The First World War broke up the oldest European organizations," Sorren replied.

"And the second war destroyed the upstart rival factions—and damn near the whole world, along with them," Donnelly grumbled. "How do you think something like Wewelsburg came about?"

I shuddered, recognizing the name of the castle where Adolf Hitler nurtured his obsession with occultism. Most people thought his fascination with dark magic was proof of insanity. But the supernatural community knew just how close the Third Reich had come to harnessing ancient energies more powerful than the atomic bomb.

"Since then, conditions haven't been ideal for collaboration," Sorren continued. "The dark covens and gangs could make more money or secure their territory better working alone, and the Alliance and our allies did everything we could to keep them apart. But what we've discovered up north is that some groups were working together more than we suspected. And now, we think Carter Etheridge sees himself as the heir apparent, the one to rally the rival factions like a supernatural cartel."

"We can't let him get ahold of that wish spirit or cozy up to the sea witch," I said, breathless with the implications.

"No. We can't." Donnelly agreed, adding a *humph* for emphasis. He glanced at Sorren. "As I recall, you've been a thorn in the Etheridges' side for more than a few generations."

Sorren smiled, letting the tips of his fangs show. "Oh, absolutely. Getting in the way of people like that keeps the job fun."

Donnelly coughed. "Bunch of entitled prats," he muttered. "They're rotten to the core—no mistake about it," he clarified for Briggs and me, "but they were never as good at it as the Pendlewoods."

I felt like I'd missed the punchline. "So they get the participation award for 'not quite an evil genius'?"

That got a laugh out of Sorren. "Jeremiah Etheridge, the patriarch back before the Revolution, was a very capable wind witch who built a shipping fleet and a fortune. He had a reputation for being ruthless, and there were whispers about magic, although witchcraft could still get a man hanged back then."

"What happened?"

"His eldest son, Daniel, smuggled a shipload of trafficked psychics and shifters into port. The Alliance was waiting for him. We couldn't shut down all enslavement, but we had hammered out accords in the supernatural community that forbid pressing people or creatures into servitude. Daniel was in direct violation. He fought back. We won. Daniel died in the battle—by my hand."

Sorren's gaze was fixed on a memory. I could see that he took no triumph from the win.

"You offered him quarter," Donnelly said. "It was his choice to keep fighting. You saved a whole boatload of people—and shut down a large-scale paranormal enslavement operation in Charleston. You don't owe that mangy piece of shit a second thought."

The shadows never left Sorren's eyes. "You know what they say about no good deeds going unpunished. The fallout from that situation is shaping the conflict now."

Donnelly sat forward, straightening his back and squaring his shoulders. "It had to be done. People like the Etheridges don't care about anyone or anything except themselves. There wasn't another option."

Sorren nodded. "You're right, of course. Hindsight is a path to madness."

"You and the Etheridges have had something of a pissing match ever since?" I asked.

"It was going to happen," Donnelly answered for Sorren. "We got in their way. If it hadn't been that night, it would have been another."

Sorren turned to look at me. "I didn't go out of my way looking to make trouble for the family. But everything they did reeked of dark magic, the kind of enterprises the Alliance couldn't ignore. We clashed again and again. I wouldn't back down, and they refused to quit."

"Did you always win?" I asked.

Sorren turned away. "Not always. But more often than not. The Alliance has cost the family several fortunes in lost opportunities over the centuries. Jeremiah and Daniel weren't the only ones to die in arcane battles on land or at sea, thanks to Dante and Gideon—and others like them."

"And they blame you." I didn't make it a question.

"Hubris is an Etheridge family trait," Donnelly said, with loathing in his voice. "Their magic is powerful, but plenty of others are just as strong. Many people with abilities choose to serve and protect the supernatural community. The Etheridges serve only themselves."

"Carter Etheridge is not the strongest patriarch in his family's history, but it would be a mistake to underestimate him," Sorren replied. "Even someone of lesser power can get lucky."

I remembered what Sorren had told me earlier. "If he's worried about being challenged for the top spot in the family, then having a Dokkaebi and a sea witch in his corner would secure his position."

Sorren waited a moment before answering. "I believe that's what's driving his obsession, and it makes him exceedingly dangerous. He'll do anything to hold on to power."

"Speaking of luck, Etheridge cannot be permitted to acquire the bottle spirit," Donnelly warned. "That would make him a far more formidable enemy. We might still beat him, but at considerable cost. It would be better not to risk it."

"We're doing everything we can to find it before he does," I said. "When we do, we'll let you know, and you can bring it here, destroy it, whatever you want."

"Good." Donnelly finished his tea and set the cup aside. "Higgins and I will contact our sources about how best to deal with the bottle and let you know what we find."

"I think I'll be staying up into the morning hours reading," I said, as my head swam with new information. "And tomorrow, Teag and I will continue the hunt for the bottle spirit." I felt in my bones that the Sullivan mansion had a big role to play in all this—I just didn't know why.

Sorren dropped me off at home with a promise to be in touch as soon as he had more information. Charleston wasn't the only city Sorren protected, but I still felt safer with him around.

"Be careful, Cassidy," Sorren warned before I got out of the car. He walked me to the door, even though it was a few feet away, and I didn't mind a bit.

"The Dokkaebi alone would be worrisome, as would any involvement by the Etheridges. But the sea witch is a disaster waiting to happen," he said. "An elemental isn't like anything you've gone up against. They're different than demons or vampires or witches. Even the weak ones are ancient and extremely powerful. They don't answer to anyone, and they don't think like humans because they've never been mortal. Don't underestimate them."

"I'll be as careful as I can," I promised. We both knew it didn't guarantee anything, but it made us feel a little better. "Ugh. It's one-thirty in the morning. So it's already tomorrow."

"I know that time is of the essence getting through Gideon's book, and I'm sorry that I'm not a morning person," Sorren said with a hint of a smile.

Gotta love vampire humor.

"Archibald will be on the call in my stead later this morning, and he'll fill me in after sunset."

"I'll talk to you tonight then," I said. He waited to see me safely inside and drove away.

I FELT like I'd barely fallen asleep before the alarm went off. Baxter yipped at me until I thought my ears would bleed, probably worried that breakfast would be late. I scooped him up and held him at eye level, letting him glare at me with all his doggy annoyance, then carried him to the kitchen and fed him, which made everything all right.

I started a pot of coffee and then took a quick shower. When I came back to the kitchen, I poured myself some java, made toast with peanut butter, and got ready for the video call. Teag would join in from the shop's office while Maggie ran the front of the store, and I planned to go in once the call was over.

There was a lot of Gideon's book left to read. I couldn't be sure that we'd get through it all in one sitting, but I intended to get as far as possible. I knew in my bones that time was running out, and we still didn't have a solution.

I brought my mug of coffee into the living room and got settled on the couch with my computer set up on a tray table in front of me. Bax followed my every move with those shiny black eyes and curled next to me. Everyone from our last call joined in, including Alicia and Donnelly, who was subbing for Sorren.

"Good morning, everyone," I greeted them as their images appeared one by one on the screen. "Ready for more adventures?" I opened the book and found where I had left off.

"A seer in Barbados told us about the sea witches that claimed the ridges and clefts at the bottom of the ocean and dwelled in its caves and deep places. Visions warned her that one sea witch in particular had risen from long slumber and decided she tired of the constant noise of the ships above her, invading her sanctuary.

"This sea witch, the seer told us, meant to wipe all the trespassers from the swath of ocean she considered hers, and rouse the others of her kind to take back their waters from the sails and prows of humanity.

"The seer sent us to a Voudon mambo in Haiti, who asked the Loa Agwe to show us a way to calm the creature. Agwe turns a blind eye to them most of the time, but this insurrection he could not allow to stand. The Loa and the sea witches, she told us, are ancient beings who were powerful before mankind walked the land. Their bargains and agreements are complicated and arcane but ironclad.

"Which is why Agwe could not deal with the rogue entity himself. He told us that if we agreed to be his champions, he would share the secret of how to bind her power.

"What choice did we have? Ramon and I had lived our lives on these waters. The waves and the winds were in our blood and woven into our essence with our magic. We swore a vow of fealty to Agwe, who promised his help in any way that did not touch off a war between the Loa and the sea witches.

"And so we went to battle. We were newly wed, and had so much to live for. As Agwe directed us, Ramon and I called to our magic and worked our spell as our valiant crews held the line against an ancient and terrible power.

"My memories are jumbled. I remember sending out all the energy that my magic could harness, heedless of the cost, intent on melding my magic with Ramon's to bind the sea witch.

"She fought us, and we struck back with all that we had. When it was over, the *Resilient* sat dead in the water, and I lay broken beneath its shattered mainmast.

"We won, but at a terrible price. The allies we called to aid us rallied valiantly, but many never made it home. Ramon, thank the fates, survived unharmed. But I was not so lucky.

"I had shattered my hip and hurt my back beyond what the doctors could fix. The strain of the magic damaged my heart. Ramon retrieved my injured body and spent his hoarded fortune taking me to physicians and witches until I put an end to it. He needed to accept what I had already realized to be true.

"I would never walk without assistance again, and my days of captaining the *Resilient* were over.

"We retreated to the sanctuary I had built, a mansion by the sea that combined comfort with solitude. It was meant to be a safe haven; somewhere we could retire when the demands of life aboard ship grew too much for us. I had not envisioned that day to come for many years. More worrisome was that Charleston lived by a different code than seafarers, and our bond, our marriage, would put us in grave danger.

"So 'Ramon Montero' ceased to exist, and Alejandro Córdoba took his place, my devoted nurse. Ramon sold the *Hidalgo* to his second-in-command, though I begged him to reconsider, and I transferred what remained of the *Resilient* to my second, save for a few pieces I kept to remember her by.

"Then Ramon brought me back to Charleston and gave me a reason to live. I offered to release him from our vows. We were both still in our prime, and he deserved better than to be bound to a cripple. But he refused so vehemently that I trembled at his ferocity. Never have I felt so loved—and so lacking. Yet when Ramon assures me that I am still all he desires, I believe him."

I looked up and found my entire video call crew wide-eyed and completely immersed in the story.

"Come on, Cassidy! You can't stop now," Simon pleaded.

I paused to take a drink of my coffee. "Don't worry—there's more."

"That explains a lot about the mansion," Teag said. "And why he had all the protective wardings."

"I want more hot pirate romance!" Maggie added, looking over Teag's shoulder with a joking gleam in her eyes. Everyone laughed, and that eased some of the tension that had built with Gideon's gripping account.

"Now we know where the sea witch comes in." Beck looked thoughtful, probably reconciling what I'd just read to what was in the old Pendlewood manifests. "Can we figure out later what the approximate date would be for that battle? Logan and I just read about two Pendlewood cargo ships that were lost in a fierce storm that the company records note as 'unnatural.' Want to bet that means magic?"

I didn't doubt that.

"Lucinda will want to know that a Loa was involved," Father Anne said, mentioning a mutual friend who is a powerful Voudon mambo. "That ups the stakes—again, and they were high enough already."

"His description fits with some records I've found in the Sinistram archive," Travis chimed in. "Now that I know what I'm looking for, I'll focus on anything I can find on binding magic—for the sea witch and the missing Dokkaebi."

I glanced down at the book and flipped a few pages. "The next bit is all about provisioning the mansion—good stuff, worth reading in detail later," I said. "He's got the planting layout for the gardens and arbor, a listing of the symbols and protections on the mansion, and some other information that is important, but not exciting."

I scanned the next few pages and smiled. "Okay, back to the action." I started to read aloud once more.

"Something changed us in that last battle—whether it was the doing of Agwe or the sea witch or a byproduct of strong blended magic, I don't know. Our bond was stronger, as if we had been soul-fused. When we became one body, we also became one mind and one power. I had never heard of such a thing, but I treasured the reality as a precious and rare gift.

"I chose the staff for the mansion, free men and women, all of them. They were people I had gathered over the years, some of whom I had done a kindness for or helped out of a difficult situation. We paid them well and counted them as family, and in return, they kept the secret of our love and magic.

"Ramon and I did not leave the grounds. Supplies were delivered, or one of the staff went to town to fetch them. We received no visitors. I cared nothing for my relations, who had shown me no regard, and Ramon had no family save for me. We strengthened the wardings on the house using all the lore we could learn. Realizing that we would live out our lives there, I commissioned the mausoleum to be built, and Ramon oversaw its construction.

"For fifteen years, we were happy. But as I neared my fiftieth year, my body began to fail me. Ramon remained strong and vital, but he would not leave my side, a wonder I never ceased to be thankful for. We spent a portion of those years learning all we could about the magic we had used against the sea witch, looking to bind her for eternity.

"I knew my time was limited. Ramon vowed to remain with me to the end. I feared how he would go on when I was gone. The bond between us burned bright and hot, an intensity I now know made up for its brevity. And I worried that when I died, it would sunder our binding on the sea witch and sweep away all for which we had paid so high a price."

As I spoke, my voice sounded far away to my own ears, and the words on the page blurred. The vision came on suddenly, and in the blink of an eye, the strong emotional resonance of the journal triggered my touch magic, making me a witness to what happened next.

I saw Ramon in a cloak with a high collar and a hat pulled low, hiding his face. He went into the city, to an alley behind one of the fancy houses where the slave quarters were located. A man blocked his way, and Ramon withdrew a pendant from beneath his cloak. I didn't get a good look at the amulet, but it reassured the other man, who stepped aside.

I saw dozens of people on the steps of their small cabins, talking quietly by lantern light. Pipe smoke curled in the air, and the night smelled of sweat and gardenias. At the end of the alley, a large woman in a white dress sat in the center of a cluster of fellow slaves. They looked up as Ramon approached, and everything went quiet.

Ramon stopped in front of the woman and bowed. "Mama Nadege," he said with deep respect. "I bring a gift—and ask for a boon." He held out a tin of fine pipe tobacco and a bottle of Caribbean rum in tribute.

One of the men seated at Mama Nadege's feet stood and took the gifts from Ramon, presenting them for her approval. She whispered and he set the items on her lap.

"I know who and what you are, Ramon Montero," she said, and he startled when she called him by the name he had left behind years ago. "I have seen the omens, and Agwe came to me in a dream. He told me to prepare to help his champions."

Ramon looked stunned. "I came to beg for your help in binding the witch of the deep."

She nodded. "So Agwe revealed to me. I have spent two nights in a trance, creating the incantation that you need." Mama Nadege reached into the doorway of the house and withdrew a small basket.

"In here are the items you will need to cast the spell Agwe gave to me. His hand wrote the words, through me, so you must speak them exactly as he spoke them in my mind." She handed him the basket.

I knew that if anyone had caught them at this moment, both Ramon and Mama Nadege risked prison or death.

"Hear me, Ramon Montero," Mama Nadege said. "Once cast, this cannot be undone. The two of you will be bound together forever—no heaven, no hell—eternal guardians."

"We are willing," Ramon swore. He made another low bow and concealed the basket beneath his cloak. "Thank you—and thanks to Agwe for his graciousness."

Mama Nadege nodded in acknowledgment, and Ramon turned away, walking down a silent alleyway under the protective stares of her people.

The vision skipped ahead, and I saw Ramon return to the mansion looking somber. Gideon waited for him, and I knew he wondered if the mambo's warning had led his partner to change his mind.

I could see that Gideon's health was failing. He was haggard, and he moved slowly as if everything hurt. Ramon looked strong and healthy, likely to outlive Gideon by many years. He could go back to sea or remain in the mansion after Gideon's passing, protected by their fortune.

Gideon said something that sent a blaze of anger to Ramon's eyes, then etched his handsome features with sorrow.

"We are already bound—bodies, magic, and souls," Ramon told him.

Gideon's eyes widened. "If we don't do this guardian magic, what becomes of you when I die?"

I knew he saw the answer in Ramon's eyes before the other man could speak. Ramon would follow him in death. It was clear from Ramon's expression that he had no intention to do otherwise. Without Mama Nadege's ritual, Gideon's death would break the binding on the sea witch, and all would be lost.

"I am at peace with this choice," Ramon told Gideon, taking his hand and threading their fingers together. "We will be together, always, and we will protect the ships at sea."

I watched Gideon's expression as his arguments crumbled, and he accepted Ramon's proposal. He lifted their joined hands and kissed Ramon's knuckles. "Always," he replied.

A torrent of strong emotions buffeted me. I felt Gideon's worry about being separated from Ramon, his fear of judgment in the after-life, or worse—of nothingness. Ramon's love gave him clarity, and the guardian spell gave him purpose.

I came back to myself just as suddenly as the vision had overtaken me and realized that my friends on the video conference were calling my name, worried at my sudden silence. By this time, they knew what had happened, but they also knew that some visions threw me more than others.

"I'm okay," I said, a little too breathlessly to be entirely believable.

"That was…wow. Give me a second." I drank the rest of my coffee and waited for my pounding heartbeat to slow and the headache in my temples to ease.

"Ramon went to Lucinda's ancestor—Mama Nadege," I told them and recounted what the vision had shown me.

"Mama Nadege was a gifted seer and a powerful mambo," Donnelly said when I finished. "I've heard Sorren talk about her, and Dante knew her too. They both sought her out for advice."

"Ramon believed that it would take both of them to work the guardian spell. I don't think he wanted to live without Gideon. Gideon knew Ramon wouldn't change his mind, and from the emotions I picked up, he was afraid that they might not be together in the afterlife," I recounted.

"When he realized that working the spell would bind them together for eternity as guardians and protect the ships and the city from the sea witch, he was all in." Putting my visions into words was always tricky, especially when it meant parsing through feelings as well as what I saw or heard.

"Etheridge thinks Gideon's book is a grimoire," Teag pointed out. "Want to bet he knows something about the guardian spell and wants to find out how to break it? Did Gideon record it in the book?"

"I don't know," I said. "We're nearly to the end. Let's read it and find out." No one complained about the time, and I had the feeling if I had tried to put off reading the rest of the memoir, my friends would have all ended up on my porch insisting I finish. I gave Baxter a belly scratch and then lifted the book to continue reading.

"We would use my remaining time to prepare. Ramon had been quietly seeking out magical artifacts, relics, and books that might be of use to bolster our casting or protect the place where we would anchor our power. We studied like schoolboys before a final examination—a very final one, to be sure.

"We chose the mausoleum as the place to work our spell since it would afford us privacy, and no one would need to enter after our deaths. Ramon added protections to it from every tradition of magic we had learned while I did the same for the house and the perimeter of the grounds. Our gardens served us well and would carry on after we were gone, but I wanted to protect our legacy as best we could.

"I met with my lawyer and confided that I did not have long to live. We worked out a chain of inheritance that would go to Edward and from there to the closest blood relative. I assured my lawyer that I would provide funds sufficient to pay the staff to stay on until the new residents moved in.

"He raised an eyebrow when I set aside the mausoleum and its land as separate from the main house and left an endowment that would provide for its upkeep and taxes for a very long time. I suspect he thought me mad when I put the caveat in my will that should my bloodline end, the mansion was to go to the new museum, and a package—this book—would be entrusted to Trifles and Folly when the mansion passed out of family hands. He questioned—but he did not argue, placating a dying man's wishes.

"When I returned, I called the staff together, who had become like family to me and each other. I broke the news of my decline, told them they could stay on indefinitely and explained Ramon's inevitable absence by saying that I was going off to die in private and his services as a nurse would no longer be needed. I don't doubt that they long knew he was far more than that to me, but we preserved the fiction for their sake.

"We said our goodbyes, and I thanked them for their service and discretion, a gift that enabled Ramon and me to have our years together in safety and peace. That evening, Ramon and I made our private farewell to one another, and before dawn, we went to the mausoleum.

"Everything we thought we might need had already been stocked in the small stone building at the edge of the property. We had also removed all magical items from the house and anything that might reveal our secret. One was dangerous, and the other far too private.

"Here is where my story ends. I cannot write the full ending, because this book must be sent to my lawyer for safekeeping before we go into the mausoleum. I am sending this to Trifles and Folly because no matter how much time passes between now and the end of my lineage, I believe that the store and its unusual proprietors will still be protecting Charleston in their own way. I have heard many stories and do not doubt the sources. If anyone can find a way to ensure that the binding on the sea witch can be renewed, it will be Trifles and Folly.

"The key to the mausoleum is fastened to the back cover of this book. Take good care of it—no copy exists.

"Do not open the mausoleum lightly. If all goes well, Ramon and I will have worked very powerful magic within its walls, and I do not know how long such power takes to fade. We have also stored relics, spell books, and other items that are dangerous in the wrong hands. Enter only when you are ready to renew the protections…at your own risk. And accept our thanks across these many years for carrying on the guardianship. We wish you luck."

For a moment, we all sat in stunned silence.

"What about the spell?" Beck said. "How can you strengthen the binding spell if he didn't leave it for you?"

"Gideon and Ramon's spirits remained bound as guardians," Alicia replied. "They weren't in the mansion—but they are probably in the mausoleum. Maybe Donnelly or I can speak to them and find out the spell that way."

"I have some ideas I want to investigate," Travis said. "I might be able to find something similar enough to work."

"Now that we know the full story, we've all got work to do," Donnelly added. "Maybe it's best to spend the day on research and consider our options tomorrow."

We all agreed, and one by one, everyone dropped off the video call.

I shut down the laptop and snuggled Baxter, trying to calm myself from the wild emotions of the story and the vision. Since I hadn't slept well and I had time before I was due at the store, I set the alarm on my phone and closed my eyes, hoping a short nap would settle my nerves.

CHAPTER NINE

I WAS NOT SURPRISED WHEN I DREAMED OF SAILING SHIPS, CANNON smoke, and sea monsters.

Then my dreams turned really dark. The images came with the clarity of a vision, and I suspected that my touch magic still picked up on the emotional resonance of Gideon's book.

Deep beneath the sapphire blue of Caribbean waters, I saw a huge underwater mountain. I sensed a presence nearby, ancient, invisible, and powerful. The ocean floor trembled, then heaved and buckled as tectonic energies shifted and tore at themselves. The mountain shook with those forces, making the water wildly choppy and sending up a haze of bubbles.

I watched in horror as tremors wracked the mountain, and then one face of the slope broke loose and slid down, tons of rock displacing tons of water.

The vantage point of the vision changed, following the enormously powerful wave. It sped away from its origin, growing wilder and infinitely more dangerous, rising into a tsunami that swept ships away like toys in its path, and left ruin in its wake.

The wave hit the Charleston coast like a thousand sledgehammers, shattering everything in its path and drowning what it couldn't break.

Not just Charleston, but up and down the coast, taking out cities, ports, homes, and military bases for miles, flooding far inland in an unparalleled natural disaster.

Hundreds of thousands of people died, and thousands more were lost to the water, unlikely to ever be recovered. Nothing could stand against that raw power, and what it didn't flatten, it dragged out with its undertow to a watery grave.

My phone alarm went off, and I woke trembling and soaked in sweat, sure that everything I saw was a true sending, a warning vision —and very real. Before I could forget the details, I jotted down what I had seen in the notebook I kept on the coffee table.

This is what Gideon and Ramon feared. They knew what the elemental could do, and it was so much worse than wrecking ships at sea. This was the future they gave their lives and bound their souls to prevent.

Now we had to figure out how to honor their sacrifice by making certain that possible future and its carnage could not happened.

I was on my way in to the shop when my phone rang. The ID surprised me—Alistair didn't usually call to chat, so that meant something was going on.

"Hi, Alistair." I forced myself to sound cheerful, although I felt certain some catastrophe, major or minor, lay behind the call.

"Cassidy. I just wanted to give you an unofficial heads up that Carter Etheridge seems intent on causing problems about the Sullivan mansion." Alistair sounded frazzled.

"How can he contest it? Gideon's will was clear, and it set this up two hundred years ago." All the rage that hadn't found an outlet surged to the fore at the idea of uber-entitled Carter Etheridge causing problems for the museum.

"He can contest it because he's not used to being told 'no,'" Alistair replied wearily. "And his family is well-connected enough that he knows most of the board, at least socially. Enough to drop hints about threatening the next fundraiser by 'having a word' with our major donors."

"Shit." I didn't doubt that Etheridge would attempt to intimidate donors or that his influence could have an impact.

"My sentiments exactly. Donors and board members are a particularly risk-averse species. They hate bad press. Etheridge is throwing a tantrum, but we have some folks who might be persuaded to give him what he wants to avoid conflict."

"Stall," I said. "We're working on it. I don't think Etheridge wants the mansion for the property value—or at least, that's not all of it. I think he's convinced himself that the book you gave me is some kind of grimoire. It isn't—but he's been stalking me, trying to intimidate me into giving it to him."

"Be careful, Cassidy. The family has a reputation for ruthlessness."

"I'm taking precautions," I assured him.

"By the way, if you're in the neighborhood, I'd love to have coffee with you and find out what you've learned from Gideon Sullivan's book. And Dr. Walker would like you to stop by her new exhibit."

"I can come over today if that suits." I knew it was a risk to show up at the museum with Etheridge on the loose, but I didn't think he'd try something around so many witnesses. And if it got dicey, I had a couple of powerful witches on speed dial who would be glad to walk me home in exchange for a chance to kick Etheridge's entitled ass.

As soon as I got to the store, I dashed off an email to a new acquaintance, Adiel Nielson, who was a historian specializing in documenting the true history of supernatural people. Even if the truth couldn't be widely known, Gideon and Ramon's story deserved to be remembered for their bravery and sacrifice. Adiel's response was immediate and enthusiastic. Once Teag and I finished with the current situation, I promised to make sure Adiel got all the details.

I worked the front of the store with Maggie while Teag teamed up online with our friend Seth to find the most likely places Wilton might have gone to ground with his wish-granting spirit. While I felt relieved that so far, Wilton hadn't wished himself to be king of the world or for a lifetime supply of pizza, I couldn't help feeling sad that his dreams were so small that we couldn't find him.

"Any luck?" I asked when I came in to refill my iced tea.

Teag leaned back. "Yeah—but it's not what I expected. I was looking for weird bursts of good luck. Instead, there've been some very unusual deaths—all people with some connection to Wilton. My bet is that Etheridge tried to find out where Wilton has been hiding, and he turned another Rawhead loose on the people he questioned when he was done."

"Yikes. Sounds like the goblin has his hands full just keeping Wilton one-step ahead."

We had fewer customers than usual, and the ones who came in couldn't stop talking about the impending storm, the tremors, and the crows. People who didn't even believe in the supernatural were still on edge from so many odd things happening at once. When they weren't asking questions about a particular item, they wanted to trade guesses on whether—or when—the governor would make the evacuation notice mandatory.

I checked the local news whenever we had a free moment, looking for weird lucky stories or more harbingers of doom. An interview with a local seismologist speculated on whether Bermuda was due for an earthquake and what was happening with the undersea fault line. Nothing looked like a tip-off about Wilton, but SPOOK's website had a lot more comments than usual on the clips Kell and his team had posted from their night at the plague church and their blog post about Brother Johan the monk ghost.

"How's it going?" I asked Teag when I wandered back for another cup of coffee.

"We're making progress. By the time you get back from your meeting at the museum, I think we'll have a good idea where to find Wilton." Teag shook his head in disbelief. "Get this—we think so far, in addition to keeping himself out of that accident and away from Etheridge, he's wished away the bill collectors and the repo man. His credit score went from dismal yesterday to well above average today. I don't care how fast you pay off your debts, it doesn't fix your score like that."

"You look stressed—more than usual," I qualified.

Teag ran a hand back through his dark hair. "Planning a wedding in the middle of averting an apocalypse is hard. They never cover that in the how-to books."

"Still looking for a venue?"

Teag sighed. "No, I think we've got that narrowed down. Alistair offered the art gallery at the museum, and Mrs. Morrissey offered the Historical Archive. They would both be beautiful—and as uncompli-cated as anything is in Charleston."

"We've been to events at both places," I agreed. "And they clean up well. Do you have a caterer and a baker picked yet?"

Teag snickered. "That's one thing I'm not worried about. Anyone who might choke about a wedding for two men suddenly discovers their moral flexibility when the name 'Benton' comes up." We both knew there was nothing funny about bigotry, but pitting an asshole's greed against his prejudice was darkly amusing.

"Family stress?" I didn't mean to pry, but I love Teag and Anthony like the brothers I didn't have, and I wanted their special day to be perfect.

"The announcement showed up in the social pages yesterday. Anthony's mom got a call from St. Philip's, inquiring whether they knew dates yet. And then the shit hit the fan."

My family wasn't part of the South of Broad crowd, but thanks to Trifles and Folly, we rubbed shoulders with them enough to understand how the "other half" lived. Combined with insights from Anthony and Beck, I knew better than to envy the complications and stifling social pressure that came with wealth.

"What's the fallout? Uncomfortable, or awful?"

Teag rolled his eyes. "How about 'deeply awkward'? I guess Anthony's parents are getting overwhelmed by calls from their Country Club pals. Some of it is real, from people who have always supported the two of us. There've been some disapproving voices who definitely will be getting dropped from the Christmas card list," he added in a wry tone.

"And then of course, there are the pearl-clutching busybodies calling to comment on how awful it is that we can't get married at St. Philips when we all know whose fundraisers they're big contributors to —and let's just say they aren't allies."

"Are the Bentons taking it okay?" I didn't know Anthony's parents well, but they didn't strike me as easily intimidated or likely to back down from social pressure.

"His family's law firm has handled enough of the upper crust's delicate business that no matter who fusses, they aren't going to walk out. Anthony's mom is super pissed, and a rich, connected woman out to avenge a wrong done to her baby boy is a force of nature." He grinned. "That's kinda fun to watch."

"So...drama but nothing actually wrong?" I asked.

He nodded. "Yeah. Still stressful—which a wedding would be anyhow even without the complications. But I think the whole situation made his parents realize that if someone with all of Anthony's advantages is running into this kind of shit, it's much worse for everyone else. Believe it or not, that's been eye-opening for them. They're good people—but sheltered."

Teag's family was solidly middle class. He'd gotten through college and grad school with night jobs and scholarships, and I knew he and Anthony had worked hard to set boundaries around money when they first got together. Compared to the Bentons, Teag's folks were low-key, but they were supportive and had embraced Anthony as one of their own.

My phone buzzed, and I recognized the ring tone. "Hi, Beck. What do you have for me?"

"We're still digging, and there's a lot to go through. But the short version is that the two families were the wicked wizard version of feuding Hatfields and McCoys, only with wands instead of shotguns, a fleet of merchant ships, and tons of money," Beck replied.

"There are more scandals and backstabbing than in any soap opera in these journals," Logan chimed in. "If you don't mind bad hand-writing and the old book smell."

"That's my partner's colorful way of saying that he's enjoying laying bare my family's unsurprisingly amoral approach to doing busi-ness," Beck said with fond exasperation.

"We don't have all the details for those few decades nailed down. But the Etheridges and the Pendlewoods did everything they could to undercut each other—like the railroad barons in the late 1800s—even if they took a loss. It was personal. We think they might have both been trying to control the sea witch to their own benefit," Beck finished.

"And if they were even partially successful at gaining that control, then they both would have been extremely put out when Gideon and Ramon bound the witch of the deep," I said.

"That's the theory," Beck admitted. "Sorry we don't have more details—we're plowing through a lot of material, and the writers don't always come right out and say things directly. There's…interpreta-tion…involved."

"Father Anne keeps bringing us donuts," Logan offered. "We need to keep up our strength for all the detecting work."

I bit back a chuckle. Logan was good for Beck, like a playful Labrador getting a too-serious Jack Russell to lighten up and play ball.

"I'm glad you've got your priorities straight," I replied with a laugh. "Keep us posted."

Finding out about a warlock war over who got to control a sea monster shouldn't have put me in a good mood, but Logan's enthu-siasm was contagious. And now I was hungry for donuts.

"I know that look," Teag said. "Better bring some donuts back for the rest of us."

"Guilty as charged." I checked the time. "Oops! I need to head over to the museum."

Teag looked up from his computer. "Want a bodyguard?"

I smiled but shook my head. "Thanks, but you're needed here so we can go after Wilton and the Dokkaebi. I'll make sure I have my wand and Alard's walking stick. And the whole route is too public for him to be able to distract everyone to send a monster running down

King Street. I'm betting Etheridge won't want to tip his witchy secrets in front of the 'normals.'"

"Just watch your back, okay?"

"I promise."

I ENJOYED the short drive to the museum, even if I did need to keep one eye out for Etheridge and his monsters. I refused to let him scare me into hiding. Bright sunshine and a deep blue sky raised my spirits. I enjoyed talking with Alistair and looked forward to getting his reaction to what we had learned about Gideon and Ramon so far—at least, the non-magical parts.

The volunteer at the front desk waved in greeting as I walked in. Habit made me brace just in case my gift decided to go into overdrive, and I was pleased to see that my control muted the resonance of the many items that had witnessed tragedy and hardship.

I had expected to meet Alistair in the public café, but he motioned for me to follow him into a more private small meeting room, where our cups and a carafe of coffee with all the fixings were already laid out, as well as a plate of the museums signature snickerdoodle cookies.

"I figured we could talk undisturbed here," he said. I guessed that he was also helping me avoid notice in case Etheridge made an appearance.

"This is perfect. Thank you."

Alistair chuckled. "I'm plying you with coffee and dessert, so you'll tell me all the juicy stories from that book."

"I will gladly trade stories for good cookies," I said, laughing. "You won't be disappointed!"

Alistair listened with rapt attention as I recounted what I'd read from Gideon's book—leaving out the magic parts.

"Do you realize what an amazing piece of history you're holding in your hands? Of course you do! It's just such a remarkable find."

"Gideon and Ramon were pretty impressive," I replied. "It's been like a spicy novel—hard to put down!"

"You know I don't really need an excuse to get together with you—we always have a good conversation," Alistair said. "But now you've got me hooked on your 'novel,' so please keep me updated if you learn more about them."

I promised that I'd keep him posted on new discoveries. We finished our cookies and headed back to the gallery area.

"Dr. Walker's exhibit is over in Gallery C," Alistair said. "I know she's looking forward to seeing you."

I thanked him, and Alistair fixed me with a look. "About that other situation…be careful, but don't worry overly about my side of things. I didn't make it this far in life without having a few tricks up my sleeve —and our board members didn't get where they are by being pushovers. We'll hold the line."

I hoped he was right. But I also knew that the type of "tricks" Carter Etheridge's had up *his* sleeve were real magic, and someone was likely to get hurt unless we could stay several steps ahead of him.

Gallery C was one of the smaller display areas, perfect for an intimate experience that allowed getting up close with the exhibits. Since I knew I was expected, I skirted the *Do Not Enter* signs and the velvet cord without guilt and walked in on the chaos and disarray that was part of putting a new event together.

"Cassidy! Good to see you! Come on over and have a look—I think you're going to like what you see!"

Dr. Lucinda Walker was a tall, slim woman with skin the color of espresso and shoulder-length hair done up into a mane of hundreds of tightly woven braids. Today she wore jeans and a T-shirt, with a bandana pulling her long braids up and out of the way, dressed for unpacking boxes and setting up displays, quite a departure from the beautiful suits she wore on campus.

Lucinda teaches folklore and mythology at the College of Charleston, with an emphasis on syncretic religion. She's also a gifted Voudon mambo, the most recent in her family's long line of practitioners. Her connection with the Loa, the Voudon spirits, had saved our bacon on many occasions.

"The display is on sweetgrass baskets and Lowcountry pottery."

She glowed with excitement as she guided me around the exhibit that was just beginning to take shape. "With a special focus on the Gullah-Geechee people, the cultural influences of the African Diaspora, and the intergenerational transmission of memories and skills through oral tradition."

Despite the academic-speak, Lucinda's passion for her subject shone in her eyes.

"You're partnering with Mrs. Teller and Niella on this? That's awesome!" Tourists prized sweetgrass baskets for their beauty and the skill of their construction. Lucinda and I fully appreciated the protective magic woven into each piece and the long history of the art form.

"She's one of the very best in the state," Lucinda said. "We highlight other basket makers as well as potters, but Ernestine has been especially generous with her time and knowledge." She sighed. "It's so important to document our elders' stories and art. We forget that they won't be with us forever, and so much of our history is still oral. There's a lot yet to be collected."

She fixed me with an expression that told me that she knew more than she was saying. "You've stumbled into some new history yourself, I understand."

I couldn't begin to guess her sources, human, psychic, or supernatural. All the more reason I was glad she was one of our most powerful allies.

"You mean like a pirate love story that might hold the key to stopping a supernatural catastrophe? Yeah, it's been a busy week." I knew she'd understand the flippancy as a cover for the heavy responsibility I felt to untangle Gideon's mystery.

"Agwe has visited my dreams," Lucinda said. "When a Loa speaks, especially a Loa with whom I am not well-acquainted, I listen. The sea belongs to Agwe. He's the patron of sailors and fishermen, and his darker presence, his petro side, is invoked to avoid bad luck or vicious storms. He is aware of your guardians."

My heart skipped a beat. "Gideon and Ramon? He mentioned them?"

Lucinda nodded. "He is concerned that their influence is waning.

That is not a good thing."

She briefly closed her eyes. "There are many immortal presences that shape our world, some good, some bad. Agwe and the Loa are just a few of those spirits. In my dream, he warned me about a 'witch of the deep' and guided me to the mouth of a cave far beneath the ocean. Something powerful and very old has been bound there—and Agwe would like to see it remain so."

"If he's a god, can't he bind her? Or power up the protection Gideon and Ramon started?"

"Sometimes the Old Ones' magics cancel each other, or they are too equally matched. In other cases, there are very old, complex, formal agreements that they have vowed to be bound by—but which permit some…wiggle room…for their champions," she replied. "That allows for a 'shadow war' of sorts fought by proxies—like your privateers."

"Ramon went to see Mama Nadege. She helped him craft the spell that bound his and Gideon's souls together to restrain the sea witch," I told her, knowing that Lucinda traced her ancestry and her mambo heritage back to the elderly woman from Revolutionary days.

"Mama Nadege was a matriarch in this city and a queen among practitioners. Sorren and Dante remember her. The rest of us have only known her spirit," Lucinda explained. "If you can find the spell, I can look it over and see how it might be reinforced without binding the living. Agwe will support us."

I knew Gideon had purposely left the spell out of his memoir, not wanting it to be misused. At some point, we'd have to open the mausoleum, and I figured that Gideon was likely to have left behind notes on the details that came after the book—like the spell.

"I'll definitely call you if I find it," I promised. "And I'd be grateful if you can please put in a good word for us with Agwe and Mama Nadege's ghost. We can use all the help we can get."

She agreed. "I'll be there when you make your move to call the Loa and work protections. Dark forces have taken note of the guardians' weakness. They will hope to act against you. Don't be afraid to gather your allies, Cassidy. We're here for you."

Although we chatted as we walked to my car, I knew without anything being said that Lucinda had taken it upon herself to be my bodyguard in case Carter Etheridge or his minions were hanging around. Either he hadn't planned an attack or changed his mind at the thought of going up against both Lucinda and me, because we didn't catch sight of Etheridge or his monsters. I appreciated the kindness, and we hugged goodbye, planning to meet for coffee once the world was safe.

"WE'VE GOT A LEAD." Teag greeted me when I walked back into the break room. "Actually, we've got five leads between what Seth and I found. Places Wilton goes when he's desperate, people he depends on. Annie Vinton is an on-again, off-again girlfriend who seems to fall for his sob stories. Between what we could hack from traffic cams and doorbell cams, we know his car was at her place two days ago."

"She's in danger if Etheridge hasn't already found her," I said, thinking of the murder spree Teag had turned up.

"That's my fear. We can warn her. Doesn't guarantee she'll listen."

Since Etheridge knew what my RAV4 looked like, we took Teag's Volvo. I filled him in on the conversation with Lucinda and the news that we had a Loa on our side. "Well, sorta," I qualified. "Agwe apparently has arcane agreements that mean he has to stay hands-off, or at least maintain plausible deniability. Whatever that means for gods."

"Just like World War One," Teag replied, threading through Charleston's traffic.

"You lost me on that."

"When the Austrian archduke was assassinated, we ended up with a world war because all the nations of Europe had a complex web of mutual defense treaties that triggered, pulling them into something that probably should have stayed a regional conflict," Teag explained, although I still wasn't following.

"And this has to do with…"

"Agwe," he said. "He's a Loa, so god-like. The sea witch is probably an elemental, a genius loci, the spirit of a place. Immortal and hella powerful. They're not the only ones, either. They all have to co-exist for millennia, and they can never really 'win' a fight against each other. So they agree to terms, stake out territories, make alliances. Some of them probably cheat, and maybe a few rogues never signed on."

"Okay," I replied, drawing out the word because I still wasn't quite following his logic.

"Then people get in the way, with their prayers and their offerings. Maybe when the sailors pray to be saved or beg for safe passage or good fishing, it doesn't threaten any of the other beings. But then people start asking to be favored or wanting to call down storms or wrecks on their rivals. They're asking for interference in human affairs. And since the beings control their territories, they have a lot of freedom to do what they want—until it crosses lines with the other beings."

"Like the Pendlewoods and the Etheridges using the sea witch against each other or competitors," I said. "Or Gideon and Ramon binding the sea witch. Even if the other beings didn't like her involvement, I can't think that sort of thing would go over well."

"Nope. Starts to seem like a threat when puny humans can retaliate against one of the immortals, no matter how well-deserved," Teag replied. "So does it escalate, like World War One, with the beings getting dragged in because of their old agreements? Or do they find ways to interfere without leaving their own 'fingerprints' on it?"

I knew from hearing Sorren and Donnelly talk that the complex social web of Charleston's upper crust had nothing on the intricate relationships that came from centuries of powerful creatures working around each other, making deals and trades and compromises.

"You worked this all out while I was talking with Alistair?" I was equally amused and impressed.

Teag chuckled. "Not on my own. Seth came up with part of it while we were tracking Wilton, and then Simon called, and we spitballed the rest. But I think it makes a damn good theory. Best we've had so far."

"It seems so very…human…of the immortals," I replied. "But then again, in the old tales, they're just like us, only with a lot more power."

"I think having Agwe in favor of restoring the protections is a good thing—don't count out his help just because he's not going to lead the charge," Teag said as we pulled up at the curb. "And I feel better with Lucinda lending a hand too."

ANNIE'S BUNGALOW was on the edge of North Charleston, on a quiet residential street. We took Teag's car again while Rowan gave my RAV4 a careful once-over for a magical low-jack since the last three attacks had happened when I was driving. I was hoping Etheridge's arrogance would make him sloppy, focusing just on my car. I kept my fingers crossed for the whole drive, and we arrived without spotting any monsters or an ominous black BMW.

The tidy house needed work, but the neat yard, flowerbeds blazing with color, and fresh paint spoke well for the owner. I didn't know how to square that with what we'd seen of Wilton, who didn't seem the detail-oriented type. We had found Annie's social media accounts, so we knew what she looked like—early thirties with dark hair in a messy bun.

Teag knocked at the door. We had already decided to pass as bill collectors, figuring that seemed like something Wilton had dealt with many times. No one answered, and my nervousness tightened into dread.

We went around to the back, and Teag knocked again. Minutes passed, and we heard no sounds from inside. We exchanged a glance, and then Teag kicked the door open.

"Oh, God." The smell of old blood and decomposition nearly made me retch.

We covered our mouths and noses and walked in with no illusions about what we were going to find. The place had been ransacked. Annie lay dead in the middle of the living room floor, and from the marks on the body, she'd been tortured before her killer slit her throat.

I stumbled and grabbed the back of a chair to keep from falling. I saw it all, like a slasher flick on fast-forward. I heard Annie's screams, smelled her blood, saw the smirk on Etheridge's face as he used magic to cause pain and then snuff out her life. She begged, told him everything she knew. Etheridge was enjoying himself.

The vision left me as quickly as it came, and I fell to my knees, barely keeping myself from throwing up all over a crime scene. I didn't want to think about how much worse it would have been without all the protective jewelry I was wearing.

"Etheridge was here. The whole place stinks of his magic. He didn't have to kill her—or rough her up. He's a strong enough witch to use spells to force her to talk or read her mind. He wanted to hurt her." My stomach churned at what my touch magic revealed.

I bolted for the back door and threw up into a plastic bag from the car. Teag followed me out a few minutes later. I figured he had made a quick check of the house, brushed away our fingerprints, and found nothing of note. He laid a hand on my shoulder, helping to comfort and steady me as I shook with the aftermath of heaving up my guts.

When we were back in the car, Teag handed me a bottle of water and a tin of mints. I accepted both gratefully, and they helped, but I knew I wouldn't be okay for a long time.

"Now what?" I asked, feeling like we had failed.

Teag started to reply and then paused as a text message he'd missed caught his attention. "Ok—we might have a break. Seth's been doing his hacker best to figure out where Wilton might be. I think his newest find goes to the top of the list."

"Yeah?"

"Vacation house owned by his maternal uncle, so the last name would be different. It would take some digging to connect Donny to that side of the family." Teag met my gaze, knowing I needed a win.

"All the other places we found were easy to connect to Wilton. If we found them, Etheridge probably did too. He's probably been and gone. We might get ahead of him if we go for the uncle's house."

"Let's do it—and hope we get a break, for once," I replied.

CHAPTER TEN

TEAG AND I WERE QUIET ON OUR WAY TO THE VACATION HOUSE. WE both have guns—a necessity dealing with dangerous situations—but we rarely rely on them because what we hunt isn't usually vulnerable to regular bullets. Silver, in the case of a werewolf, or iron for the fae, but those are unusual situations. Cunning and magic—and a lot of help from our talented friends—have kept us alive, coupled with good research and a dollop of luck.

Then again, we don't usually go up against regular humans.

"Are you sure the spelled net will work?" I asked Teag. "If Wilton is aware enough to make a wish—either to escape or to fend us off—we're toast if the Dokkaebi is listening."

"The net should work great—in theory," Teag replied. "It also includes a spell to dampen the magic of the person being restrained. Since Wilton doesn't have any magic of his own, as far as we know, that should stop him from summoning the bottle spirit to help him. Then we conjure the goblin to trap him and call it a day."

If the Dokkaebi had been keeping Wilton—and himself—safe from Etheridge, there was a slim chance the spirit might see us as protectors and go willingly. If the bottle spirit didn't want to serve a dark witch, it might decide we were the lesser evil until it found another chance to escape with a new weak-willed fool, like it had done with Wilton.

We both knew it wouldn't be that easy, but we weren't willing to just shoot Wilton or risk a tranquilizer, and getting close enough to hit him over the head seemed like an equally poor solution.

"We've got a lot of protective amulets on us, which should help to deflect the Dokkaebi's power," Teag added. When dealing with magic, few certainties existed. For my part, I'd prefer not to be zapped into a time rift by a pissed-off gin goblin.

"If Wilton doesn't wish for the spirit to attack us or protect him, do you think it'll feel any duty toward him on its own?" I asked. Would a creature like that feel gratitude toward the person who freed him, even if his savior just wanted to drink the gin?

"From what Rowan knew, the Dokkaebi are pretty transactional in their thinking. If the request isn't a formal wish, phrased the right way, the magic doesn't activate. As far as the spirit feeling like he owes Wilton...I'm not sure they reckon those kinds of things like we do. But the goblin probably does have a drive to protect itself—and we might look like a better option than Etheridge," Teag replied, echoing my thoughts.

"I hope you're right."

The vacation home sat on a rise above the Ashley River, with a nice view of the water and marshland. We parked off to the side, far enough back that the sound of the engine wouldn't alert Wilton.

A dock and ramp into the water suggested that Wilton's uncle liked to fish, although no boat was tied up right now. The one-story house was a modest cottage with a blue shiplap exterior and gray shutters. It had a wide porch facing the river, nicely situated for catching the breeze and watching the sunset. Sandy soil made for a patchy lawn, and the empty flower beds and overgrown foundation plantings suggested that Wilton's aunt and uncle no longer visited often enough to maintain them.

I nodded toward the carport, where the car we'd seen on the traffic videos sat barely concealed beneath a tarp. Teag gave me a questioning look, and I knew he was asking if my touch magic picked up on anything. I shook my head. The house didn't give off any haunted vibes or the negative energy that often lingers when bad things have happened in a place.

In fact, the resonance seemed *too* quiet, and I worried that perhaps the bottle-spirit had given Wilton the slip and taken advantage of its freedom, but then I felt its odd magic like a background hum so persistent it was easy to overlook. I hoped that the amulets Rowan had given us would make it harder for both the Dokkaebi and Etheridge to sense us.

We'd decided that the least complicated option presented the fewest opportunities for disaster. Teag had wrapped an empty box in brown shipping paper, and now he brought it up on the porch, out of easy reach of the door. He plastered himself against the wall on one side of the entryway while I did the same on the hinge side. At his signal, I rang the bell.

I heard mumbled cursing, and then the door opened. "I didn't order anything," Wilton said as Teag and I held our breaths, waiting for him to move. Curiosity got the better of the man, or else he figured the least he could do since he was squatting in his uncle's house was to bring in the mail, because he headed for the box.

Teag flung his woven net, dropping it over Wilton in one move. I shook the dog collar looped around my left wrist, and Bo's ghost materialized, barring the doorway in case Wilton tried to run back inside. I leveled my wand at him, ready for trouble.

Wilton went down in a heap, crumpling beneath the net. He twitched for a moment, eyes wide and glassy, and then relaxed. A loud snore made me jump.

"Shit. Let's get him off the porch. Don't let the net fall off—it's maintaining the spell." Teag pulled Wilton's arms up so that the net remained over his face and shoulders, and I grabbed his ankles. We handled him carefully to keep the net from slipping and so that we weren't affected by the spell.

Together, we maneuvered Wilton inside, and I ran back to bring the box. We didn't need to attract any nosy, helpful neighbors. With the door locked behind us, I used a spelled cord Teag had woven to bind Wilton's ankles and wrists, then we arranged him on his back with the net solidly over his head and chest.

"How long is the spell good for?" I asked, glad we had managed to do all that without getting accidentally whammied ourselves.

"At least half an hour," Teag replied. "Maybe longer if the net stays in place. I'm hoping we'll be hell and gone long before that."

The inside of the cottage looked like it had been furnished with comfortable cast-offs, giving it a homey feel. I wondered if Wilton had permission to be here or if he was imposing on his uncle's goodwill. I saw the keypad for a security system and figured that either Wilton had the code or his uncle hadn't bothered to set the alarm.

"So where's the hitchhiker?" I asked, not wanting to name the Dokkaebi. I could sense another presence, something subtly changing the energy around us, but I had no idea what to look for to stuff it back in the bottle. Good thing we had a summoning ritual.

I kept an eye on Wilton, with my wand in hand and Bo's ghost seated at my side, a goofy grin on his face. Wilton hadn't moved, and from his loud snores, he slept soundly. I looked all around, and the number of empty liquor and beer bottles suggested that Wilton had been drowning his sorrows. I wondered if the Dokkaebi had been tempted by any of the alcohol. The labels made it clear Wilton chose his liquor by price, not quality; maybe the gin goblin had better taste.

Teag set up the ritual space in the dining room with the items in his backpack, withdrawing the *sikhye* punch, soju, rice cakes, and finally the good gin—altered with a few extra ingredients to lull the spirit into a tipsy drowse so we could stopper the bottle and bind it with sigils.

I held my breath as Teag set down a protective salt circle around me, a separate circle around Wilton, and then another around his work-space, with the offerings to the goblin outside the boundary. He drew a few marks I didn't recognize that looked vaguely Korean, and I wondered if they were an ancient form of the alphabet. Then he lit a black candle and waved his hand through the smoke toward the north and south and then to the east and west.

He poured the rice punch into a wide mouth cup, lifted the cup with both hands in front of him, like an offering, and spoke what I guessed was an invitation in a language that sounded like Korean. Around the foot of the cup, Teag had wound a thin braided thread, likely imbued with his Weaver magic.

Next, he popped the top from the bottle of soju and repeated the gesture and phrase. The bottle also had a thin braid looped around the neck like a tie. Finally, Teag revealed the rice cake, and opened the bottle of slightly-altered gin, which also was wound with a magical braid. Once more, he lifted the cake and the bottle in supplication to the goblin, inviting him to partake, before pushing the small pastry into the gin and setting it down just outside the circle.

Teag spoke a final few words and sat back on his haunches as if he were inviting a guest to the feast.

We waited in silence, broken only by Wilton's snores. I knew that Teag had Mrs. Teller's woven bottle basket to help secure the Dokkaebi in its new prison, as well as paint made with silver and holy water to mark the glass with binding sigils. I kept my main focus on Wilton, but he was still out cold.

The strange vibe I'd felt before grew stronger, and while I was careful not to handle anything, my touch magic picked up on an over-whelming sense of emptiness. *Does the goblin meddle to amuse himself? Are the "pranks" his idea of a distraction?* The thought of an immortal, magically powerful creature toying with humans was disquieting.

The gold beads on the bracelet the lady at the grocery store gave me warmed rapidly, quickly becoming uncomfortably hot. I knew something was in the room with us, but it hadn't taken physical form. Then motion drew my attention to the candle smoke, which wavered oddly in a room without a breeze.

My gasp made Teag look up, and I pointed toward the rising wisp that distorted as *something* moved through it. For just a few seconds, the shadow became a profile—a short, squat creature with a gaping maw filled with sharp teeth and strong, clawed hands.

I heard the faint *skritch* of nails on the wooden floor and caught a pungent whiff of old fish. My eyes widened as I watched the rice punch slowly vanish, although the cup never moved.

The slam of car doors nearby drew me to the window. Peering out from behind the drapes, I saw Etheridge's black BMW and a black SUV.

"He's here. With backup."

Teag shrugged and jerked his head toward the ritual preparation. I knew without words that he needed to concentrate on the ritual and containing the goblin. That meant I had to pull up my big girl pants and keep a dark warlock at bay.

I trusted in the protective amulets I wore, but they didn't make me completely magic-proof. The four guys who got out of the SUV looked more like muscle than mages. I was still out-gunned, but at least they didn't all appear to be witches.

Teag worked the summoning in the dining room, which was sandwiched between the living room at the front of the house and the kitchen at the back. If I held my ground and Bo guarded the kitchen, we could buy Teag time to finish the ritual.

Since I couldn't retaliate with overwhelming force, I'd just have to be sneaky.

Etheridge spoke to his goons, so I stole a glance to see how Teag was doing with the ritual. I held my breath as the soju level slowly decreased in its bottle. Teag stayed completely still, not wanting to distract the Dokkaebi or the ritual.

I shook Bo's collar, and the ghost materialized. When I pointed toward the back door, he trotted off in that direction. I glanced out the window and saw that two of the enforcers were gone, probably going around back. I trusted Bo to keep them at bay.

That left me with two goons and Etheridge.

When the front door opened, I sent a stream of magical fire from the walking stick before anyone had a chance to set foot inside. From the cursing, I figured that I'd hit someone.

The door slammed open again, and I fired with my wand this time, sending a blast of force strong enough to knock two grown men completely off the porch. The trick wouldn't work too many more times, but I doubted Etheridge wanted to get his expensive suit rumpled. In the kitchen, I heard the door splinter, then Bo's vicious growls and barking, and a pained yelp that told me someone had discovered that ghost teeth could still bite.

"Let's talk about this," Etheridge called from the porch. "There's been a misunderstanding. Give me the bottle. He stole it from me."

"Stole it *for* you, don't you mean? And then decided to keep it?" I shouted back, taking cover behind a sideboard. It wouldn't hold against any real magic Etheridge chose to unleash, but it beat standing out in the open like a target.

"Well, well. Cassidy Kincaide. You show up in the most interesting places."

"The bottle was stolen from a friend of ours," I yelled back. "It doesn't belong to you—or Wilton."

"I'd say it belongs to the person who can keep it," Etheridge replied. "I'm coming in there, and you can't stop me."

I glanced over to Teag. The scratching sound came again as the creature shifted, and the only thing that remained was the gin trap. For a moment, nothing happened, and I feared the goblin had gotten wise to our trick. Maybe he was just mellow with his favorite foods and the little extra "kick" the magic had added. I glimpsed his silhouette as he passed in and out of the candle smoke, and then the bottle shook as the spirit entered it.

Teag dropped a spelled silver net over the bottle and then reached beneath it quickly to cork the container. He dripped candle wax around the opening to keep the seal in place and pressed fine silver threads and a thin braided woven cord to strengthen the binding. Next he withdrew the special paint and marked sigils I recognized and more of the archaic Korean symbols before placing the bottle in Mrs. Teller's woven holder. He shoved it all into his backpack and nodded.

I leveled another blast of flame through the doorway and lunged, pushing the emergency button on the security keypad.

The alarm started to whoop, deafeningly loud. The house might not have close neighbors, but that alarm went directly to the police. I gambled on Etheridge not wanting to be found here.

Teag cut the ties binding Wilton and took back his net and cords. The thief groaned as he started to wake. Teag shouldered his backpack.

"Wait," I said and splayed my hand across the canvas. "I know you're in there," I said to the Dokkaebi. "And unless you want an eternity of servitude to a warlock family, you need to help us get out of here—without the bad luck twist."

Through my touch magic, I sensed the Dokkaebi. *Ancient. Alien— like all supernatural creatures that didn't begin as mortals. Sentient.*

I felt the goblin's silent assent, and then an explosion outside shattered the front windows.

Bo's frantic barking from the kitchen told me it was time to go.

"You're going to regret this, Kincaide," Etheridge shouted before I heard the SUV roar away.

"What do we do about him?" I asked with a nod toward Wilton just as he let out another deafening snort.

"Let him wake up and wonder what the hell happened," Teag replied. "Given all the empty bottles, that might not be unusual for him."

We needed to get the hell out of there.

Bo's ghost joined us in the kitchen. Teag and I had weapons at the ready, but the goons had fled, no doubt worried about the alarm and the explosion. I didn't want to get arrested, but given the choice between waiting to get bailed out versus going head-to-head with a dark warlock, I felt like we'd gotten a reprieve.

I snickered when I realized the goblin had blown up Etheridge's BMW.

Sirens wailed in the distance. We were running out of time. The black SUV and its occupants were gone, and we needed to put space between us and the house. Teag and I piled into his car, and he threw his backpack with the goblin bottle into the back seat. Bo's ghost disappeared when we slammed the doors, and Teag made his way down the driveway, then pulled out onto the road and drove in the opposite direction of the sirens, careful not to speed.

"Wow," I said, unable to manage a better response with my heart pounding so hard.

"Yeah," Teag replied, sounding equally gobsmacked. "'Wow' kinda sums it up."

Teag hadn't had time to clean up his circles and markings, so I felt sure we were going to see panicked news reports about "Satanists loose in Charleston" if Wilton's aunt and uncle found the salt and trappings of magic.

"Did Rowan help you come up with the ritual?" I needed to talk to stay grounded as we wound our way through side streets, taking an indirect route and trying to "fly casual."

"It was like a weird group project. Rowan worked out some of it, but then Mrs. Teller brought in a friend of hers, Mrs. Jeong, who is a Korean *mudang*—it's a type of shaman. Turns out, she knew about Dokkaebi, although she hadn't dealt with many. She didn't want to do the ritual herself—she's retired—but she had no problem teaching me how to strengthen what we'd already figured out. Lucky for us."

That went a lot better than I thought it would.

"Clyde Kenner did the right thing. He hid the bottle and ignored it. Since the goblin never got out in all those years, people like the Etheridges didn't even realize it was here," I said.

"Well somehow, Etheridge found out," Teag said. "He just had lousy judgment when it came to hiring a thief."

I turned to the backpack that held the goblin bottle. "Thank you," I told the Dokkaebi, although I reasoned that the spirit had its own self-interest in mind more than ours when it came to fighting off a warlock like Etheridge. "I wonder if Clyde frustrated the hell out of the goblin? He couldn't hear the spirit once the bottle was in the safe, and he didn't care. Which made him the perfect guardian."

We hadn't talked about where we were going, but we both knew that the safe at Trifles and Folly, within the shop's strong wardings, was the only secure place to store the bottle until we could hand it off to Sorren or maybe to the Briggs Society. *Unless...*

A crazy idea occurred to me. "If the goblin has enough power that Etheridge sensed it and wanted Wilton to steal the bottle, could we tap into that energy somehow to re-charge Gideon and Ramon's spell against the sea witch? Like some sort of...supernatural goblin battery?"

"I hadn't thought of that...but it might," Teag replied. "Let's get that bottle into a lead case inside the safe, and then we can figure it out."

CHAPTER ELEVEN

I CALLED SORREN AND DONNELLY TO TELL THEM WE HAD THE
Dokkaebi trapped and ask for advice on what to do next. If the goblin
had to remain trapped, then using it to power up Gideon and Ramon's
binding on the sea witch really appealed to me—providing it didn't
create new and different potentially world-ending issues.

That was the problem when it came to messing with magic. Little
changes could cause big, unexpected, and very scary repercussions.

Teag and I debated whether we should "guard" the bottle that was
in the safe. The shop had a little apartment up above, and we used it
sometimes in dire circumstances, but we realized that anything that
could get through the shop's wardings would be more than we could
handle without serious backup. We finished out the day, and sent
Maggie home early since we owed her big-time for covering for us so
much. She's amazing, and I make sure her paycheck reflects how much
she's appreciated.

Anthony had another continuing ed weekend class since he was
trying to get all his requirements done before the wedding. Kell was
doing a follow-up with his SPOOK team, filming at the Battery to see
if they could get more information about the monk ghost and then back

at the plague church. That left Teag and me on our own, and so we ordered Chinese food and headed to my place for the night.

"So listen to this," Teag said, looking up from his laptop as I put Baxter's kibble in his dish. "I found an ocean geologist who knows a lot about the area around Bermuda. Apparently, that part of the sea floor is…odd. There are very deep caves underneath some of the Bermuda chain of islands, and something called the 'agonic line,' which is where true north and magnetic north align."

I finished with Baxter and went to open a bottle of Shiraz, then I set out bowls of chips, salsa, guacamole, and other snacks. "Interesting. Back in the day, didn't some of the Bermuda Triangle stories claim that compasses and airplane guidance systems went wacky in that area?"

Teag nodded. "Yep. And they do—especially older ones. So the magnetism is a natural explanation for some of the phenomena. But with that area being one of the deepest points in the Atlantic and all the caves, plus the magnetic aberration…there's powerful energy for magic—a strong genius loci would fit right in."

I was about to comment when I got a message on my phone. "Beck wants to video call. Can you please set it up?"

A few moments later, Beck and Logan popped up on Teag's screen. After a couple of minutes of greetings and pleasantries, Beck got to the point.

"From the old ships' manifests we found, it's pretty clear that the Pendlewoods from Gideon Sullivan's period—and probably the Etheridges too—were not just shipping magical relics and haunted or cursed objects. They were trafficking shifters and people with magical abilities," Beck said, looking like he wanted to be sick. Logan slipped an arm around him.

That squared with what Sorren had told us at the Briggs Society about the fight that cost an Etheridge ancestor his life.

"Your family isn't you," Logan murmured. Beck twined their fingers together, but he still looked upset.

"Piecing together what we could find, I think both families were working with Huntsmen. The families probably had a network of informants who would identify people with special abilities. Then they'd hire the Huntsman to capture them and transport them to buyers on the mainland. In the case of shifters, probably for sport hunting," Beck said, loathing clear in his voice. "Those with other psychic abilities were probably pressed to serve the interests of their masters. It's sick and fucked up, but it happened."

Teag glanced at me. "Dante and Coltt and the crew of the *Vengeance* went gunning for those types of 'cargo' ships. I wouldn't be surprised if Ramon Montero didn't go after them too."

Unfortunately, that kind of trafficking hadn't stopped completely when sailing ships became obsolete, despite the efforts of the Alliance. We'd cracked down on one long-standing kidnapping ring in Charleston not too long ago, and there'd been enough incidents up in New York that Sorren and Donnelly had set up a small group of researchers to figure out the details.

"Clairvoyants might have come in handy to foretell bad weather at sea. Not everyone had the kind of wind and water magic that Gideon and Ramon had—or that Dante possessed," I mused.

"If they were mucking around with magic to control the sea itself, that might have gotten the attention of the local elemental," Beck continued. "Especially if they were trying to use their magic to sink their rivals. And if the families were willing to kidnap people with paranormal abilities, they certainly wouldn't have any qualms about trying to either sweet talk or outright force the elemental to do their bidding."

"And maybe it did, for a while," I conjectured. "Creating the stories about the 'sea witch' and the 'witch of the deep.' But they could have pushed too far or forgotten that they weren't really the boss of an ancient, immortal, high-powered spirit."

"Sounds like something my relatives would do," Beck said.

"The ocean geologist told me that there've also been undersea earthquakes not far from Bermuda," Teag picked up the tale. "That's what was on the news last night."

"Briggs said genius loci were located all across the ocean, protecting the areas they claimed as their own," I said. "Can we find out if the place where those undersea quakes are happening is near where Gideon and Ramon had their first showdown with the sea witch?"

"I can probably figure that out," Beck replied.

"I saw a geologist on the news, talking about the kind of disaster scenarios he studies," Teag said. "One of those sounds a lot like the dream that you had, Cassidy. If a quake hit just so, it could shear off the face of one of the seamounts. That would create exactly the kind of tsunami you saw from Gideon's vision, and in theory, it could not only wipe out Charleston but the whole Southeast coast."

"Shit," I muttered. "I hate when the dreams are right."

"There's something else Seth and I turned up." Teag looked at me. "I don't know whether it will be important…but I figured you'd want to know. You're a distant relative of Gideon Sullivan—from an indirect line."

My eyebrows shot up in surprise. "I am? Really? How?"

Teag walked me through the genealogy. I listened intently, with all sorts of questions circling in my thoughts. "But I don't have water magic. My psychometry is nothing like that."

"Dante was a water witch," Teag pointed out. "The relation to Gideon is a few generations later, on that side of the family."

"What does that mean for the guardian magic? Gideon's spell waned when the last of his direct descendants no longer survived. I'm not related that closely, but could it give us an edge in restoring the protections to full power?"

Teag shrugged. "I don't know. But Gideon must have known something about the magic that already ran in the family to entrust his book to Trifles and Folly—and maybe he even knew about Sorren and the Alliance."

Beck and Logan promised to keep digging, and we thanked them for their help. After the call ended and we finished eating, we cleaned up the kitchen and took the rest of the wine into the living room.

Bax jumped up on my lap, I settled onto the couch, and Teag curled into his favorite chair. I re-read Gideon's book aloud, and this time, I looked for details I might have missed as well as emotional impressions.

"Cassidy? You drifted off. What's the matter?" Teag asked after I'd been reading for a while. I realized that I'd stopped in the middle of a sentence.

I shook my head to clear it. "Nothing's wrong. It's just that last time, I got so caught up in the story that I skipped over some parts, and I tamped down on the touch magic reactions so I could follow what was going on. This time, I'm trying to pay more attention, in case there's something important I overlooked."

"Have you picked up on anything?"

I was quiet for a minute, processing my feelings. "I'm struck by the depth of emotions Gideon conveys in his memoir. He isn't trying to look like a hero, or get credit for what they did, or make them seem perfect. There's a raw honesty that's very refreshing. That all comes through to my psychometry in a way that goes beyond the actual words."

Teag nodded. "What else?"

"When it's time to recharge the guardian spell, I'm convinced we need to do it at the mausoleum. And I agree with Gideon that we need to be cautious about opening the crypt. So we'll need help from Rowan. Since Lucinda had visions from Agwe about all this, she needs to be there too."

An alert sounded on Teag's phone, and he checked an incoming message. "That's from Travis Dominick," he said. "Sent a bunch of files. We'd better take a look."

Travis was an ex-priest and a former member of the Sinistram, a shadowy secret Vatican special ops group that was, literally, the "left hand" of the Holy Father, taking care of supernatural problems with extreme prejudice.

When he became disillusioned with both the Church and the Sinistram, Travis got out and now he runs a halfway house in Pittsburgh. He still has access to a vault of arcane information in a hidden Vatican library beneath Duquesne University, and that trove of knowledge has saved our asses numerous times.

Teag pulled up the email on his phone and I read it over his shoulder.

Teag and Cassidy,

I found more in the archives than I expected about guardian spells and binding elementals—or as you've called them, genius loci. From what I've uncovered and the dates of some of the records, the Sinistram suspected that some sea captains were manipulating the sea elementals and using water and wind magic.

I'm not surprised to find that certain parties within the Church were working with old magic families to gain advantages, which undoubtedly included the Pendlewoods and Etheridges, among others.

What follows is a spell and detailed ritual for binding guardian spirits to the pledge of containing a particular dark entity. From the notations in the manuscript, I don't think the Sinistram attempted to work the spell—perhaps because it required blood sacrifice and bound the eternal souls of the one or ones who cast it.

If this spell works as I think it must, then Sullivan and Montero first worked magic to bind their souls together and then committed their immortal essence to the guardianship. There would be power in such a vow even if the two making it were not magic practitioners. It draws on primal energies—blood, breath, and sex—and teeters on the edge of forbidden magic. Please be very careful.

I haven't found as much on Dokkaebi, but what I did, I included. Brent said to ask your ex-C.H.A.R.O.N. contact about some of their secret equipment to capture and contain spirits. He thought he'd heard they had something that might help, but he does his best to stay the hell away from those people, so he can't ask for more information.

If we find anything else out on this end, I'll email. Let me know if you've got other questions. Good luck. Try not to get hexed.

I could picture Travis replying to Teag's message with a mix of scholarly excitement and friendly worry, which made me smile. Brent Lawson, Travis's demon-hunting partner, had been a soldier, a cop, and an FBI agent and now ran his own private investigation firm with an eye toward dealing with supernatural cases. His skill brought frequent, unwelcome invitations by C.H.A.R.O.N., a black ops government organization that dealt with the paranormal—and was known for dubious moral choices.

The spell itself was an encrypted attachment.

I looked at Teag, who studied the email like it might reveal the secret of the universe. When he finally looked up, he grinned. "Let's call Chuck. He always has the best toys."

Chuck Pettis didn't like to talk on the phone, and he didn't trust any email that wasn't heavily encrypted and sent via a complex set of secure relays. In-person conversation just made everything easier. He was happy to come to my place because he knew how strong the wardings were.

"Good to see you," he growled when he entered. "Been a while. 'Course, I've been off with Uncle Robert taking some time away… figured with all the omens, there must be trouble brewing."

Chuck is in his mid-fifties, average height, and a little too thin. It's easy to tell that he's ex-Army just from the way he holds himself and how his eyes never stop scanning for threat. Back in the day, Chuck was supernatural special ops, and now he hates C.H.A.R.O.N. as much as Travis loathes the Sinistram. His uncle had also been a C.H.A.R.O.N. operative even longer ago, and the two of them chose Charleston to retire in large part because Sorren's influence dissuaded relentless secret government agencies from trying to renew their claim.

Chuck looks like he chewed nails for breakfast, and his gravelly voice suggested an old smoking habit. But when he picked up Baxter, scratched his ears, and rubbed his belly, Chuck's Terminator image took a real hit.

"How's your uncle?" I asked. Robert used to run a shop like Trifles and Folly—down to the world-saving hidden abilities—in Cape May, but had sold it to our friend Erik Mitchell and then retired, coming down to spend his golden years with his nephew.

"Full of piss and vinegar, like always," Chuck said, his tone fond despite his choice of words. "Still a force of nature—and I hope he stays that way."

Even from a few feet away, I could hear the quiet ticking of the watches Chuck always wore tacked to the inside of his vest, coat, and jacket. His belief that he'd die if the watches and the clocks that fill his house all ran down was an odd superstition. I figured that, like the rest of us, Chuck had seen some horrors in his life, and if the watches gave him a little peace of mind, I wasn't going to quibble. He seemed to be a bit less obsessed about the timepieces since he'd been working with us, and I wondered if Sorren might have had a hand in that.

"So…whaddya need?" Chuck wasn't much for small talk. I offered him a beer, and we went to sit in the living room.

"Saving the world again, one weird crisis at a time," I told him. Chuck's been through some really strange shit with us, and he's always come through. "This time, it's pirate ghosts, a sea witch, a prep school warlock, and an alcoholic Korean goblin."

He cracked a smile at that. "You've got a Dokkaebi on your hands? Lord have mercy. How did that happen?"

Chuck drank his beer and listened carefully as Teag and I took turns filling him in. For as much as Chuck likes to come across as a grunt, he has a head for strategy and covert ops, and he didn't survive his tours of duty by being dim. I valued his insights and appreciated him having our backs.

"Nice job bottling up the goblin," Chuck said. "I only ran into one in the field—and that was enough. Unfortunately for us, its owner knew what one of those could do and used it against everyone who came at him. We lost a lot of good men locking that damn spirit up." He took a long pull from his beer, and for a moment his thoughts were clearly far away.

"The kicker is that Carter Etheridge hired a thief to steal it for him —and then the thief took off with it. We barely beat him to the thief… and the bottle," I told him.

The name "Etheridge" snapped Chuck out of his thoughts. "That stuck-up, entitled, trust fund prick? What's he got to do with this?"

I explained the bigger problem, with the waning guardian magic, Gideon and Ramon's brave sacrifice, and Etheridge's obsession with the memoir, ending with the fight at Wilton's place.

"Once we got the goblin trapped again, I wondered if there was some way to tap its energy like a battery. That way, it could help renew the magic that Gideon and Ramon worked to keep the sea witch bound. We were talking with Brent Lawson, and he said to ask you," I added.

Chuck pondered that for a moment. Teag got him another beer, and Chuck accepted it gratefully. "Maybe," he said, with a look in his eyes that told me he was quickly scanning his memories. "We were just focused on locking that damn goblin up that other time, but we didn't need a 'battery.' It's not like you can ever let the spirit free without causing big problems. It can't die. So if it's got to be locked up, might as well be useful."

"How would we 'plug' the guardian spell into the energy source?" I asked. "From everything Gideon says in his book, the spell started to fade when his last direct descendent died. That was about three months ago."

Chuck tapped his fingers against the arm of the couch as he thought. "It's a blood spell then. That would make sense."

"How would the spell decide which descendants counted as being 'direct'?" I asked. "He had one son, and the Sullivans weren't exactly prolific. When we checked into Gideon's family, there's no one left who's closer than a third cousin."

Chuck nodded. "There are witches you could ask who'd know better than I do—I don't have a lick of magic myself. If you can find the exact wording, we'd know more about what Gideon meant to do. While we're re-energizing the spell, it might be possible to tweak it a bit, assuming there's any family left."

"It turns out that I'm distantly related to Gideon," I said. "It might mean nothing—"

"Or it might," Chuck said. "Worth looking into. But what would you make of it? You fixing to move into that mansion of his?"

I bought my parent's home when they moved to Charlotte. It's a Charleston "single house," the kind where the door to the street opens at the side of the building, onto a long porch instead of into the house itself. I grew up here, and the house has been in my family for a long time. Plus, thanks to our talented friends, it's one of the most warded places in Charleston. Moving wasn't an option.

"No, but if the Sullivan house is properly cared for by the museum and the mausoleum is securely warded, we might have a bit of wiggle room. Was the spell focused on having someone spend time in the house or actually living there? How closely did they have to be related?" I mused aloud. "If we could figure out what's essential, we could reinforce the important parts and ignore the others."

"Sounds like we need to talk with Rowan tomorrow," Teag said. "But back to the battery idea…how could we connect the energy of the Dokkaebi to the spell, and also make sure that the goblin can't somehow twist the connection and use it for its own purposes?"

"We had tech at C.H.A.R.O.N. that was designed to do something along those lines," Chuck said. "It was supposed to contain the source while diverting a steady flow of energy somewhere else."

He grimaced. "The bastards at high command commissioned something that could siphon off the magic of a captured demon. A Dokkaebi can't die any more than the genius loci can. It might just work."

"How are you going to get the tech from C.H.A.R.O.N.?" Teag asked. "I didn't think you were exactly on good terms."

Chuck laughed. "We aren't. And I already have it—because I stole it." He paused. "That's a harsh word, 'stole.' More like I took some 'parting gifts' with me when I left, in compensation for what they owed me—like my sanity. And then I reverse engineered the shit out of them and made some modifications of my own."

"Will the device hold up over time? The last thing we need is having the goblin get loose again." I feared the power of a wish-granting goblin in the hands of someone like Etheridge as much as I did the sea witch's tsunami.

"Yeah. It should hold. It did with every demon they tried it on. The clever part is that the entity can remain bound. The sensors that touch the containment unit—in this case, the bottle—have sigils that pick up on the energy the spirit radiates. It's also spelled and engineered so the entity can't reverse the flow."

For the moment, I refused to think about the diabolical uses such a device might be put to—although I felt certain those had been uppermost in the mind of the C.H.A.R.O.N. engineers who created it.

"How long will it take to have one ready?" Teag asked.

"Give me a day," Chuck replied. "Now that I know I'm calibrating for a goblin and a pair of ghost witches, it shouldn't take much to make the adjustments and tweak the spell that goes with it. The device channels the bound entity's magic, and it requires a witch to receive that magic and use it. Although…the ghost part is a new one for me."

I trusted Chuck. He'd never failed us before—and I'd seen what kind of tech he could cobble together from stolen bits and contraband pieces. "Okay. But work fast—the binding is slipping, and the storm is coming—that many omens can't be wrong."

CHAPTER TWELVE

THE NEXT MORNING, MY PHONE RANG BEFORE I'D FINISHED MY FIRST cup of coffee.

"He's suing." Alistair's sigh said everything he couldn't put into words. I had plenty of reasons to dislike Carter Etheridge, but going after the museum to get his hands on Gideon Sullivan's mansion and memoir became top of my list.

"Can he win?" I held my breath.

"Our lawyers doubt he can win in court. He has no standing—he isn't related to Sullivan, and there's no reason for him to have a claim on the property. It would be a pretty dangerous precedent to set, that someone who wants to grab up properties and resell them at a profit can challenge the legitimate beneficiaries," Alistair said. "And yet..."

If it comes down to the wire, my distant relationship to Gideon might beat out no relationship at all.

His voice drifted off, and I knew what he was thinking. Etheridge had money and magic on his side. Even people who didn't believe in the latter could still be influenced by it—or intimidated by the rumors about the warlock family.

"I don't think it will go to court," Alistair added, sounding worn. "He's gambling that the Board of Trustees will balk at the expense of defending the bequest and at the bad PR. He'll offer a lowball payoff, betting that they'll take it and think they got the best end of the deal."

"Do you think the Board will?"

"I hope not. I think they're made of sterner stuff. But it's always a possibility."

"Can you stall? Drag it out? I can't explain…but it's really important." I didn't want to reveal the whole sea witch problem to Alistair if I could avoid it—we tried not to expose our full abilities to more people than necessary—but I had the feeling that he'd believe me even if I did.

He's asked Teag and me—and some of our friends—for help with cursed and haunted objects enough times to suspect that there's more we aren't saying. Still…Etheridge was dangerous, and Alistair didn't have natural defenses.

So we'd have to make sure he was protected, and some of that safety lay in not knowing the whole truth.

"I'll do my best," he promised.

"Thanks for letting me know," I told him. "Keep me posted, please." I ended the call and let out a long breath. Baxter looked up at me hopefully, and I tossed him a little bit of my toaster waffle.

"I bet you'd bite Etheridge, and I'd let you," I said to Bax. "But it would probably turn your stomach."

Baxter's happy snuffling noises as he ate made me smile, despite Alistair's bad news.

I called Sorren and left a message about the new problem at the museum. Just in case, I called Donnelly as well, although I'm never sure how phone calls work with a building that phases in and out of time. Maybe they could threaten Etheridge enough to make him back off the museum.

If he wanted to come after us, fine. We could handle him. I was looking forward to it.

I finished my coffee and poured another cup, fixing it just how I liked it, with cream and sugar, fortifying myself for a hard day.

I felt certain that Etheridge wasn't pursuing the Sullivan mansion because he wanted to turn the land into pricy condos. There were plenty of other properties he could get for less trouble—and without a potential public relations headache.

No, Etheridge had either figured out that the Sullivan manor held powerful magic, or he had done some research into his own family history and discovered the sea witch story—and the role Gideon and Ramon played in binding her and throwing a monkey wrench into the profitable occult trade.

He may have even figured that all the cursed and haunted items the two of them 'liberated' from the Pendlewood and Etheridge cargo ships had ended up in the mansion. It would never occur to him that Gideon and Ramon might have destroyed the pieces to keep them out of the wrong hands.

Whatever Etheridge knew or didn't know, he was dangerous—not just to Charleston, but to everyone in the path of the destruction the sea witch could unleash.

We were the only ones who could stop the elemental...a fellowship made up of a few witches and psychics, some stubborn ghosts, and a clever vampire. The task seemed impossible, but we'd managed against other forces with less warning. I believed in us, but I also knew to take nothing for granted.

Teag had started driving me to the shop in case Etheridge tried to grab me at the house. I knew he couldn't get through the wardings, but despite the protective Hoodoo on the sidewalk, I didn't want to take a chance on being nabbed by his goons.

"Want to stop for coffee?" he asked. Given how crowded Honeysuckle Café was early in the morning, Etheridge would be a fool to make a move on us there—he'd find a video of his attack on YouTube before he got a block away.

"You're singing my song," I moaned. "Good coffee makes a bad day manageable."

"Are you planning for it to be a bad day?" Teag asked, and while he kept his voice light, I heard the undercurrent of worry in his tone.

He listened as I told him about Alistair's call and Etheridge's latest maneuver. "We need to strengthen the guardian magic before Etheridge somehow gets his hands on the mansion and its lands," I told him. "Renewing the magic might hold him off too."

Teag nodded. "Maybe. We still don't know whether he hired Wilton to steal the spirit bottle because he sensed the power or because he actually knew it was a Dokkaebi. If he can pick up on the strong wardings around the Sullivan mansion, then he might conclude there's something inside worth protecting."

"Could be. But why is he so desperate to level up? He's the head of the main branch of the family. Does that mean he's also the strongest?"

"Maybe Sorren's right about rivals," Teag replied. "There's always someone who wants to move up. If so, he might want to supercharge his magic, especially if he knows or suspects that someone could be stronger. Or maybe too much is not enough, and he wants power for power's sake. Does it matter?"

"Not really, I guess. We still have to stop him." I knew it wouldn't be easy. But we had two seafaring ghost witches on our side, and I wasn't ready to count Gideon and Ramon out before we saw what they could do.

Trina had the TV on as usual when we walked into the café, but everyone staring in rapt attention at the screen definitely wasn't the norm.

"Storm's moving in," Trina said when I looked puzzled, and her words sent a chill down my spine because that was true in a way and on a scale she didn't realize. "The governor is expected to announce a mandatory evacuation within the hour."

"Hurricane?" I tried to sound nonchalant. Charlestonians take storms seriously—we've been hit by some big ones—but we don't panic. Hurricane season comes every year, so we have our preparation routines down pat.

The city could handle high winds and normal storm surge, but a tsunami of the sort Teag's oceanographer described wasn't remotely "normal." I shivered, remembering the images from my nightmare that had been all too real. My friends and I needed to make sure those predictions never came true.

Teag elbowed me, and I realized I'd drifted into my thoughts after we stepped away from the counter. I looked up at the screen once more, expecting to see more talking heads keeping ceaseless chatter over when the storm might hit.

Instead, I saw a reporter doing a stand-up next to one of the ghost bikes about all the calls the station had received from people who swore they saw the bike wheels spinning without being touched.

The broadcast cut away to the Battery, where "witnesses" were giving their breathless stories about seeing either the monk ghost or the Fort Moultrie Light—a phantom lighthouse that hadn't existed in more than one hundred and fifty years. Video of crows were interspersed between the cutaways, including a gathering large enough to blanket all of Whitepoint Park that definitely had an apocalyptic feel to it.

"That doesn't look good," Teag murmured, the understatement of the year.

The news show went back to the anchor at her desk, with a map of the Charleston area marked with several red concentric circles.

"Scientists reported a new wave of tremors throughout the Lowcountry today, marking the fifteenth day in a row of seismic activity. The events have slowly grown in frequency and strength over the last three months," the reporter said. "What they mean—if anything—remains to be seen. Stay tuned, and we will provide the most comprehensive updates of any station in the region."

The news cut away to commercials, which meant everyone went back to doing what they'd been doing, and Teag and I headed for the car.

"When the people who know nothing about magic start talking about omens, we've got a situation," Teag said as he pulled away from the curb.

"No wonder Etheridge is on high alert," I replied. "Anyone with a lick of magic has to read those signs and know trouble is coming."

"Want to bet that the ones who don't have the juice for a big battle are already heading out of harm's way?"

"Maybe that's not a bad thing."

Charleston's witches had their own complicated social categories based on power and pedigree. Over the past year, after a near-uprising by the witches of lesser native talent and no family connections, Sorren and Donnelly had begun brokering discussion and facilitating change. That boded well for a future where those with magic presented a more united front against common enemies and reduced their pointless bickering. But most of those folks couldn't help us with the sea witch problem, so it was just as well they stayed safe and got out of town.

We parked behind Trifles and Folly. I carried my latte and the one we bought for Maggie. Teag unlocked the back door and disarmed the security system. I made a beeline for the coffee maker. The latte I'd nearly finished would only hold me for so long.

"Rowan's here," Teag called from the front as I filled the coffee pot. He let her in and then came back to the break room to join us once Maggie arrived.

"Hi," I greeted Rowan. "Thanks for coming so early."

She shrugged. "Figured we might as well touch base before things get busier." Rowan gave me a sly look. "Word on the street is you blew up Carter Etheridge's Beemer."

"Much as I'd like to take credit, I didn't do it. The Dokkaebi did. Although if Carter looks a little singed around the edges, that's totally on me." I leaned against the counter and took a long pull from my latte.

"He had it coming," I added, although I knew Rowan wasn't faulting me. "Etheridge sicced his lawyers on the museum over the Sullivan mansion, and he's killed people trying to get the spirit bottle."

I couldn't help glancing toward the office, where the lead case containing the Dokkaebi still rested in our spelled safe. Neither the tremors nor the impending storm of the century worried me as much as what kind of fuckery Etheridge would get up to with the goblin doing his bidding.

"Lucinda, Donnelly, and I have been talking," Rowan said, settling in at the table. "We went over the information Travis sent—and it's solid."

"No surprise there," Teag replied, getting out three mugs from the cupboard. I took Maggie's latte to her and came back to sit with Rowan.

"We think the plan to power up the original spell will work.

Chuck's device could certainly help, but Donnelly's necromancy alone might be able to pull back the two faded spirits if they're willing," Rowan said.

"I'm sure they will be," I replied. "They intended their bond and the spell to last forever. It didn't just stop the sea witch—it also ensured that the two of them couldn't be separated in the afterlife."

"The spell requires a bonded pair—and death," Rowan continued. "Which makes them the eternal guardians." She smiled and shook her head. "Pretty damn ballsy."

"Do you know how to re-charge the magic?" I found myself holding my breath.

"Yes—at least, we think so. But we've got to hurry. Etheridge's legal maneuvering aside, the omens are a warning that time is running out," Rowan replied. "If the tremors predict a quake near the elemental's seamount, and the sea witch slips her bonds, a tsunami like that would wipe out the Southeast coast and miles inland."

I swallowed hard. "Yeah. I've seen that in my nightmares. It doesn't go well." Rowan's expression told me that she also suspected —as Teag and I did—that those dreams were really warning visions.

"So you think the hurricane is related?" Teag asked, looking up from his screen.

"The timing is too perfect to be a true coincidence," Rowan said. "Especially when the storm formed right over the part of the ocean where they did the first binding spell."

"We realized that too," I said.

"As the genius loci gets more wiggle room from the spell Gideon and Ramon cast, more of her energy can 'bleed out' of the bindings and influence a naturally-occurring storm, increasing its strength."

The past few times Charleston had been hit by a powerful earthquake or a strong hurricane, the damage and death toll had been huge. To have both strike in short succession, driven by an angry elemental with a grudge, would be even more catastrophic. I flinched, seeing those images from my dreams again, real and horrific.

"All right," I said. "How can we help?

"Can you get us into the mausoleum? Because Travis and Donnelly and I all believe that's not only where Gideon and Ramon worked the final spell—that's where their bones are. From what you've shared of Gideon's book," Rowan said, "they did everything they could to create a supernatural fortress in there. I'm hoping that they also left us a copy of the original spell, just in case they needed help from the future."

I nodded. "I have the key. Apparently, the only key. But it came with a warning that strong magic was worked inside, and it should be opened only in dire need."

Rowan gave a bleak laugh. "I think we meet the criteria."

THE DARK CLOUDS and wind-whipped trees predicted a storm, and the governor's mandatory evacuation order emptied the coastal areas. As always, there were hold-outs. They would get rounded up by the police and forced to leave until the situation got bad enough that those remaining would have to get by on their own. Some hunkered down where they were, taking pride in having ridden out many storms in their solidly built, historic homes. Most heeded the warning and fled on the crowded roads that had all been turned one-way outgoing to speed the exodus. Maybe the stronger, more frequent tremors convinced the skeptics even more than the storm warnings.

The people were right to be frightened—they just didn't know to be afraid of the right threat.

The Sullivan mansion's remote location promised that accidental human interruptions were unlikely, although the incoming storm itself might throw a wrench into our plans.

We expected Carter Etheridge to make a move. Like there wasn't already enough to worry about.

"The storm isn't going to make this any easier," Teag muttered.

"Not sure it's going to make it any harder," I countered. "Other than it's like someone ordered up 'spooky horror movie atmosphere.'"

"Wind, water, and rain are part of this spell," Lucinda said, rejoining us. She had walked to the edge of the sea to call Agwe, using a white conch shell embellished with blue painted *veves*. In the midst of the storm, an air of preternatural calmness surrounded her. "Ramon, Gideon, and Agwe wielded them with their magic."

"Spell or no spell, I've got no desire to get hit by lightning, so let's try to get inside as soon as we can," Rowan grumbled as the wind whipped her hair into her eyes.

We had our crew together, along with the spells and materials that might help us avert catastrophe. Donnelly, Rowan, and Alicia were here to communicate with the ghosts of Gideon and Ramon and bind the Dokkaebi to be the guardian spell's backup battery. Lucinda and Sorren came along as our protectors since we had no idea what entities might be attracted when we opened up the crypt. Teag and I were here on behalf of the Alliance and Trifles and Folly since the store and its history were bound up in this at a bone-deep level.

Kell didn't accompany us this time. While he's a mean shot with a shotgun, courage alone wouldn't be a match for the forces we were dealing with. Hell, I wasn't even sure that the rest of us would come through this unscathed.

Early in our relationship, Kell would have argued the point. Now that he knows more about the kinds of threats we handle, he understands that staying at my place with Maggie to have food and first-aid ready was still an important way to support the team, something he could do without putting himself—and me—at greater risk. I missed him, but knowing he was safe let me concentrate on the problem without distraction.

I carried the lead case with the gin goblin in my left hand. Bo's old collar was wrapped loosely around that wrist, and the dog tags clinked against the metal briefcase. In my right hand, I had my wand, and I had Alard's walking stick thrust through my belt. An agate spindle whorl felt heavy in my pocket. Sorren had given it to me—a long-ago gift to him from a Norse demigoddess that enhanced the magic of the bearer.

Teag had a bag with the items for our ritual to restore the guardian spell, as well as the curled silver whip, nets of magic-woven rope soaked in salt, holy water, and colloidal silver, and a few other helpful things. He wore a dagger and a short sword in sheaths on his belt, weapons he had trained for years to wield with dangerous precision.

Both of us wore amulets and bracelets of silver, agate, and onyx, as well as cords woven with Teag's magic to protect us and enhance our abilities. I saw that Alicia was equally protected. Rowan was dressed in a flowing shirt and loose pants, all in midnight blue, with silver rune jewelry.

Lucinda wore white for her role as a mambo. Her swirl of elaborate braids was woven with shells and blue beads as a tribute to Agwe. She had a small bag with the items necessary to prepare an altar and make an offering to the Loa. The rest of us wore regular T-shirts and jeans, practical for hard work—or moving fast in a fight.

I'd heeded Gideon's warning and hadn't tried to visit earlier. I didn't want to tip off Etheridge or rile up the sea witch before we were ready. While it might have helped to see the interior instead of going from the floor plans and the architect's renderings, it wasn't worth the risk.

The longer I'd studied the plans, the more convinced I became that Gideon built the crypt with the intention to make it the anchor for their magic. I'd seen my share of mausoleums, even some of the opulent resting places built by the robber barons of the Gilded Age, and none were set up like what Gideon commissioned. I had a pretty good idea of what to expect once we finally were able to enter the crypt.

The Sullivan mausoleum was the size of a one-story fortified bungalow with stained glass windows. Protective trees and bushes surrounded the building, as did an iron fence. Sullivan and Montero did not leave anything to chance.

The single iron door opened into a large foyer. Maybe Gideon told his architect that he wanted a space to hold a private wake or cere-mony, or perhaps he suggested it as a keeping room for the family cemetery. I suspected it was a defensive buffer between the outside world and the ritual area beyond.

The next room was labeled "chapel" on the plans, but I doubted that it resembled the churches downtown. The final room, all the way in the back, ostensibly held the crypt drawers—six of them. I checked burial records and found no documentation that anyone other than Gideon was entombed in the mausoleum. Montero, known then as

Córdoba, vanished from all records at the same time of Gideon's reported death, although I felt certain we would find his bones inside. None of the other family was put to rest in the crypt, instead choosing a small graveyard on the mansion's property.

Now that I thought about it, I wondered if those Sullivan-Montero family ghosts might be part of the layers of protection designed around the mansion and the mausoleum. Gideon and Ramon might not have been trained witches, but they had obviously sought out good counsel and done their homework for their guardian spell to have lasted nearly two centuries.

I had studied the drawings, but that hadn't prepared me for the size of the granite-walled building.

"I've seen smaller houses," Teag said, looking at the mausoleum with surprise. "That's a big place for two bodies."

"I think in the case of Gideon and Ramon, it's more of an antechamber between life and death," I replied.

"You're exactly right." Archibald Donnelly spoke up. "Even without opening the door, I can sense that this has become a liminal space, a borderland in the Veil."

"Kinda gives a whole new meaning to Dead Man Zone, doesn't it," Teag murmured.

"Indeed it does," Donnelly replied to Teag's snarky comment. "And not just the spirits of the two gentlemen inside. As I'm sure Alicia can attest."

Alicia is a powerful medium. She knows how to ward her séances and protect herself from ghost possession, and I'd seen her fight her way free from spirits that refused to leave. We'd faced down some pretty creepy revenants, so she was no newcomer to an arcane battle. Even with all that experience, Alicia looked a bit twitchy.

"What's wrong? What are you picking up?" I asked.

"There are at least twenty spirits between us and the mausoleum," she said, and Donnelly nodded his confirmation. "Family ghosts, so the resonance among them is particularly powerful. If we want to get to the crypt, we have to get past them."

I glanced at Donnelly. "We don't want to fight them. We're here to extend what Gideon and Ramon did, not bring harm."

"Then we need to convince them that we're on their side," Donnelly replied. "I could probably banish them…maybe. But they'd return vengeful, and we don't need that—plus it would drain me, and I'm of better use repairing the guardian spell. So I advise diplomacy."

"Why are they riled?" I turned slowly to look around us. "They couldn't have known we were coming."

Low growls came from the left and right, and four large, red-eyed barghests slunk from the shadows, teeth bared and heads lowered for a fight.

Two dozen ghouls came at us behind the mausoleum. Their waxy, corpse-pale skin glowed in the moonlight, and their emaciated bodies hid the creatures' unnatural strength. The stench twisted my stomach.

"That explains why the ghosts were upset," I muttered, slipping my wand back into my sleeve and drawing Alard's walking stick from my belt. I gave the dog collar a shake. Bo's nearly-solid ghost materialized at my side.

The ghouls parted, and a man strode through the break in the ranks of the monster army, making an entrance, even now, like the narcissistic son of a bitch that he was.

"That's far enough." Carter Etheridge said. With him were six other men, two that were clearly muscle, and four others I figured had magic. Four more men emerged from the darkness to plant themselves between us and the mausoleum.

It didn't surprise me that he'd made it past the perimeter of protective trees. That was a passive barrier to deflect rogue spirits and malicious novices. Magical wardings around the mausoleum and mansion were stronger and dangerously active.

"Go home, you miserable little puffed up cockalorum," Donnelly huffed. "Be gone. You've got no business here."

"Give me the key to the crypt, and I'll let you live," Etheridge's cold smile made his lie clear.

"I gave you fair warning." Sorren stepped forward. "This is none of your affair. Leave now, or we will destroy you."

"If you had that power, you'd have done it centuries ago," Etheridge taunted. "One vampire and a bunch of magical misfits against a warlock dynasty? Don't flatter yourself. Now give me the key. Or don't," he added, "And I'll take it off your bleeding corpse."

Etheridge twitched his right hand, and the creatures ran for us at full speed.

Game on.

Sorren went after the barghests to the left while I blasted the two barghests on the right with a stream of fire from the walking stick, setting the creatures ablaze. Sorren bested the hellhounds in speed and strength. He twisted to avoid their fangs and dodged the sweep of their clawed paws, then ripped heads from bodies and emerged from the battle covered in the monsters' blood.

Donnelly focused on the ghouls. He thrust one hand out toward the onslaught of undead attackers and clenched his fist. A shouted a word of power ripped away the predatory spirits that had seized control of the stolen corpses. They formed a sickly green, glowing cloud above the pile of bodies until Donnelly spoke another word and set the cloud afire from within until nothing remained but embers that darkened as they fell and then vanished.

Rowan raised her hands, palms out, and sent a shockwave of magic strong enough to knock Etheridge and his bodyguard flying through the air to land—hard—several feet away. Bo's ghost lunged after them, snapping his teeth and growling.

I sent a stream of fire at the second witchy guy, and as soon as he stopped, dropped, and rolled, Rowan's muttered curse had him on his knees puking up his guts.

Sorren moved in a blur, fast, strong, and silent, a blood-soaked terror. He put two goons on the ground, still breathing but out cold, while Rowan's magic sent the third witchy guy tumbling toward where she'd tossed Etheridge and his bodyguard onto a heap guarded by Bo's ghost.

Teag's right hand flicked out, and the coiled silver-coated metal whip snapped, wrapping around the fourth witchy guy's wrist, cutting nearly to the bone. The man curled in on himself in pain as Teag flung a weighted, woven net that draped over the man's head and shoulders. He went down like a sack of rocks.

I feared that at any moment the men who stood between us and the crypt would launch a counterattack. Then I heard their screams.

A tide of angry ghosts washed over them, pulling them down into the vortex of a gray maelstrom. In seconds, their cries were lost amid the shrieks and howls of the angry, protective spirits.

Alicia's lips quirked—just slightly—and I figured she had orchestrated the attack.

Wild wind shook the tree branches like dry bones, and with a deafening crack of thunder and a brilliant streak of lightning, the heavens opened, pouring down cold, drenching rain. The ground shuddered beneath our feet, reminding us—as if we could forget—that this was no normal storm.

Etheridge rose to his feet, soaked, dirt-streaked, and furious. "What did you do to me, you bitch?" he screamed at Rowan. His companions stayed down, guarded by Bo's ghost.

"It's a Tribunal spell," Rowan answered, her expression as cold as a hanging judge. "Blocks your power long enough to be held accountable."

"You have no right," Etheridge raged. "I demand you release me."

His monsters were dead, and so were most of his allies, except for a few that remained twitching and moaning on the ground.

"Guess that just leaves you, sonny." Donnelly faced Etheridge with a feral smile.

"You can't touch me. I'm not dead."

Donnelly shrugged. "You have a soul. I could rip it from your body and turn it inside out. But I think someone else has already staked a claim."

Lucinda stepped forward. The wind snapped her braids like serpents writhing around her head and billowed her loose, white clothing. I could have sworn I saw a faint glow suffuse her dark skin. Then I saw her fiery red eyes.

Etheridge fell back a step. His fingers twitched with spell work, but nothing happened thanks to Rowan's magic.

"*What* are you?" Etheridge's voice betrayed his fear.

Lucinda favored him with a toothy, vengeful smile, and the expression on her face looked nothing like her usual self. "Agwe cannot leave the sea, so he sent me. I am Erzulie Dantor. You are not welcome here."

My breath caught. We'd encountered Erzulie Dantor before, and she was a fearsomely protective Loa who claimed the outcasts as her beloved children. I welcomed her as an ally even as my hindbrain recognized the mortal danger of her presence.

"Go back where you came from. This is none of your business," Etheridge snapped.

"Oh, that's where you're wrong." Lucinda's voice was poisoned honey. "Your family's meddling with the sea witch troubles my husband, Agwe. That troubles me. He favors strengthening the sea witch's bonds, but my husband is not without compassion," Erzulie Dantor spoke through Lucinda. "He deserves an offering—and he might save a bit to give her a last meal."

I could hardly believe what I saw, but my touch magic assured me that the vision was real. Although we were a good distance from the coastline, ghostly waves swept toward Etheridge and his downed helpers at frightening speed. The waves weren't solid, but they were real.

Etheridge's eyes widened, just now truly realizing he was outmatched. "Wait! We can work this out. Let's talk—" His bargaining ended in a scream.

The surge crested and knocked him to the ground before the phantom undertow claimed him and his supporters and dragged them out to the depths.

The spectral tide vanished, leaving no mark behind to prove it had ever existed. The bodies of the ghouls and barghests, as well as those of Etheridge and his men, were gone.

I stared in horrified fascination and finally got a grip. When I looked back to Lucinda, the red eyes and otherworldly glow had faded. She looked tired, but determined.

"We still have work to do," Lucinda said in her normal voice. That snapped us all out of our incredulous staring. "Let's get it done."

We crossed into the inner courtyard without incident, although I felt a bone-deep chill and a rush of frigid air that was out of place on a temperate night. We had seen what the protector-ghosts were capable of doing and did not take our safe passage for granted.

I willed my hand to be steady as I used the key from the book to unlock the mausoleum. The heavy iron door needed two people to drag it open, and the metal tingled beneath my hands from the spells protecting it.

Rain sluiced down in sheets, thunder rumbled, and the wind rattled in the trees. The granite walls and slate roof muted the fury of the onslaught but couldn't silence it completely.

Despite the dust, the air inside the crypt still held faint traces of sage, rosemary, mint, and lavender, all plants prized for protection. They mingled with a whiff of cinnamon, myrrh, cedar, and anise, powerful for spells involving death, resurrection, and the afterlife.

The antechamber looked like what I expected from the building's plans, but nothing in the drawings suggested the profusion of symbols, runes, and sigils covering the walls, ceiling, and floor. Some were painted, others etched into the granite. A few were carved and then filled with silver, onyx, obsidian, and opal.

I didn't touch anything, but I felt the pulse of the magic in play here. It raised the hair on the back of my neck and prickled against my skin. Testing me, sussing out my intentions.

This wasn't a foyer—it was a supernatural airlock designed to challenge anyone who dared enter and trap unwelcome visitors. I shivered, hoping that the old magic judged us to be worthy.

"They're still here."

Teag and I glanced sharply at Alicia. Her eyes were closed, and she stood completely still, deep in trance.

"Can you communicate with them?" I asked. "Are they still strong enough to remember who they were?"

"They have faded, but they remain." Her voice took on a sing-song cadence and odd breathiness that sent a chill down my back. "They request that we come closer."

Behind us, Lucinda pushed the iron door nearly shut. "You go do what you need to do," she told us, "and I'll be here, making an offering to Agwe."

Rowan, Sorren, and Donnelly were still outside in the storm, ensuring Etheridge didn't have reinforcements. I knew Donnelly and Rowan would eventually come inside to renew the guardian ritual, while Sorren promised to keep watch.

Lucinda turned, scoping out the chamber, and chose a spot to set out her candles and make her offering, a location that placed her as a bulwark between the inner chambers and the outside world.

She spread a blue and white cloth, placing white candles at the four corners. Next, Lucinda poured rum into a scrimshaw cup, raising it in tribute before setting it down. Seashells and turquoise fish figurines joined the cup, along with a wooden bowl filled with rice cooked in coconut milk. Finally, she took the conch shell marked with Agwe's *veve*, his sacred mark of a boat, and looked to us again.

"We will make sure you are not disturbed." She blew a note on the conch, and it echoed in the confines of the granite-walled room.

CHAPTER THIRTEEN

I FELT A NEW POWER SWELL AS THE NOTES OF THE CONCH FADED. Sometimes I'd glimpsed Loa like Papa Legba and even Baron Samedi during our battles when Lucinda had called on them for wisdom and protection. Now, I smelled sea air and thought I heard waves.

"He does not leave the sea," Lucinda said, guessing my thoughts. "That is why I went to the water's edge and made a gift. His attention is upon us. Agwe watches the sea witch. She is restless. Best to do your work quickly." She didn't sound like herself, and I knew from her stilted phrasing that she was linked to the spirit of the Loa.

Alicia, Teag, and I crossed the threshold from the antechamber into Gideon's chapel. Paintings and icons of Saint Elmo, the patron of sailors, hung beside those of Saint Sebastian, protector of the plague-ridden, Saint Ulrich of Augsburg, and Raphael the archangel, all of which were identified with Agwe. The three saints and the Loa also appeared in the stained glass windows, lit by brilliant flashes of light-ning. Relics and magical items sat on shelves or inside carved niches.

"The symbols are different here," Teag murmured, his voice quiet and reverent.

I scanned the markings and searched my memories. Where the

sigils in the outer room were protections and traps, those in this room were associated with binding and locking.

"I think Gideon and Ramon tried to amplify their spell the first time with all the occult items they collected," I said. "Their 'battery' helped the protections last almost two centuries—not too shabby."

On the other side of the room, a doorway opened to a small nook with two burial drawers, side by side.

Now I knew that those final resting places would remain forever empty. Gideon and Ramon's desiccated corpses lay in this room, in the center of an elaborate ritual space.

Guttered candles marked the four quarters of a complex ritual circle inlaid into the stone floor. Several magical items were inside the warded space—a boline knife with a pearl handle, a silver chalice with a residue of darkened flakes, and a shallow bowl filled with the ashes of incense, along with a scrimshaw pipe.

I forced my gaze back to the mummified bodies. Darkened skin pulled tight over the skeletons beneath, and dry patches of hair clung to the scalps. Neither wore clothing, and I remembered a comment in Gideon's book about how being together in every way increased their shared magic.

"Can you speak to them?" I asked Alicia.

She frowned, then shook her head. "They are present but weakened. Perhaps Donnelly can lend them some of his power."

"Cassidy—look." Teag pointed to a yellowed envelope that lay just outside the ritual space. Spidery, old-fashioned handwriting in faded ink provided a still-legible addressee—Trifles and Folly.

Teag spread one of his woven-magic cloths on the floor outside the warded workspace, and I set down the case, flexing my hand and arm, which had strained with its weight. Even through the layers of magical wardings and the lead shell, my touch magic could still sense the goblin spirit trying to break free.

"I'll set up the ritual items and get the bottle and that freaky contraption of Chuck's ready. Better take a look at what's in that envelope," Teag said as he dug into his pack.

I knelt next to the envelope, careful to stay outside the ritual space, and let my hand hover, palm down, over the old parchment. The letter "felt" like Gideon's book, confirming that they had the same author. So many strong emotions resonated from the note—grief, weariness, love, determination, acceptance. The contents might break my heart, but I felt sure that no harm would come to me from handling the paper itself.

I recognized the same careful penmanship from Gideon's memoir, and I read the letter aloud.

"To the Proprietor of Trifles and Folly. I trust that however far in the future this finds you, the store continues to protect Charleston and the coast from unusual dangers. Because of our endeavors at sea, I have become aware of your particular abilities, which is why I am entrusting my book and the information in this letter to you.

"If you are reading this, it is likely that the spell Ramon and I worked to overcome the sea witch is fading. We did not vanquish her as much as we bound her for a period of time. I don't think such a creature can be destroyed, but the entity is too dangerous and malicious to be allowed free rein.

"I am dying, and Ramon will not be dissuaded from joining me, so if we are to make our lives and deaths mean something, we choose to strengthen the binding for as long as possible. As I wrote in the book, we have sought counsel on how to do so. The magic is dark and difficult, and it ties our souls to this world as guardians, so we have not undertaken this lightly.

"I did not dare to entrust the specifics of the spell work to the book in case it should fall into the wrong hands. If you have reached the interior of the crypt, then all the sentinels and wardings have deemed you worthy.

"When the spell we have crafted wanes, if it is within your power, please strengthen it indefinitely with us as the willing anchors. We will be sentient and together and have no wish to be parted or to rely on the whim of a deity, if such exists, for our eternal disposition.

"Protect the guardian spell and this mausoleum, and grant us our request to remain together. Please accept our deep gratitude, though lifetimes may have passed between when I set pen to paper and when you read this. Go in peace. Gideon and Ramon."

A second sheet of paper provided a detailed list of ingredients—some of which were rare, arcane, or of dubious provenance. Below that was the incantation and the explicit instructions for working the ritual.

I looked up and blinked away tears. "They didn't just want to save the world—they wanted to make sure their souls remained together forever."

"If you have the spell they worked, then we should be able to reinforce it, right?" Teag replied.

"We'll know as soon as Rowan and Donnelly can join us. By the way, the stuff in the pipe is cohiba, from the Caribbean. It was listed in the spell components. Used for shamanic visions."

I wondered if the drug had eased Gideon's pain, or if as mystics believed, it made it possible for spirits to travel beyond their bodies to recreate the spell on both sides of the Veil.

We heard the iron door squeal against stone as it opened just enough for Rowan and Donnelly to slip through. A gust of cold wind accompanied them, guttering the candles. The torrential rain plastered Rowan's hair to her head, and water dripped from her soaked clothing.

"Sorren is keeping watch," she said off-handedly, as if a witch, a necromancer, a Loa, and a vampire hadn't just wiped the floor with a warlock hit squad. "I can feel the energies starting to shift. Even with Agwe's help, the guardian spell is dangerously weak."

"Agwe has heard our petition," Lucinda said, looking up from where she knelt in front of the offerings to the Loa. "But he cannot hold the sea witch back forever."

"He won't need to," Rowan said with certainty.

She passed through the antechamber, careful not to disturb any of Lucinda's preparations. Rowan spared a glance for the markings on the walls but did not slow to examine them.

When she reached the ritual room, Rowan paused to take stock of the protections, eyes narrowing in calculation. She appraised the working space Teag had arranged and Chuck's contraption. Then her attention turned to the lead case. Teag had opened it, revealing the bottle that held the trapped goblin, still encased in woven seagrass. He had attached the sigil-marked sensor pad that would channel that energy through Chuck's contraband black ops tech and then, linked by spell work, feed that power to the guardian spirits.

"Even with the sigils, and half encased in lead, the bottle reeks of power," Rowan said, keeping her distance.

When the case was locked in the safe, I could force myself to ignore its faint buzz. The longer it was open and close by, the more uncomfortable the resonance became. The goblin wasn't screaming in my mind, but then again I hadn't been near it for seventy years like Mr. Kenner.

Donnelly joined us then, as bedraggled as Rowan but managing to look cavalier despite the drenching. "This is quite the crypt, isn't it?" he said, with an appreciative glance around. I handed him the yellowed parchment letter.

"Gideon left this for us—it's the original guardian spell. He made it clear it's their desire to be bound as protectors for all eternity," I told Donnelly.

His gaze fell on the bones, and his expression shifted to a combination of concern and sorrow.

"Well now, there they are." Donnelly moved toward the skeletons while Rowan shifted to be closer to the ritual materials. I took a half-step closer to the case and bottle, which made the strange prickle of its energy even stronger.

None of us entered the area within the warded workspace on the floor.

"What do you make of it?" Rowan asked Donnelly.

He walked slowly around the outside of the inlaid circle and its symbols. Rain beat against the stained glass and pounded on the roof. Wind whistled and howled past the carved figures on the corners of the mausoleum, reminding us that our chance to restore the guardian protections was slipping away.

"I can strengthen the two ghosts while you work Travis's spell," Donnelly said. "That will redirect the connection to Cassidy's descendants—securing an anchor to the world of the living without placing any burden on them," he hastened to add at my concerned look.

"What about *that?*" Teag asked with a nod toward the bottle with the trapped Dokkaebi and the odd steel chamber of Chuck's secret tech that looked like a cross between a small jet engine and a high-tech coffee Thermos.

"Ah, yes. Our goblin battery. Chuck supplied all the information Travis needed to make sure the spell he found accounts for tapping into its energy as well. Once it's activated, Rowan and I can work the spell Gideon provided. I think our plan will do nicely." Donnelly glanced up as the sound of the storm grew louder. "We'd best be getting started."

We had discussed the ritual ahead of time in great detail, so we all knew our parts and places. I moved closer to the goblin bottle and Chuck's gadget. Rowan raised wardings inside the chapel to protect us from intrusion—by people or by the storm that still raged outside. I could feel the prickle of potent magic, and when I concentrated, I spotted the iridescent scrim of power coruscating around the perimeter of the room.

Alicia and Teag faced the doorway to the antechamber. I strongly doubted anything would get past Sorren and Lucinda, but in case it did, Alicia and Teag were prepared to fight off intruders, human and otherwise.

Donnelly stood just outside the large inlaid circle and symbols on the floor and looked on the intertwined skeletons with compassion. Then he stretched out his right hand and took a deep breath.

"Gideon Sullivan and Ramon Montero—receive this energy and show yourselves."

The bones shimmered, and gradually the figures of two men formed, standing beside what was left of their physical bodies. They resembled their portraits, though decades older. The years and declining health had gone harder on Gideon, who looked more like a plump grandfather than the daring captain of his youth. Ramon's dark hair had threads of silver, and he had lines at the corners of his eyes, but he still remained a dashingly handsome rogue.

The two men held hands, unafraid and unashamed. Gideon's gaze sought me out.

"You are Evann's heir."

I nodded. "Yes. And your distant kin."

Gideon looked at me with surprise. "Interesting. I presume since you and your friends are here—and dressed very strangely—that my close family is dead and the land has passed on as we willed it?"

"That's true," I answered, feeling a bond with Gideon from reading his memoir. "We believe we have a way to extend your guardian spell and keep your spirits together—with a long-term energy boost that might mean never having to go through this again."

Ramon's gaze flickered upward as the wind howled around the crypt, and the rain battered the stained glass. "How is it you bring so many with power to aid you? Is magic no longer forbidden?" His voice held longing, wonder, and hope.

I smiled. "Nobody cares about whether someone has magic anymore, although we still tend to keep it quiet. Lots of things have changed. You and Gideon could be married at the courthouse in Charleston, just like everyone else."

Gideon squeezed Ramon's hand, and Ramon looked at his partner. The emotion in their gaze took my breath away.

"Hard to believe—but good to hear," Gideon said. "What do you require of us to strengthen the spell? It felt like a torrent of flame when we did the working, and now it's barely a glow."

"Tap into the magic as it rises," Donnelly told them. "Let it fill you and restore you. And when that strange contraption lights up," he added, pointing to Chuck's pilfered secret gadget, "accept the extra energy, but don't ever let out what's sealed in that bottle."

A strong tremor shook the ground. "The sea witch is rising. We must do this now," Donnelly warned.

Gideon and Ramon shared one longing glance and then turned toward the necromancer, hands joined. Rowan began a quiet chant under her breath, strengthening the wardings around the chamber. Teag had drawn his short sword in his right hand and held a spelled net in the other, determined to hold the entrance from any intruder.

I was within arm's reach of the bottle, which Teag had carefully removed from its lead case. It stood upright, still inside the sweetgrass holder, on a mat woven with Teag's magic. A sigil-marked contact wire connected it to Chuck's purloined mad scientist gadget, waiting for the spell that would activate the psi-tech and channel the magic to Gideon and Ramon.

Donnelly's deep, resonant voice carried as he started to speak the original invocation—slightly altered to focus on Gideon and Ramon instead of himself. Rowan chanted Travis's second spell, and the two wove together like melody and descant.

My touch magic registered the new, rising power from the guardian spell replenishment, along with Rowan's wards, the dregs of Gideon's old magic, and the captive Dokkaebi, which had become more active in its prison as if it knew something was about to happen.

"Gideon Sullivan and Ramon Montero—what is your intention?" Donnelly asked the two ghosts.

"We wish to remain guardians against the malice of the sea witch, sharing the burden together for all time," Gideon replied.

"Our intention is to remain together and to protect the land and its inhabitants from danger forever," Ramon answered.

I felt the energy in the room stir as Donnelly reached the part of the spell that activated and channeled the goblin's magic. Donnelly's clever phrasing and Travis's incantation kept the geas of the guardian spell on the two ghostly protectors instead of shifting it to any living person.

The storm winds shrieked, and hail pounded the roof like relentless, rapid gunfire. I knew that the mausoleum and the mansion had survived the fury of many hurricanes, but I couldn't completely stifle the primal fear that rose in response. A tremor shook the crypt, stronger than before, and I feared it would send some of the relics tumbling from their ledges.

"Finish the spell," Teag urged. "Don't stop."

Inside the spelled bottle, lights flashed as the Dokkaebi fought the confines of its prison. Maybe it sensed a chance for escape since it had been removed from its lead tomb. Perhaps the storm's wild energy called to it. Whatever the cause, the goblin's new, frantic activity worried me.

Chuck's gadget remained dead silent, sending panic surging through my veins.

The steel cylinder sat dark and unresponsive, unchanged despite the magic that raged around it. *What if Chuck was wrong? Maybe he stole a dud—or a decoy. Shouldn't it be doing...something?*

As Donnelly and Rowan's incantations reached their climax and magical energy crackled and sparked in the air, another tremor rocked the mausoleum. As if in slow motion, I saw two things happen at once. The bottle started to fall, and a hairline crack threatened the integrity of the symbol surrounding Gideon and Ramon's bodies.

I didn't have time to think as I threw myself into the gap, arms stretched wide. I grabbed the bottle with my right hand to keep it from breaking, while the palm of my left hand slapped down over the edge of the workspace circle on the floor, sealing it.

Seconds too late, I realized I had just closed a magical circuit with my body and touch magic.

White-hot pain lanced through me, igniting every nerve. My body froze. I couldn't breathe. Energy surged along my spine and through muscle, sinew, and bone as if I'd grabbed a live electric line.

Everything became *more.*

I didn't just *hear* Donnelly and Rowan working their magic—I saw the swirls and eddies of power. The spark and glimmer of energy in every sigil and artifact merged together into a blinding flare. Gideon and Ramon stood real and solid at the center of the spell work. The circle on the floor and its markings glowed with inner fire.

The howl of the wind and the percussion of hail underscored the song of the interweaving spells.

The goblin bottle clutched white-knuckled in my right hand, thrummed like a dirge. I saw the creature's true form, full of teeth and malice. The Dokkaebi threw itself against its glass prison, trying to break free and consume the bounty of energy contained in the crypt.

Chuck's stolen tech lit up and blinked like a Christmas tree, whining as if it might explode. Maybe my touch jumpstarted it, or it might have just taken a while to warm up, but it was now part of the unholy circuit that flowed through me. The inlaid circle burned beneath my palm, but either the tremor's cracks hadn't broken the outer ring, or my flesh bridged the gap.

I felt the conclusion of the spells like a tide rushing through my body, filling me too full and threatening to drag my soul away with the undertow.

The magic settled to a strong new baseline, and now I could feel the goblin's energy routing through the gadget as intended, flowing into the perimeter of the inlaid circle and feeding its power.

Would I burn up from inside or be sucked dry like a husk? My body refused to respond when I tried to move, like being electrocuted and unable to let go of the live wire.

I didn't want to die, but if I went out helping to save people, I could move on in peace.

Suddenly, Sorren was there, gripping my shoulders with both hands, kneeling next to me. His words cut through the fog of magic, pulling me back where I had started to fade, as if he bridged the gap between both sides of the Veil, anchoring me.

Teag shouted in panic, and then Donnelly spoke in a deep, authoritative tone I couldn't ignore even as the pain dragged me under. That voice and Sorren's presence reached me in the darkness when nothing else remained.

CHAPTER FOURTEEN

"Cassidy? Can you hear me?" Kell's voice pulled me from a restless sleep. Something was off about his tone, but the haze in my brain wouldn't let me figure out what.

I tried to answer, but the words wouldn't come out, and all I could manage was a moan.

"Is that a yes?" He sounded hopeful and heartbroken all at once. "Cassidy?"

Kell's voice faded as the mental fog grew thicker, and I didn't have the strength to fight the tide.

When I woke again, the haze had thinned. Despite my sluggish thoughts, I was aware enough to realize that I wasn't completely myself, and I wondered how long I'd been out.

Judging from Kell's thick stubble, I realized I was missing several days of my life.

"Kell?" My parched throat threatened to close, and his name came out as a squeak.

He jolted awake, eyes wide, hair mussed. Kell didn't look like he'd slept soundly for a long time. I was starting to figure out that the days I didn't remember had been really bad.

"I'm here," he said, managing to hide his worry and give me a reassuring look. That just confirmed this was worse than I first thought.

Kell reached out to push my hair back from my forehead, gently trailing his fingers down my cheek. "How do you feel?"

Clarity brought pain. My body throbbed, but the persistent fogginess made me wonder if medication hid the true extent of my injuries. Baxter nestled beside me, and at the sound of my voice, he lifted his head and moved to lick my face.

"I hurt."

Kell flinched. "How bad?"

That required a silent, internal triage. I couldn't explain some of the things that hurt, so I started with the basics.

"I don't think any bones are broken." Managing words worked better if I kept sentences short. "I feel...cooked."

The blood drained from Kell's face. "Actually...that's not far off. Do you remember?"

Thinking taxed my throbbing head and felt like wading through cold molasses. We had gone to the mausoleum, fought Etheridge, and worked magic. There'd been a storm, and the ground shook. Gideon and Ramon were solid and almost alive. Then something went wrong.

"We were in the crypt...it almost worked."

Kell helped me sit up enough to drink water, which soothed my throat and took the roadkill taste out of my mouth. I realized that somehow I was back in our bedroom in my house, dressed in a T-shirt and loose sleep pants, with an IV in my hand.

"It did work—but we nearly lost you." Sorren stood in the doorway, and his silent approach made both of us jump. "Donnelly and Rowan were almost done with the spell, but a tremor broke the circle and made the goblin bottle fall. Chuck's gadget took a while to start up. You jumped in to save the day and...almost died."

Kell reached out to tangle our fingers together. The exhaustion and grief I saw in his face told me more than I knew he could easily put into words. It must have been really bad.

"The circle—"

"They fixed it."

"How did I get here?"

Kell hesitated as if he wasn't quite sure how much to say, although I felt certain the others had filled him in. Sorren continued the story.

"You kickstarted the gadget and kept the bottle from breaking while closing the ritual circle. But it was like drinking from a firehose —or a flamethrower. It was more than your body could take, and it started to burn you up."

"I think I died."

Kell turned away and swiped the back of his hand over his eyes.

"You did—or near enough," Sorren said. "Donnelly kept your soul tethered to your body while Rowan did what she could to heal you, but the damage was too extensive. I fed you my blood. Not enough to turn you—just enough to heal. You are still human. It was the only way to keep you here with us."

I'd rarely seen Sorren look fearful, and it took a moment for me to realize he didn't know how I'd react to what he had done. He had saved Teag's life once in the same way. That was one of the reasons we were both likely to live to an unusually ripe old age.

"Thank you," I said. Sorren's expression cleared when he realized I accepted his gift.

"I'm just glad it worked," he admitted. "For a while, we still weren't sure you'd make it—even with my help and Donnelly's. Once we stabilized you, I called my private physician and had him waiting here at the house. I'd had him on standby—just in case."

"I'm sorry," I whispered. "I didn't think before I dove for the bottle."

Kell shook his head. "How can you be sorry for maybe saving the world? Donnelly and Rowan aren't sure the spells would have worked if you hadn't done what you did. But dammit, Cassidy, you scared the shit out of me."

Time to change the subject. "Where's everyone?" I asked.

Kell took a deep breath, and his shoulders released. "Maggie's on the couch. She refused to go home, and so she's been making sure there's always something to eat. Teag, Sorren, and I took turns sitting with you."

"Thank you." I reached toward the bottle of water, and Kell helped me drink a little more. "The shop?"

"Chuck and his Uncle Robert pitched in since Robert used to run the store for the Alliance in Cape May," Sorren replied. "Everyone else comes and goes to check on you. They'll be glad to know you're awake."

He managed an encouraging half-smile. I figured it must have been even worse than Sorren let on if I had managed to panic a vampire and a necromancer. "I'll go let them know the good news," he added and left Kell and me alone.

I lifted our clasped hands to my dry lips and kissed Kell's knuckles. "I love you."

"I love you too."

I knew he meant it, and I also knew that the danger and risks took a toll. I felt very lucky that he was brave enough to stick around.

"Need to sleep more," I said, as the haze began to roll back in, making it difficult to keep my eyes open. Baxter snuggled in, keeping vigil in his own way.

Kell made sure the pillows were arranged just right and leaned forward to kiss my forehead. "Get some rest. I'll be here when you wake up."

TWO DAYS LATER, my mind had cleared, and I was off the IV and able to eat again. Maggie made spaghetti, so there was plenty to go around when Teag and Anthony joined us. I still didn't feel completely back to normal, and Sorren insisted that both his doctor and Rowan check me over. They concluded that rest, food, and time would patch me up good as new.

"This is the best spaghetti I've ever eaten," I told Maggie, barely keeping myself from shoveling food into my mouth. Now that I could eat again, I was suddenly famished. Baxter slept on my feet beneath the table. He hadn't let me out of his sight.

"I figured having your favorites might help make up for lost time," she said with a broad smile. "Glad it's working."

"So what else did I miss?" I asked after taking a bite of garlic bread.

"Beck found records that suggest the pirates who repeatedly attacked Gideon's ship were hired by the Etheridges. Presumably because he and Montero were interfering in their occult relic trade," Teag replied. "We believe that both the Pendlewoods and the Etheridges were using their magic to manipulate the sea witch. Lucinda thinks we're right, based on what she picked up from Agwe through the link she shared with him."

After what happened at the crypt, I didn't want to make a supernatural link with anyone or anything for a long time. Just the thought sent a shiver through me. Kell picked up on it and nudged closer, setting a reassuring hand on my thigh.

"Simon called the night we did the ritual," Teag continued. "Dante wouldn't leave him alone until he checked on how things went. Simon wanted to drive down when he found out you were hurt, but we finally talked him out of it since he couldn't do anything to help. So when you feel up to it, he—and Dante—would appreciate it if you returned the call."

"Tomorrow," I said, figuring that between dinner and socializing, I wasn't going to be burning the midnight oil tonight.

I heard a knock at the door, and Maggie went to let Sorren in. He greeted everyone, but I could feel the weight of his gaze on me, trying to assess my recovery. Sorren can be a little overprotective of his human allies since he is very aware of how "fragile" we are compared to the strength and healing abilities that come with being a supernatural creature.

"Glad to see you up and about, Cassidy," he said, joining us in the living room. "You gave us all quite a scare."

"So I've heard. Scared me too," I replied and leaned into Kell, taking comfort from his presence.

"Chuck sends his apologies about the psi-ops tech," Teag added. "It did work, but the time it took to 'warm up' was badly underestimated. To say the least."

"And the Dokkaebi?" I'd been so worried that the bottle would shatter and set the goblin free, I'd overlooked all the rest of the danger to prevent that from happening.

"Still safely trapped," Sorren replied. "Now that the gadget and its spell set up the connection, the device isn't needed anymore. Rowan checked all the sigils on the bottle, and made sure it's secured so there's no danger of it falling if we get more tremors," he added with a pointed glance toward me.

"Since the renewed guardian spell restored the energy Gideon and Ramon needed to continue their protection, drawing on the goblin is more like an emergency generator," Sorren continued. "He's as safe in the crypt as he would be at the Briggs Society and useful in a pinch as well."

Teag looked to Sorren. "With everything that happened, I never asked if anyone noticed that Carter Etheridge disappeared. Did they?"

Sorren chuckled. "Alistair and the museum board members certainly did. Without Etheridge, the whole lawsuit falls apart. Rumor has it that Etheridge might have been under investigation for tax fraud and skipped town ahead of the Feds." His smile showed just the tips of his eyeteeth, a hint that he was the one who had started that very convenient bit of gossip.

"He's not the last of his family," Teag said. "What's to stop them from picking up where he left off?"

Sorren shrugged. "Nothing—except that I paid them another visit to let them know that the guardians are back at full strength and that the Alliance would take an extremely dim view of any interference. It would be inconvenient for them if we were to take even more of an interest in the family's affairs."

While Sorren treated his allies with fond protectiveness, he was a badass vampire, an apex predator, and anyone who messed with him or the people under his protection quickly found out just how lethal he could be. Having him personally involved could certainly make the Etheridges reconsider their meddling and seek less dangerous opportunities elsewhere.

Anthony looked to Teag. "I don't want to know."

Teag smiled. "I wasn't going to tell you, sweetie."

We'd talked shop enough for one night. "What's up with the wedding plans?" I asked Teag and Anthony. Time for what I hoped would be good news.

The two men shared a fond smile. I was glad to see them happy. "The announcement about my parents pulling their endowment from St. Philips Church worked out for the best," Anthony replied.

"As it turns out, other people weren't happy with the church's choice to exclude people. There's been a debate for a while now about owning up to the role that wealthy members back in the day played in the slave trade and owning enslaved individuals. Heaping the marriage equality issue on top of that will probably cost them members and donations beyond just his parents," Teag said. "It's too early to know if that will lead to any changes, but I think they finally heard the message, loud and clear."

Anthony had his arm around Teag's shoulders and pulled him a little closer. "My folks have been asked to take a role in a couple of LGBTQ charities. They're definitely considering it—as well as redirecting the money from the endowment. They never hid the fact that I was gay, but they never announced it from the rooftops either. Taking a much more visible advocacy role will draw the attention of their social circle to the issues. So I guess there's a silver lining, after all."

"And the rest of the plans are going smoothly?" Maggie asked. "If you run into any nasty cake bakers or photographers, let me know. My knitting club takes a dim view of that kind of thing. We'll roast them on Yelp."

Anthony shook his head and Teag grinned. "Thank you," Teag said. "We appreciate it. But so far, everyone other than the church has been wonderful about working with us. And while we can't tell Anthony's parents the whole truth about Father Anne's work outside of her parish duties, she's got them completely wrapped around her little finger."

I've met Anthony's folks at various fundraisers and charity events. They're gracious and friendly, in the staid Old Charleston manner. Imagining them hitting it off with Father Anne was charming—and something I couldn't wait to see in action.

"Before I forget—" Teag said. "I kept an eye on your email while you were recovering. There's one from Adiel Nielson about his supernatural histories project."

I nodded. "Great. He's working with the Fox Institute to document the history of people with magic and supernatural creatures—with all the proper precautions—and I thought that Gideon and Ramon had earned a mention. I'll send a reply once I get my second wind."

The group broke up early, and while I knew it was in deference to me being not quite back to normal, I also realized I was rapidly running out of energy. I hugged Anthony, Teag, and Sorren at the door and thanked them again for all their help. When they were gone, I turned to the kitchen, expecting to do clean up, only to find Maggie was way ahead of me.

"It's finished," she announced with a satisfied smirk. "I'm going to sit up reading for a while, but you've had a busy day. Get some sleep, and if I wake up in time, I might have bacon ready for you in the morning."

I gave Maggie a big hug and thanked her profusely. Then I let Kell lead me off to bed. I was still too wiped out for anything more risqué than sleeping, but I always slept better with him beside me.

"Thanks for saving the world," he murmured as we cuddled beneath the covers. "It's the only one we've got. But it wouldn't be the same without you, so be more careful, please?"

I snuggled against his chest and slipped an arm around his waist. "I promise. I want to stick around."

Once again, the odd little fellowship of friends and allies we had cobbled together managed to stop a major catastrophe. Most of the world would never know—but recognition wasn't the point. Whether we were lucky or cursed, we had the rare skills and opportunity to make a real difference. My friends and I wouldn't have it any other way. Tomorrow would bring new dangers, and there were no guarantees.

That just made every win and every good moment all the sweeter.

AFTERWORD

Every time I write a new book in a series, it's like visiting old friends. It's always a joy to come back to Cassidy, Teag, and her Charleston crew. Since all the modern books written under my Gail Z. Martin name and Morgan Brice name interconnect, it's also fun to see where characters you've met elsewhere might pop up! For me, it just seems natural that people playing an active role in the supernatural community would know each other, and I love the way it makes the larger fictional world feel more real and complex.

St. Philip's Church in Charleston did actually change its denomination because of marriage equality/gay clergy. That saddens me greatly. I don't know for sure the impact that decision had on membership and donations, but I don't think it's a stretch to suspect that some folks chose to make changes.

St. Sebastian's plague church is a figment of my imagination. I visited a similar church in New Orleans that was built to handle Yellow Fever victims, and since Charleston also suffered recurrent epidemics of both Yellow Fever and Malaria, I figured the addition made sense, although I can't find any documentation of that type of church actually existing in Charleston.

Earthquake activity on the fault line near Bermuda is possible but unlikely, according to the sources I found. There are actually undersea caves and mountain ranges near Bermuda, so that part is real. Dokkaebi are part of Korean mythology, although, as usual, I took a little editorial license with the details.

At some point, we have a wedding to look forward to! I'm not sure when, but it will happen—and when it does, you'll definitely be invited.

I hope you enjoyed this visit to Charleston—there will be more to come!

ACKNOWLEDGMENTS

Thank you so much to my editor, Jean Rabe, to my husband and writing partner Larry N. Martin for all his behind-the-scenes hard work, and to my wonderful cover artist, Lou Harper. Thanks also to the Shadow Alliance street team for their support and encouragement and to my fantastic beta readers and the ever-growing legion of beta and ARC readers who help spread the word, including: Andrea, Anne, Ben, Chris, Christi, Darrell, Dawn, Debbie, Dino, George, Glen, Jason, Justin, Kara, Karen, Karolina, Kathryn, Kimberly, Laurie, Leonard, Michael, Miki, Robin, Sandra, Sharon, Sherrie, Sue, Susan M., Susan S., Teri, Trevor, and Vikki! And of course, to my "convention gang" of fellow authors for making road trips fun.

ABOUT THE AUTHOR

Gail Z. Martin writes urban fantasy, epic fantasy, and steampunk for Solaris Books, Orbit Books, Falstaff Books, SOL Publishing, and Darkwind Press. Urban fantasy series include *Deadly Curiosities* and the *Night Vigil* (Sons of Darkness). Epic fantasy series include *Darkhurst, The Chronicles Of The Necromancer, The Fallen Kings Cycle, The Ascendant Kingdoms Saga, and The Assassins of Landria*. Under her urban fantasy MM paranormal romance pen name of Morgan Brice, she has five series (*Witchbane, Badlands, Kings of the Mountain, Fox Hollow,* and *Treasure Trail*) with more books and series to come.

Co-authored with Larry N. Martin are *Iron and Blood*, the first novel in the Jake Desmet Adventures series and the *Storm and Fury* collection; and the *Spells, Salt, & Steel*: New Templars series (Mark Wojcik, monster hunter), as well as *Wasteland Marshals* and *Cauldron: The Joe Mack Adventures*.

Gail's work has appeared in more than forty US/UK anthologies. Newest anthologies include: *The Weird Wild West, Gaslight and Grimm, Baker Street Irregulars, Across the Universe, Release the Virgins, Tales from the Old Black Ambulance, Witches, Warriors,& Wise Women, The Four ???? Of the Apocalypse, Christmas at Caynham Castle,* and *Trick or Treat at Caynham Castle*.

Join the Shadow Alliance street team so you never miss a new release! Get the scoop first + giveaways + fun stuff! Also where Gail and Larry get their beta readers and Launch Team! http://www.facebook.com/groups/MartinShadowAlliance

Find out more at www.GailZMartin.com and on her blog at www.

DisquietingVisions.com. Join the newsletter and get free excerpts at http://eepurl.com/dd5XLj Gail is also a con-runner for ConTinual, the online, ongoing multi-genre convention that never ends. www. Facebook.com/Groups/ConTinual

Support Indie Authors

When you support independent authors, you help influence what kind of books you'll see more of and what types of stories will be available because the authors themselves decide which books to write, not a big publishing conglomerate. Independent authors are local creators, supporting their families with the books they produce. Thank you for supporting independent authors and small press fiction!

ALSO BY GAIL Z. MARTIN

Darkhurst

Scourge

Vengeance

Reckoning

Ascendant Kingdoms

Ice Forged

Reign of Ash

War of Shadows

Shadow and Flame

Convicts and Exiles: Collection

Chronicles of the Necromancer / Fallen Kings Cycle

The Shadowed Path: Jonmarc Vahanian Collection

The Dark Road: Jonmarc Vahanian Collection

The Summoner

The Blood King

Dark Haven

Dark Lady's Chosen

The Sworn

The Dread

Watch for the new Legacy of the Necromancer series, which picks up 17 years after the end of The Dread.

Deadly Curiosities

Deadly Curiosities

Vendetta

Tangled Web

Inheritance

Legacy

Trifles and Folly: Collection

Trifles and Folly 2: Collection

Assassins of Landria

Assassin's Honor

Sellsword's Oath

Fugitive's Vow

Exile's Quest

Night Vigil

Sons of Darkness

C.H.A.R.O.N.

Other books by Gail Z. Martin and Larry N. Martin

Jake Desmet Adventures

Iron & Blood

Storm & Fury: Collection

Spells, Salt, & Steel: New Templars

Spells, Salt, & Steel: Season One

Night Moves

Monster Mash

Creature Feature

Wasteland Marshals

Wasteland Marshals

Witch of the Woods

Ghosts of the Past

Shutdown Crew

Joe Mack: Shadow Council Archives

Cauldron

Black Sun

Chicagoland

www.ingramcontent.com/pod-product-compliance
Lightning Source LLC
Chambersburg PA
CBHW020623110726
47899CB00002B/633